"I wouldn't change a thing."

As Eli said it, they turned their heads at the same moment and touched noses. His eyelashes brushed Christie's brow when he blinked in surprise. For a moment she'd thought he'd been about to…

Softly, he pushed back the damp tendrils clinging to her forehead.

The gentle pressure of his hand lingered against the side of her face, his fingers cupping her chin so tenderly that it made her heart ache. Would she ever learn to accept that friendship was all there was to her and Eli?

Here was the chance to ask the million-dollar question. "Even Jacqueline walking out?"

"Especially that." He leaned closer, their noses touching once more. "Because then I couldn't have met you."

Her lips parted as she breathed in the moment and the man.

There was no denying her feelings for him. But did she dare risk the chance that he might get sick again? That she'd end up hurting him somehow? She cared too much for him now.

"Eli, I don't know."

Dear Reader,

I learned at a young age that love is an energy that cannot be destroyed. When it is true, love endures, regardless of what life may bring.

When I first learned of my grandmother's cancer, I wanted to leave college and spend every minute with the incredible woman who'd taught me to be compassionate of others, to have high standards for myself and the men I dated, and that crackers and butter are actually the best snack while watching 1950s horror movies.

Needless to say, her will to have me graduate on time won out, and I finished college just as her life ended. Although we had a chance to say goodbye, and for her to remind me to wear lipstick in public, a window in my heart stays open. Her light will shine through it for the rest of my life.

I've met many couples who have touched me deeply with their unflagging devotion during challenging times. Loving another, regardless of what the future may hold, plays a large role in *Wish Me Tomorrow,* when Christie Bates, a grief counselor, meets cancer survivor Eli Roberts. Together they learn that love and family are worth any risk–even if tomorrow may only be a wish.

I would love to connect with you and hear your inspiring stories. Please visit me at www.karenrock.com.

Karen

HARLEQUIN HEARTWARMING

Karen Rock

Wish Me Tomorrow

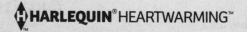
HARLEQUIN® HEARTWARMING™

Recycling programs
for this product may
not exist in your area.

ISBN-13: 978-0-373-36641-5

WISH ME TOMORROW

Printed in U.S.A.

ⒽHARLEQUIN®
™ www.Harlequin.com

KAREN ROCK

An English language instructor, Karen Rock has adored romance since her grandmother first gave her Harlequin Presents books. When Karen learned of Harlequin Heartwarming, she was inspired by the opportunity to write unforgettable, deeply romantic, tender love stories that mothers could share with their daughters. When she's not writing, Karen loves scouring estate sales for vintage books, cooking her grandmother's recipes, hiking the "high peaks" and redesigning her gardens. She lives in the Adirondack Mountain region with her husband, daughter and two Cavalier King Charles spaniels who have yet to understand the concept of "fetch," though they know a lot about love. For more information on Karen's upcoming books, check out her website at www.karenrock.com or follow her on Twitter @karenrock5. She'd love to hear from you!

To those I've loved who are here or gone.
You are ever in my heart.

CHAPTER ONE

ONE EMPTY FOLDING CHAIR. Christie Bates stared at the vacant seat then checked her iPhone to make sure the wall clock was accurate. Yep, still 6:35. Everyone in the cancer support group she led was here except one, the one who'd been coming the longest. Her insides twisted. He hadn't missed a meeting in three years.

And the sight of an empty chair in a room like this was always…ominous.

She exhaled slowly and squashed the negative thought as her eyes roamed over the chatting group. The world needed positive energy. And *they* needed it most of all. She jumped when a hand squeezed her shoulder.

"Would you like me to close the door so you can begin?" asked Anne, the West Side YMCA's receptionist. Pool-bound children shrieked in the stairwell outside.

"No!" Her voice sounded more forceful than she'd intended. It carried over the noise and quieted her group. Seven pairs of concerned eyes turned her way. So much for keeping things upbeat.

She pinned on a bright smile and patted Anne's hand. "We're not quite ready to start yet, but thanks."

Anne studied her for a moment then shrugged. "I'll be out front if you need me."

Her heels clicked across the wood floor and echoed in the high-ceilinged room. Overhead fans stirred the muggy June air, the humidity so thick Christie felt as though she wore it. At least she'd had time to change out of her nurse scrubs and shower before the meeting. After a twelve-hour hospital shift, the mini-break had made her feel human again.

"Why are we waiting?" a newer member asked around a mouthful of chocolate-chip cookie.

Another pointed at the clock. "We always start at 6:30."

"You're right." Christie swallowed her fear and widened her smile. Her clients had enough stress to handle. They didn't deserve more. "But let's give it a few more minutes in case someone's late. You know how hard it is to get a taxi in the rain."

The group nodded sagely then resumed their conversations. She sagged against the back of her chair. *Phew.* Her quick excuse worked. It was a logical reason for the delay given Manhattan's traffic issues and she wouldn't imagine another possibility. There was power in positive thinking. She shredded a napkin in her lap. Not that it had saved her brother. If only she'd been there when… She shook her head. Nope. She wouldn't get on board that dark train of thought.

She bent to pick up her juice cup and discreetly knocked on the wooden floor, no-bad-luck, an Irish superstition passed down by her gran. She'd witnessed enough medical miracles to know that science couldn't explain everything.

Christie crossed her legs, smoothing her gray pants and rumpled white blouse. Forcing her eyes from the empty chair, she surveyed the assembled group members for changes in skin color, weight and discomfort levels. Everyone seemed stable. But where was her absent client? Perhaps she would ask Anne to call and check on him. She might be overreacting, but knowing he was okay would help soothe her nerves.

Before she could stand, a tall stranger wheeled the missing man through the door. She drew her first easy breath of the night. He'd come after all. The group called out greetings to John, relief evident in their voices.

"Hello. Hope I didn't hold everyone up," the

latecomer declared, as his helper—a very handsome helper, Christie noted—wheeled John into the spot beside the empty chair. Where were John's canes? Her heart sank. His condition must be deteriorating.

"Lousy weather out there, huh? My neighbor brings his kids here a couple of times a week, so I asked him to help me catch a cab." He gestured to the dark-haired gentleman wearing a navy polo shirt, jeans and a polite smile. "Eli Roberts, this is Christie Bates and—" he waved a veined hand "—everyone. You'll like them. Oh. And would you get me one of Christie's raisin-oatmeal bars? Been craving one all week."

The man nodded then helped John out of his coat, shook the rain from it and placed it on the back of the chair. His face reminded her of a Roman soldier on one of her father's ancient coins—he had a powerful jaw, straight, prominent nose and a strong brow.

"May I get anyone anything?" he asked once he'd locked John's wheels in place. After taking a few requests, he strode to the snack table. It was a good night when the group ate. Sometimes the number receiving chemo was so high the side table went untouched.

She noticed that he grabbed John a napkin and a cup of juice along with the snack. *Thoughtful*.

After giving John a quick hug, she straightened and looked up into the bluest eyes she'd ever seen. Her grin faltered at the man's piercing stare.

"Eli. If you'd like to join us—" She extended a hand to guide him to the seat, but he jerked back. Caught off balance, Christie stumbled, her black Keds trampling each other. Heat flared in her cheeks.

"Sorry," he muttered, righting her with a quick, efficient hold on her elbow before seating himself.

O-kay. Not a touchy-feely guy. Heard and understood.

She sneaked another glance at him, registering his tense shoulders along with his guarded expression. He'd done a nice thing by bringing John in, but cancer support groups were a lot for healthy people to handle. She should give him a graceful excuse to leave.

"The Yankees' pregame coverage is playing on TV in the lounge down the hall if you'd like to wait there, Mr. Roberts."

"Call me Eli," he said in a gruff voice, his eyes inscrutable. "And I promised John I'd stay." A look passed between the two as he took his seat.

She forced a welcoming grin and nodded. If John wanted him here, that was fine. But if he didn't lighten up soon, she'd send him on a coffee run so he wouldn't put a damper on the meeting.

When she got back to her seat, she glanced his way and caught his intense gaze again. What was it about his stare that flustered her? She was a twenty-eight-year-old professional, not a schoolgirl sneaking peeks at the cute new kid. Time to get a grip.

She looked at the clock and grabbed her clipboard. Fifteen minutes behind schedule. A first. Eli was throwing her off her game, but at least John was here and the seats were full.

"Today's inspirational quote is by George Herbert," Christie began. "'Storms make oaks take deeper root.' Let's practice our relaxation breathing as we contemplate its meaning and how it applies to our lives."

Her bowed head snapped up at a muffled snort. While everyone else closed their eyes, Eli stared at the ceiling and shook his head.

"Do you disagree, Mr. Roberts?" she burst out before she could think better of it.

"I do," replied the impertinent outsider. Shooting to his feet again, he circled the group, gathering their garbage and carting it to the wastebasket.

"No matter how deep trees dig, bad storms can knock them down anyway."

Well, sure. Of course they could. Although she'd spent her early childhood in Woodlawn, an Irish-American neighborhood in New York, her family had eventually relocated to Kansas—one of Tornado Alley's hardest-hit states. There, she'd learned to weather storms, not dwell on them. When tempests hit, neighbors pitched in to put back the pieces of shattered lives.

A high-pitched sound rattled through a nearby client's tracheotomy tube. Christie grabbed the woman's shaking hand and squeezed. Elizabeth had Stage IV esophageal cancer. She didn't need a reminder of the dangers she faced.

"We focus on the positive, *Mr. Roberts.*" She laced her fingers with Elizabeth's, relieved when the woman's trembling eased.

His square jaw clenched. "And ignore reality? That seems a bit misleading, doesn't it, Miss Bates?"

"It's Ms.," she corrected, mostly because she was getting good and riled now. What did this man think he was doing? These people lived with far too much reality as it was. They came here for fellowship and support, not a lecture.

"Well, *Ms*. Bates, the truth is that all trees

want to live. It's just the luck of the draw that some make it and others don't."

Heat spread up her chest and rose to her neck. She glanced down. *Darn.* Those red splotches betrayed her at the worst times. If only she looked as cool and controlled as Eli. She forced herself to meet his eye and caught a brief, tortured look before he averted his face. *Interesting.*

A ruckus in the corridor distracted her, reminding her that they hadn't shut the door. A pack of kids rushed past on their way from one activity to another.

"Daddy, Daddy." A young escapee wearing wet swim trunks raced inside. He launched himself onto Eli's lap, the smell of chlorine clinging to him.

"I swam without my floaties today." With his missing front teeth, the child's grin was irresistible. Christie joined in the group's chorus of oohs and aahs.

Deep dimples appeared as Eli's face relaxed into a broad smile. Where was this side of the man moments ago when he'd rained doom and gloom on her meeting? His joyful expression and the affectionate way he ruffled his son's hair did something strange to her heart. She checked out his ring-free left hand. Had his wife died? That could explain some of his behavior, as well as why John wanted him to stay at the meeting. But he looked young to be a widower, no older than his early thirties.

"Sorry," an older woman called from the doorway. "I went to get Tommy a towel, and when I came back, he was gone."

She barreled into the room and gave Christie an apologetic wave.

"It's all right, Mary," Eli said. "He does that to me, too."

Tommy squirmed at his father's stern expression. "What do you say to Mary?" he prompted and took Mary's proffered towel.

Tommy studied his swinging flip-flops. "Sorry, Mary," he said, a lisp turning his *s* into a *th*. "I won't do it again."

"Right." Eli hugged Tommy then began drying him.

Tommy pointed at Christie. "That's how I met her."

With his hair no longer plastered to his face, the youngster looked familiar. She took a moment to recall how she knew him. Since her meeting was so off track, she couldn't see the point in forcing the group back into meditation anytime soon. Besides, Elizabeth was smiling and happy, clearly enjoying their energetic visitor.

Eli's face tightened once more. "You know Ms. Bates?"

The towheaded dynamo wriggled off his father's lap and scampered over to her. "She gave me an oatmeal bar with raisins." He scanned the treat table and turned from his father to Christie, face bright and expectant. "Can I have one?"

"If your father says so." Why hadn't she recognized the adorable imp earlier? A couple of months ago, he'd burst into their meeting and wolfed down half the pan. She matched Tommy's grin. "But be careful—last time you almost took out a tray of Jell-O."

"You stopped me before I crashed." Tommy flapped the sides of his towel and jumped up and down. "But that lady with the blue hair was mad. She said I had to leave."

Christie stifled a laugh. Tommy had a point. The former receptionist had been a bit of a grump. "Not to worry. She was angry at everything."

Tommy's blue eyes grew round. "Even Jell-O?" He lowered his terry-cloth wings. "But it wiggles."

Elizabeth's tracheotomy made a humming sound, her warm smile about to steal Christie's heart. No way she was letting Tommy out the door yet. Kids had a more positive effect on people than a whole book full of inspirational quotes.

"Exactly." She nodded solemnly. "Now hold on to one end of the towel. I'm going to show you something grand before you get your dessert." She sent Eli a questioning look. Tommy had been very patient waiting for his answer.

"How did you two meet?" His light tone held an undercurrent of tension. "And, yes, Tommy, you can have the oatmeal-raisin bar." He held up his index finger. "Just one, though."

Christie pulled the other end of the towel, spinning Tommy free of the absorbent cloth.

"Again!" Tommy shouted when he rewrapped himself.

"Answer your father first, Tommy." She turned him to face his parent.

"I ran away from Mary 'cause I wanted to show Becca my drawing of Scout. Only I got lost and came here instead." Tommy scratched his freckled nose before turning back to her. "Please spin me, Miss—" He shook his small head, brow furrowed. "Miss—"

"It's Christie. Hey, everyone." A preteen girl with brown hair in a tight bun wandered into the room and returned the group's waves. She wore jeans over a black leotard and had a bag embroidered with sequined ballet shoes slung across her shoulder. "I met her when we picked you up, remember? So why did you run away? *Again.* You know how much it upsets Dad and Mary." Despite her admonishment, her tone was mild.

"Becca!" The boy wrapped his arms around his sister's legs. "Did you see me swim without my floaties? Do you want an oatmeal bar? It's healthy and Dad said we could."

"I didn't see you because I was still in dance. But that's awesome, Little Man." Becca fist bumped Tommy. "And, yeah. I'll have a snack. So starved."

"How was dance, Becca-Bell?" Eli's arms opened wide, his gaze expectant.

Some members of the support group began speaking in low-pitched voices, the word *Yankees* punctuating their discussion. No doubt they were debating the team's chances tonight. It was a crucial game that Christie was interested in herself. Yet this family fascinated her, as well.

"The same," Becca mumbled, fidgeting with the latch on her bag. "And please don't call me that anymore. Remember?"

He slowly lowered his arms, a crease appearing between his brows. "Does that fastener need to be fixed?"

Becca shrugged before she turned away.

Christie glanced between the two; their tension was palpable. Although it could be a teenage thing, it seemed deeper than that.

Elizabeth stood and brought treats, another member following with Dixie cups of juice. After taking the proffered snacks, Becca said, "Thank you," nudging Tommy to do the same.

"All right, kids." Eli rose to his imposing height. "Time to go."

He held out his arms once more. Tommy flew into them while Becca hung back and tightened her shoelaces. "I'll be home in a little bit," he promised.

"Sure," Becca replied, her voice flat. She gave Christie and the smiling support group a small wave, wrapped a protective arm around her brother and followed Mary through the exit.

"That was nice, Mr. Roberts." Christie's smile faded at his glower. She cleared her throat. "Does anyone have something they'd like to share?"

She looked pointedly at Eli, who stared back, arms crossed over his broad chest.

Why the sour mood? Even though there didn't appear to be a woman in his life, and his relationship with Becca seemed strained, he still had what was most important—his health and family. But his bleak expression made her wonder.

Perhaps he didn't have everything after all.

ELI FORCED HIS eyes away from *Ms*. Christie Bates as everyone in the group took turns recounting their week. He knew his staring bordered on rude, but something about her fascinated the photographer in him.

She wasn't beautiful in the traditional sense. Her nose had a slight upward tilt that spoiled its classic lines. Her green eyes, his favorite color, were set too deep, the dark circles under them belying her carefree attitude. Her forehead was a finger's breadth too high and her delicate, pointed chin reminded him of old-time movie stars, not modern-day bombshells. Her hair, a shimmering auburn waterfall, would meet the fashion industry's standards, though.

Despite the imperfections, or perhaps because of them, her face captivated him. Even the splatter of freckles across her nose made him long for his Nikon, something he hadn't picked up since— He forced his mind away from that memory. It was one he wanted buried, cremated, even.

He peeked at Christie once more and met her jewel-toned eyes. *Busted.* But the quick glance confirmed his instincts. All her flaws added up to an arresting face. It was a shame her personality was so over the top. All that phony stuff about cancer making you stronger, giving people false hope. It bordered on criminal. He hated to call her out on it, but these people needed to know the truth, to be prepared.

"Elizabeth, that is a lovely scarf. Is it new?" he heard her ask the woman beside her. Her soft voice had a unique, musical lilt. Where had he heard that accent before?

The woman lowered the silk paisley covering her tracheotomy and reminded Christie she had bought the scarf for her last Christmas. Christie laughed, her bowed lips curling. He dragged his gaze away and bolted down a cup of lukewarm juice. Why was this woman getting under his skin?

"Well, then, that was grand of me, wasn't it?" Christie asked.

His mind clicked. Irish. The accent was subtle, as though she'd grown up around people from the old country. No wonder she bought into all that hope and faith stuff. Maybe she believed in rainbows with pots of gold, as well.

Her white teeth flashed at a man with an oxygen tube. "That's wonderful," she responded to something he'd said. "You've nearly doubled your white-blood-cell count."

Eli glanced at the clock, glad to see that there were only twenty minutes left. With any luck, they'd get a cab and be home in plenty of time to relieve Mary. She'd been a loyal friend and employee through these difficult three years.

No matter how much John nagged him to go to the White Horse Tavern, he'd be home by eight. Mary had been telling him for the past two weeks that she and her husband had reservations at one of Manhattan's best restaurants to celebrate their anniversary.

"And, John, I've noticed you've got some new equipment. How is that going?" asked Christie. Eli glanced down at his buddy. John's head rested sideways and back against the chair, his eyes closed. That figured. John dragged him to this meeting, made him promise not to leave—as if he would—and then fell asleep.

Christie rushed toward them, her face creased in concern. She grabbed John's wrist and held up her watch, checking his pulse with a medical professional's efficiency.

"Someone get Anne," she called, all business. "Everyone else, stay seated."

Eli dashed out into the hall, his heart thudding. Why had he assumed John was sleeping?

He skidded to a stop before a woman whose desk nameplate read Anne Cartwright.

"Come quick," he urged. "Christie needs you."

Despite his long strides, the diminutive woman kept up with him.

"John. Blink if you can hear me," Christie was saying when they returned. "Good. Now, can you squeeze my hand? No. Okay. Don't worry. We'll get you fixed up, good as new." She looked relieved at Anne's appearance.

"Anne, call 911. Tell them we have an ependymoma patient who's had an arrhythmia-induced stroke that's affected the left half of his body and speech. He's conscious but in atrial fibrillation."

Anne rushed off, phone already in hand. She stopped at Christie's next words.

"Where is the center's AED Unit?"

After spending hours in medical clinics, Eli knew these were machines that used electricity to jump-start failing hearts.

Anne whirled, her face ashen.

"It's down the hall near the gym." Her voice was a notch above a whisper. She turned back to her call for the EMTs and hurried out of the room.

"Mr. Roberts," she began, but he cut her off.

"Got it." Eli bolted for the door. After scouting the hall, he spotted a couple of guys leaving what looked like the gym and raced that way. In a locked cabinet marked AED he saw a gray plastic box. But where was the key?

"Hey," Anne called from down the hall, the phone pressed to her ear. She threw a set of keys to him. His hands shook as he tried three before finding the right one.

Back in the meeting room, he passed the AED to Christie. She thanked him with a faint smile before turning her attention back to his friend. Who was this capable, take-charge woman?

"Would you lift him to the floor?"

Eli scooped John from the chair and laid him down, sliding his jacket beneath his friend's head. Christie pulled up John's shirt and pressed two adhesive pads to his chest while the rest of the support group sat in a worried huddle. An automatic voice rang out that it was assessing the patient. Eli's heartbeat thundered in his ears.

After a moment, the voice warned all to stand clear; a shock was advised. Christie pressed an orange button and stepped back, her eyes meeting Eli's. Her calm expression slowed his racing pulse. Clearly, she knew what she was doing.

A jolt shuddered through John and his lids fluttered open. "Wharrrr—" he slurred.

She smoothed John's glistening forehead then pressed her fingers to the base of his throat. Behind them, seats shifted and creaked as the group strained to see what was happening.

"Is he going to be okay?" someone whispered.

"John, stay with me. The ambulance will be here any minute," she said, but John's eyes closed once more.

"No!" Eli burst out. This was not happening.

She took her fingers off John's neck. "No pulse. Starting chest compressions," she announced to no one in particular. "The AED needs two minutes to recharge."

He scrambled over to John's other side and grabbed his friend's limp hand. *Hang on, buddy,* he pleaded silently. *You can do this.*

Christie began rhythmically pressing John's chest. "Is he breathing?"

Eli gawked at her. If John wasn't breathing, that meant he was—

"Put your ear next to his mouth."

He bent toward John and felt a faint rush of air against his cheek. "Yes. Still breathing."

Thank you, God.

She checked his pulse again. "Still no pulse."

The whimpering behind them gave way to all-out crying as she resumed her chest compressions with cool precision. A minute later, the AED announced its readiness. She hit the button and they moved away before it zapped John again.

Eli and Christie exchanged a worried look. She probably felt as scared as he did, but she hadn't panicked under pressure. She was a competent professional and he'd made all the wrong assumptions about this strong woman.

After the unit completed its round of electricity, Christie felt for John's pulse. His breath caught when her eyes squeezed shut, a tear slipping through her lashes. He rubbed a hand across his eyes. *No. No way. Not now, John.*

"Pulse is faint, but it's steady," she whispered and opened moist eyes. Suddenly, she rocked back on her heels. Without thinking twice, he ducked over to her side and slid an arm around her waist for support.

She'd saved John's life.

Christie blinked up at him but made no move away from his touch. "Thank you," she said, a blue vein standing out on her pale forehead. "I'm not usually so…" Her voice trailed off as she looked over at John again.

She really was something—unflappable when

it counted most, when he could hardly see straight. Eli's fingers tightened around her slender waist.

"Coming through," hollered one of the two men pushing a stretcher. She gave herself a small shake then took off the AED unit before he helped them lift John onto the lowered gurney. While they checked vitals, Christie summarized what had taken place.

"Good work." An EMT nodded to her before tucking a chart under his arm. "Who's coming with John?"

"Me," Eli and Christie said.

"Only one rider, up front with the driver. Decide fast and meet us outside in thirty seconds."

Eli's shoulders drooped. Without a babysitter he'd have to renege on the vow he'd made John to stay with him, see him through whatever happened. But asking Mary to stay was out of the question. She deserved this special night with her husband.

"I guess it's you." He folded John's wheelchair and picked up his coat. "I promised John I'd be there if the end came, but I don't have child care."

She studied him for a moment then surprised him. "Obviously you and John are close. If you feel comfortable with it, you could give me your address and I'll watch Tommy and Becca."

"You would do that?"

She nodded. "But I'd want an update every half hour. Deal?"

The children had met her twice. And he'd seen her in action. They couldn't be in safer hands. Besides, Mary would give Christie the third degree before she'd even let her into the apartment. Mary would make it work. "Thank you. It means more than you know."

When he rattled off the address, she pressed something furry into his hand and closed his fingers around it. "Trust me. I know how important it is to be there for your friend. And that's for good luck."

He called Mary from the ambulance then unfurled his other hand to reveal a rabbit's foot. *Seriously?* He tucked it into his pocket, wondering how someone who dealt with loss all the time could believe in something like that.

"Lucky for this guy a nurse was there. She saved his life," the EMT said.

Eli peered out of the ambulance's passenger window at the disappearing YMCA. He imagined Christie in full-on pep mode, offering hope and comfort. The platitudes hadn't been an act. And the EMT was right—she did save lives.

But as his fingers dug into the lucky rabbit's foot, he knew firsthand that no amount of comfort, luck or medical skill could rescue some people.

CHAPTER TWO

AFTER CONCLUDING THE support-group meeting with reassurances and hugs, Christie huddled beside Eli's brick prewar apartment building on a narrow SoHo street. Streetlamps glowed to life as the purple dusk deepened, illuminating pavement shining from the evening's drizzle. A few buildings away, a Korean deli's green awning stretched over flower-filled buckets. She inhaled the sweet scent, desperately needing some grounding after tonight's ordeal with John.

Her insides still shook, but at least her hands had quit trembling. The need to save John had gone beyond professional, firing through her with a desperation stirred up by ghosts from her past. Maybe that was part of the reason she'd been unable to simply go home afterward. If she couldn't be at the hospital, she was glad, at least, to be here, where she was guaranteed updates.

John should have arrived at Bellevue by now, and the critical-care team would be working hard to stabilize him. Given his already-compromised health, the group faced a serious challenge. But didn't they always? And John's strong, larger-than-life persona would help him conquer this setback. It had to.

She shifted her weight to her right foot and pulled her damp shirt from her shivering body. How much longer would Mary keep her outside? She had promised to watch Eli's children so he could stay with John. And if she didn't get inside soon, she might miss hearing the latest on John's condition.

"Ms. Bates?" Mary's voice crackled through a brass speaker.

She pressed the talk button. "Yes. I'm still here." Emphasis on the *still*. She shifted to her left foot.

"My husband ran your license number and it seems you're all clear."

"Your husband?" Mary had some serious connections. Getting inside Eli's building was tougher than gaining clearance at the Pentagon.

"He's a sergeant at the Sixth Precinct on West Tenth Street," said Mary, pride ringing in every word.

"A man in blue? He must be handsome, then."

"There's nothing like a man in a uniform," Mary gushed, the sound of the buzzer ending her sentence.

Christie's sneakers squelched across a white marble floor to elevators with wrought-iron gates. A bronze art-deco light fixture made of scalloped glass dangled from a fifteen-foot ceiling with crown moldings.

This was the glamorous New York she'd envisioned back when she'd sat on her front porch swing in Kansas, dreaming of the day she'd rejoin Gran in the big city. Visiting her widowed grandmother had fueled her desire to become part of this vibrant, cosmopolitan world once more. She'd never forgotten her old neighborhood's Irish street festivals and specialty shops, and its fine-dining and family-style restaurants.

She pressed the elevator button and stepped back to watch an ornate dial twitch closer to the lobby. When the elevator dinged, the familiar panic about entering an enclosed space clutched at her throat. An image of her brother's casket flashed in her mind before she could block it. Where had that memory come from? She thought she'd locked it up and thrown away the key.

She searched her purse with trembling hands. Where was her lucky rabbit's foot? She'd had it for ages. Wait. She'd given it to Eli. She squeezed her eyes shut and pictured John. He needed it more than she did. She pulled the crisscrossed metal gate open and forced herself inside.

"One hundred, ninety-nine, ninety-eight..." she counted, a coping trick her psychologist friend and roommate, Laura, had taught her. She whispered "ninety-four" before the doors swooshed open, the lit button indicating the top floor. *Impressive.* Whatever Eli did for a living, he must be very good at it.

"Christie!" Tommy yelled as he burst through the double doors of his apartment. He wore dinosaur-patterned pajamas and massive green claw slippers. His wet hair and clean scent suggested a recent bath.

"Hey, Tommy." She strained to keep her voice calm as she tugged at the stuck elevator gate.

"I'll get you out, Christie. Daddy says I'm strong." Tommy wrapped his small fingers around the metal strips and pulled. A golden retriever bounded out and barked.

"Scout. Tommy. Back inside." Mary appeared, shooed the two into the apartment and turned to Christie. "My dear, are you all right?"

Christie slowed her breathing and dropped the hand hovering over her chest. Blackness crept around the edges of her vision.

"I can't get the gate open," she gasped. How much longer before she passed out? How mortifying if she did.

"We've asked the condo board to replace this

thing a hundred times but they claim it's too valuable." Mary yanked the gate upward and sideways, applied a light kick to the bottom left corner and pulled. With a grating squeal the apparatus came loose. "Looks like a piece of scrap metal to me."

Saved! Christie stumbled out and dragged in a deep breath.

"Thank you." She tried to pull it together. The ambulance call and the high emotions of the night had shaken more than just her claustrophobia.

"We should thank you. Eli would have been crushed if he couldn't be there for John."

"Has he called?"

Mary nodded. "While you were outside. He said to tell you that John's condition is stable but still critical. Oh. And that he'll call you again soon."

She smiled in relief. John's life had hung by a thread at the YMCA. Thank goodness for Eli's quick-thinking aid. She might be a trained RN, but she hadn't been on a code response team in years. She wasn't used to the adrenaline rush that came with that kind of pressure. Having him beside her had helped keep her steady.

"Christie, are you coming?" Tommy called.

He held out a silver purse. "And you forgot this, Mary."

Mary took the purse and put an arm around Tommy. "I would have been sadder if I'd forgotten your good-night kiss." Tommy tipped his bright head back, his dimples so like his father's.

"Goodbye, Becca," Mary called through the doorway.

Tommy waved a dismissive hand. "She's in her room talking to her boyfriend." He clamped a hand over his mouth. "Oops, I wasn't supposed to tell."

"We'll deal with that tomorrow, dear." Mary ruffled Tommy's hair, stepped into the elevator and gave a last wave.

Tommy grabbed Christie's hand and yanked her inside. An excited Scout wove in and out of their legs, halting them to beg for an ear scratch before moving aside.

"Want to see my dinosaur? His name's Rexie and he's awesome."

"Sure." She smiled as the youngster scampered down the hall to her right, Scout hot on his heels. She turned to survey the rest of the apartment and— Wow.

A mammoth open space, so unlike the illegally sublet SoHo loft she and Laura shared, yawned before her. Despite the vintage exterior, the apartment had an ultramodern aesthetic that blended rather than clashed with its Corinthian columns. Square light panels alternated in a checkered pattern across the vaulted tin ceiling. A woven beige area rug covered gleaming maple floors. Floor-to-ceiling windows encompassed an entire wall, commanding a panoramic view of the neighborhood and city. The neutral color palate, repeated in black leather couches with white and beige accent pillows, was broken by vibrant artwork and framed photographs. The apartment could have graced the cover of a decorating magazine…if it wasn't completely and utterly trashed.

Holy cow.

She leaned against the closed door and gaped at the mess. It looked as if a Kansas twister had barreled through the room, scattering papers, books, toys and, of all things, a sewing machine covered in fabric pieces, feathers and open bags of sequins and rhinestones. Not that the place was dirty. In fact, every uncovered surface shone. No doubt Mary was doing her best to keep things clean, but why leave it so untidy?

She twitched at the lack of organization and bent to pick up a paperback.

"Dad doesn't like anyone touching his stuff," Becca said behind her.

Christie put the book on a recessed shelf and turned. "I can see that." She smiled at the young girl, who wore a pink tank top and gray sweatpants. Her dark hair hung past her shoulders in loose curls. "How are you, Becca?"

"Good. A little hungry, though," Becca laughed. "I can never eat enough after dance class." She looked around and lowered her voice. "Is Mr. Vaccaro going to be okay?"

"He's getting the best possible care," Christie assured the girl. Good thing her voice sounded steady. When she'd seen John sitting so still in his wheelchair, she'd felt as if her own heart had quit beating. "Now, let's find you something to eat."

"Oh. Me, too. Me, too." Tommy burst from behind his sister and dropped his plastic *Tyrannosaurus rex*. Scout snatched the toy, trotted to a plaid dog bed beside the door and settled down to gnaw on the dinosaur's tail.

"It looks like everyone's starving." Christie eyed Scout. "Give," she commanded in her firmest nurse voice. The dog's mouth slackened, the toy dropping to the floor.

"Wow." Becca tucked her hair behind her

ears. "He never listens to anyone. How did you do that?"

She grabbed the toy and sidestepped a shoe pile on her way to the kitchen. "I have a dog, too." She turned on the hot water and washed the dinosaur in a double sink set in a black granite countertop.

It felt good to clean. Create order. There was nothing like busywork to distract her from worries. She took her first solid breath since she'd noticed John was unconscious.

"What kind of dog? Is he big like Scout?" Tommy and Becca seated themselves in beige leather stools at the counter that separated the kitchen from the rest of the living space.

"*He* is actually a *she* and her name's Sweet Pea." She handed Tommy the slobber-free *T. rex*. Scout trotted over at the toy's reappearance but scuttled back at her stern look. She glanced at a stainless-steel microwave over a matching cooktop. It was 8:15. How much longer until Eli called again?

"Sweet Pea." Becca spun in her seat. "That's such a cute name. What kind of dog is she?"

She smiled, picturing her small, white-and-tan dog. On her way to the apartment, she'd phoned Laura, who'd agreed to walk Sweet Pea. How lucky to have such an amazing roommate.

She'd pick up Laura's favorite frozen yogurt, Pinkberry's chocolate with honey-almond granola topping, on her way home.

"She's a Cavalier King Charles spaniel." She thumbed to a photo of Sweet Pea on her iPhone and passed it to the kids. She headed to the fridge. "How do grilled-cheese sandwiches sound?"

"Are they the healthy kind?" Tommy's fingers traced Sweet Pea's long ears and their curly fur.

Christie paused on her way back to the counter, organic cheese and butter in hand. "Do you have whole-wheat bread?"

Becca grimaced. "That's the *only* kind we have. Dad's been a complete health-food nut ever since—" Her face froze and she fell silent.

Christie located the bread behind a stack of unopened mail while her mind turned over the possibilities of Becca's unfinished sentence. Although Eli had sounded annoyed at the cancer-support-group meeting, she'd glimpsed pain, too. Was his decision to be more health conscious related to that?

"This is seriously the cutest dog ever." Becca held up the iPhone, Sweet Pea's tilted head and tiny snout on display.

"Is she a puppy?" Tommy got to his knees and stretched toward an overhead pot rack.

"Here." He handed her a frying pan as Becca steadied his stool.

"Thanks." Christie hunted for a spatula and a butter knife. "Sweet Pea's almost ten, which is old for a diabetic dog."

Becca came around the counter, pulled open a couple of drawers and located the utensils. "Need a hand?"

"Sure. Would you turn on the cooktop while I butter the bread?"

"What's tiabetic mean?" Tommy hopped off his stool and stood next to Christie. "I can help, too."

"It's *di*abetic, Little Man." Becca grabbed a buttered sandwich. "It means she needs shots." The frying pan hissed as she placed it inside. "Insulin, right?"

Christie nodded, impressed. "Twice a day, breakfast and dinner." She handed Tommy two cheese slices, which he lined up with careful precision, tongue sticking out between his teeth. "Becca, I'll take over the frying, okay?"

"Why do you do that?" Tommy placed the last piece of bread on top and followed her to the range. "Shots hurt."

Becca pulled Tommy away from the hot pan and wrapped her arms around him. "Because if she didn't, Sweet Pea would die. We learned that in health class."

"Die?" Tommy looked stricken. He ran back to his stool and picked up the iPhone.

Christie turned from the stove and gave Tommy a reassuring look. "Not until it's her time, Tommy. Her medicine keeps her healthy and I make sure she gets it every day."

Tommy's quivering lip stilled and Christie flipped the browned sandwich.

Why had Becca said that? The bluntness of teenagers. Her veterinarian had advised her to euthanize Sweet Pea years ago, saying that she'd go blind (she hadn't) and that it would be difficult to keep up with the shots (it wasn't). Sweet Pea's life expectancy was shorter than other dogs, but it only made their time together more precious. She would rather have ten years with Sweet Pea than fifteen with another dog.

"My daddy got medicine so he wouldn't die," Tommy blurted.

Christie nearly dropped the cooked sandwich as she slid it onto a plate. Was he saying his father had been treated for a terminal illness? Her insides clenched.

"Tommy!" Becca scowled and passed him the dish. "Eat."

"Well, it's true." Tommy ignored the steaming

food. "And Christie understands 'cause she helps other people with cancer, like Mr. Vaccaro."

"Yes, I do." The spatula slipped from her grip and clattered to the floor. She bent down and rested her forehead against a lower cabinet, hiding her surprise. So it *was* true. Eli was recovering from cancer. Her stomach twisted in empathy for him and his children. What they must be going through, and by the look of things, without a wife or mother to help. No wonder he sounded bitter. She grabbed the utensil and rose, her face as composed as possible.

She turned off the stove and handed a scowling Becca the last grilled cheese. "Becca, eat something."

"Dad doesn't want people knowing." Becca pushed the plate away. "He won't let us talk about it with anyone. Even each other. Ever."

Becca's frustration touched a chord, her distant behavior toward her father suddenly making sense. Becca didn't ignore him out of anger—she avoided him out of fear. And Christie should know; she'd done it to her own brother.

She hated thinking about that painful time in her life. But Becca's reaction to her father's illness reminded Christie so much of herself at that age. Confused, hurt and lost.

She waved the grilled cheese under Becca's

nose until the girl gave her a reluctant smile and grabbed the sandwich. "Please don't worry," she said. "Everything will work itself out."

"So you *can* help Daddy!" Tommy's blue eyes were wide and bright.

"I can't promise you that." She looked from a crestfallen Tommy to a narrow-eyed Becca. "But if he gives his permission, you can call me anytime to talk."

"Anytime?" Becca looked at her intently. "Even really late?"

Her heart squeezed tight at the thought of Becca—scarcely more than a child herself— scared for her father with nowhere to turn.

"As late as you need," she promised, hoping she wasn't getting too involved in Eli's personal life.

Then again, helping kids deal with cancer was her job. If only Eli could see how much his kids needed to talk through their fear, she'd be happy to help. Besides, it wasn't as if she was getting involved with him. His handsome, anguished face came to mind. Now that was a risk she didn't trust her heart to take.

The phone rang, breaking the silence. Becca grabbed the cordless. "Hello?" She listened for a moment then shoved the handset to Christie. "It's Dad," she said, her voice hollow.

"Thanks, Becca. Hello?" She clutched the phone and paced. The children's eyes followed her.

"Ms. Bates, it's Eli. How are the kids doing?"

"They're great." She grinned at Tommy as he polished off his sandwich. His gap-toothed smile was really too precious, especially with cheese squirting out of it. "They're eating sandwiches, and then I think we'll watch a little TV before bed."

Becca finished her last bite and carried the dirty plates to the dishwasher. When she returned to the counter, she helped Tommy climb onto her back and carried him to the living room.

"That sounds perfect." A feeling of lightness overcame her at the husky cadence of his voice. "But bedtime's at nine, so not too much TV, okay?"

"Nine o'clock. Got it." She heard cartoon voices from the living room, where Tommy and Becca sat watching a talking sponge on a flat-screen TV.

"How's John?" She cradled the phone between her ear and shoulder and began cleaning the countertop.

"The same. Stable, but still critical. We're waiting for some test results. How much longer can you stay?"

She eyed the snuggling siblings, grateful for the company they'd given her tonight. "As long as you need."

"Thank you, Ms. Bates, for everything— helping with the kids, letting me stay with John." His voice thickened. "Saving his life. I think I gave you a hard time tonight, and I'm sorry."

Warmth rushed through her at his admission. "Don't give it another thought. And please call me Christie. Would you let me know when John's condition improves?"

"When or if?"

"When. Think positively."

His laugh wasn't exactly warm and fuzzy, but then again, it didn't sound bitter. "You never quit with that faith and hope stuff, do you?"

She grinned as she swiped a damp paper towel across the cooktop. "Nope."

"Then you'll have to hope for the both of us."

"I can manage that. And, Eli?"

"You know. That's the first time you've called me that, Christie."

Her heart did a little flip. "Oh."

He cleared his throat. "Sorry. What were you going to say?"

She turned her back to the living room and lowered her voice. "Take care of yourself." A quiet moment passed. Then another. "Eli, are you still there?"

"Yes," he breathed. "It's been a long time since anyone's said that to me."

Despite her best intentions, things *were* getting personal. "Just part of my job," she said offhandedly, not feeling casual at all.

"Oh. Right. Of course." His gruff voice returned. "I'll call you soon. And, Christie?"

"Yes?"

"I'll see you when I get home."

For a moment, she warmed to the image. A strong, caring man coming home—to her. Then she shook off the ridiculous sentiment. After tonight, they'd never see each other again. And it was for the best.

She'd vowed to care for support-group attendees. Falling for them, however, was not an option.

ELI CLICKED OFF the phone and slumped in an upholstered chair in the Bellevue emergency-department waiting room. Beside him, a young mother jiggled a wailing toddler. A large family huddled on a nearby couch, some weeping while others paced. A young man hollered and punched a soda machine until uniformed security officers dragged him away. The air was thick and smelled of antiseptic, illness and despair.

Was it possible to feel both glad to be somewhere and wish you were anywhere else?

He watched the harried nurse at the reception desk briskly sort patients. Her calm, nononsense manner reminded him of Christie and the impressive way she'd managed John's emergency.

He leaned his head against the wall and replayed his conversation with her. The way she'd said his name had loosened something balled up inside him. For a moment he'd imagined himself in another place and time, able to date a woman like her.

He strode to a glass vending machine and glimpsed his reflection.

Fool.

He was a single father recovering from cancer…not exactly the catch of the century.

Hadn't the desertion of his ex-wife, Jacqueline, taught him anything? Cancer infected more than bodies. It destroyed relationships, too. He might be in remission now. But what if his cancer returned? To protect his children, he'd never let another woman into his life or theirs.

Eli dropped some coins in the slot and grabbed the bag of trail mix that fell to the bottom. He glanced at the clock. How long since the nurse's last update on John? There was no lineup at her desk. Now was the perfect time to ask.

She looked up from her computer with a weary expression.

"Mr. Roberts, you're still not allowed to go inside. Family members and caregivers only," she repeated patiently for the umpteenth time.

"I rode in the ambulance with him."

The nurse inclined her head, the harsh light casting shadows on her gaunt cheeks. "I'm afraid that's not enough."

Eli smiled politely and handed her the un-opened bag of trail mix. He'd lost his appetite. "It's all right. I understand."

But he didn't. In what universe did biology count more than humanity? Despite repeated calls, John's sons hadn't bothered to show to-night.

He crossed to the window and watched rain blur the city's lights into a colorful kaleidoscope. Ninety minutes had passed and he needed to re-assure John that he wasn't fighting alone. But how could he get by security? He paced, each step taking him nowhere fast.

A half hour later, his cell phone buzzed.

"Eli?"

Christie. He sat in the nearest chair and gripped the phone. "Are the kids okay?"

"Fine. They went to bed like angels. Listen, I was wondering if you preferred your books alphabetized or lined up according to size?"

What? Was she organizing his apartment? He liked it the way it was. Jacqueline had never allowed Tommy's toys or Becca's dance gear around, the regulated order a constant reminder of how he'd never fit into her picture-perfect world. Nowadays, the chaos kept them from remembering their past.

"Christie. Please don't touch anything."

"Oh. Okay. Did the test results come back on John?"

He pulled out her rabbit's foot and ran his fingers along the soft fur. "I don't know. They won't let me see him."

"Who's on the front desk?"

He peered at the nurse. "I think her name tag says Rachel Smith-something."

"Smitherson." Her voice rose. "I know her. Put her on and tell her it's me."

"You're not related, either."

"No. But I'm also not a defeatist."

"Or a realist," he said dryly.

"Please give her your cell, Eli."

How could he say no when she said his name

like that? He walked over and handed Nurse Smitherson the phone. "Christie Bates for you."

The woman listened for a moment then smiled up at him. Was Christie making some headway?

"Of course, Christie. If I'd known, I would have kept the gentleman apprised. I'll have him come back right now." She handed him the phone and pointed to wooden double doors that separated the waiting area and the emergency room.

A buzzer sounded and the doors opened.

"Follow me." She led him to a room filled with beeping machines and uniformed professionals. "Dr. Landon, when you have a moment, would you please update Mr. Roberts? He's Mr. Vaccaro's health proxy."

"What's going on?" Christie's faint voice sounded. He brought the phone back to his ear.

"How did I become John's health proxy?" he whispered. "And I'm not sure what's going on. The doctor's coming out soon."

"You take care of John, right?"

"Right." He dodged a gurney wheeled by a medical technician.

"Then that's close enough. By a stretch. But we're desperate here."

He chuckled. "You are something."

"I might say the same of you."

"The doctor's here. I've got to go."

He punched off the phone and followed a middle-aged woman in a white coat to a nearby alcove.

"We've just gotten Mr. Vaccaro's test results, so your timing is perfect." The doctor opened a chart and perused its contents. After what felt like an eternity, she looked at him once more, her face grave. His fingers tightened around the rabbit's foot.

If nothing else, it prevented him from digging holes in his own palm, right?

"I'm afraid Mr. Vaccaro has suffered a thrombotic stroke from a heart arrhythmia. It does not appear related to his cancer nor does it seem to have aggravated it. In fact, the MRI shows tumor shrinkage."

He rubbed his eyes. Was he hearing good news?

"Although I can't predict how completely he'll recover from the stroke, he's regained seventy percent of his mobility and all of his speech. As for his heart, a pacemaker will control the arrhythmia." Dr. Landon's mouth twitched in a wry smile. "It seems he'd like a glass of whiskey."

He could have kissed her. John was a fighter.

He would recover from the stroke, and better yet, his cancer was responding to treatment. He squeezed the rabbit's foot, for real this time, feeling like the luckiest man in the world.

He thanked the doctor and strode to John's room. A nurse removed a blood-pressure cuff and made space for him.

"John. It's Eli." He squeezed John's hand and was relieved to feel the pressure returned. "The doctor says your tumor shrank and the stroke is under control."

"James," John murmured, his eyes opening and closing.

"No. It's Eli."

John pointed a plastic-encased finger. "Jameson."

Eli grinned. John's favorite whiskey. "I'll bring it when I visit tomorrow." He lowered John's hand to the sheet.

"Put it in my IV." John's chuckle turned into a cough.

A nurse rushed in. "I'm afraid it's time to go, sir." She steered him out of the room.

In the hall, he spotted John's sons and tensed. They strolled his way in no apparent hurry.

"How's old Pop doing?" the older son, Brian, asked.

"See for yourself," he called over his shoulder and sprinted outside. A taxi jerked to a halt at his raised hand.

He had someone much more important with whom to share this good news. And once he'd done that, he told himself sternly, he'd see Christie into a cab and out of his life.

No matter that she was the first woman to make him smile in too long to remember.

CHAPTER THREE

CHRISTIE TOSSED ANOTHER magazine on the floor and stepped back to study the effect. She dragged a hand through her hair. Still not messy enough. Eli would know she'd organized his apartment if she'd didn't put it back to rights—or wrongs—but still. She should have listened to Becca's warning but hadn't believed anyone would prefer a messy house. After speaking to Eli, though, she understood she was wrong. It was his home and the way he wanted it. She respected that. In fact, there was a lot about the gruff Mr. Roberts she was starting to admire. He was a loyal friend, protective father and considerate employer.

If only he understood that shielding his children from his cancer did more harm than good. They needed to talk about their feelings, not bottle them up. Becca barely spoke to him. How much longer before Tommy followed suit?

Her gran always said, "There are no unmixed blessings in life." Eli had regained his health but was losing his family. How could she help him understand? And was it her place to? He hadn't asked for help, though his children had.

She tugged some books from a shelf and checked her watch—10:00. Why hadn't Eli called? Surely he had John's test results by now. Maybe his cell battery had quit? Or he and John were visiting? She scattered pillows on the floor. If only he'd give her a quick call and reassure her.

Without warning, the lights went out, plunging her into complete darkness. The soft hum of the refrigerator quit along with the whirring central air conditioning. She froze, a tingle of alarm running up her spine. The building was old. Had its power failed? Her claustrophobia returned with a vengeance.

Everything felt close, the heavy blackness pressing all around, dragging her down like... She clutched a pillow to her galloping heart, the remembered sound of thudding dirt on a lowered casket echoing faintly in her ears. She inhaled and exhaled slowly. No. She hadn't had those nightmares in a long time. Why were so many memories resurfacing today? Perhaps John's close call had shaken them loose.

Christie felt her way to the glass wall and raised the shades. Light glowed softly from covered windows across the street, the overcast sky obscuring the moon. No help there. She sank into a nearby chair and focused. Laura had taught her that if she altered her thoughts they'd change her emotions and behavior. Instead of cowering like a scared mouse, she'd find candles. Yes. Hadn't she seen some tapers in pewter holders on the mantel? There must be more.

No sense sitting in the cloying murk. She needed to open the windows and strike some matches.

Eli's home was overdue for some fresh air and light.

"HERE WE ARE, SIR," the cabbie announced at the Broome Street address.

"Thanks." Eli thrust a twenty at the driver and jumped out of the cab.

He peered up at his dark building. What a wild night. He'd attended his first cancer-support-group meeting, met a woman who both frustrated and fascinated him, helped save his best friend's life, and now this—a building power outage. So much for the promised update to its faulty electrical system.

He shook his head. Christie probably had a fanciful saying about life having some sort of plan. But he knew better. Everything, every single thing, happened by chance without consideration for timing or convenience. Random events could be kind or cruel. And meeting someone who piqued his interest, at this point in his life, felt like a little bit of both.

He unlocked the building's leaded glass door and shut it behind him. For once he was glad the super refused to update the antiquated entrance. A key in a lock always worked, regardless of an overtaxed electric system. The thought of his children alone in the dark made him take the stairs two at a time.

A sixth-floor penthouse was as safe as you got in a power failure. But still. His kids were all he had. And nothing bad would happen to them as long as he lived. If he lived. His chest tightened.

Exactly how long would that be? Would he teach Tommy and Becca to parallel park? Admire them in their graduation robes? Walk Becca down the aisle and shake Tommy's hand when each of them got married…hold his grandchildren? His eyes stung at the thought.

He paused on the fourth-floor landing and rubbed his aching calf. It'd never been the same since they'd replaced his diseased fibula with titanium. In fact, nothing seemed the same. Surviving cancer felt like living in a house of cards.

At any moment, everything he'd built could fall apart.

A couple of minutes later, he found his door and fumbled for the lock, the metal key scraping against the wooden panels. After several attempts, the tip of the key slipped in. He slammed through the door in an instant.

"Take one more step and it will be your last," warned a voice in the dark.

O-kay. Not exactly the homecoming he'd looked forward to. He wasn't used to knocking on his own door.

He peered into the dim room and saw the outline of a slender woman standing on a chair.

"Christie?"

"Eli?"

She clutched something large over her head, the chair wobbling. He lunged as the object— a hefty volume from his bookshelves, he realized—fell from her grip.

"Ouch!"

"Oh, my goodness. Did that hit your foot?"

"Yes," he grunted, sliding off his shoe to rub his big toe. "Lucky you didn't get my head."

She took his offered hand and stepped lightly to the floor. "*Lucky* you still have my rabbit's foot." Her white teeth flashed in the dark.

"I would have preferred steel-toed boots." He

limped into his living room. His very tidy living room, he noticed, now that his eyes were adjusting to the dimness. Had she organized despite what he'd told her?

"How about an ice pack instead?" she called from the kitchen. He heard the freezer door open. "It's a little melted, but still cold."

"Sounds fine." He looked around the candlelit room. "I like what you've done with the place," he said, meaning it, to his surprise.

She'd lined up their shoes and arranged Tommy's action figures in dramatic poses. The sewing area resembled a tailor shop with Becca's costume materials sorted and folded. Wow. He'd never spend another hour searching for lavender sequins again. Christie's version of order felt homey rather than sterile. Perhaps he'd been wrong to insist on the chaos.

"Oh, about that—" She leaned close to place a cold bag across his toes. "I clean when I worry. When you asked me not to touch your things, it was too late." She sat beside him on the couch. "But since the kids went to bed, I've been making it messy again." She gestured to a few books and pillows on the floor.

This was her version of a mess? He almost laughed until he took in her apologetic expression.

"It's fine." He spread his hands, glad she

hadn't headed out the door as soon as he returned home. He was way too keyed up to sleep, and he couldn't deny he just flat-out wanted to know more about her. "Actually, it's great. Really."

Her soft sigh whispered past his ear as she settled deeper into a corner of the sectional. "That's a relief. How's John?"

"Good. He's gotten back most of his movement and all of his speech." He inhaled her wildflower scent, the subtle aroma wreaking havoc with his senses. *Stay focused.* "In fact, he asked for some Jameson."

She laughed, the jubilant sound infectious. He couldn't remember the last time he'd enjoyed sharing a laugh with a woman. Strange. He'd won back his life, but he hadn't really been living it, he realized. There was danger in wanting things, in dreaming of a future when you couldn't guarantee tomorrow.

"John will be asking to go to the White Horse Tavern, then."

"Have you been there?" It was a popular neighborhood pub. Did she live in SoHo?

"My gran lives on Bleecker and I'm on Spring. I take her there every Sunday after church."

The contradictory nature of cities, living near people you never met, surprised him anew.

What would have happened had they run into each other years ago?

"Is she Irish?" he asked. A breeze from an open window blew her fragrant hair against his cheek.

"To be sure," she said with an exaggerated inflection then laughed. "Gran immigrated when she was twenty." She pulled her hair back and began braiding. "How did you know?"

He resisted the urge to touch the soft strands tickling his neck. "Something in your voice. And this." He held out her lucky rabbit's foot.

Her fingers brushed his as she took it.

"I wished I'd had it when your elevator trapped me."

He frowned. His super would get a call tomorrow. First the power, now this. That gate was a menace. "How long were you stuck?"

Her laughter sounded again in the softly lit room. "No more than a minute. But it was enough. I'm claustrophobic. And a bit dramatic, if I'm honest. Perhaps I should have gone into acting instead of nursing—well, pediatric grief counseling now."

"No," he exclaimed. Her face reflected the surprise he felt at his outburst. Well, now he'd need to explain. "You're so good at what you do. Trust me. You'd never want to go into entertainment."

She cocked her head and toyed with the fringe on a pillow. "And why is that, I wonder?"

"I've photographed actors and models. It's an artificial world and you, you're so—" He grappled with how to finish his thought.

"It's all right." She looked down at her hands. "I know I'm no beauty."

What? He studied the adorable tilt of her nose and the curve of her generous lower lip, the shadowed light enhancing her unique looks. She had occupied his thoughts the better part of the night and didn't have a clue.

"You're real," he said, figuring it was safe to admit that much. "That's the only difference."

"Oh." Silence stretched between them. "Don't you like working with beautiful women every day?"

"It was a paycheck." Makeup and hair extensions didn't add up to beauty in his eyes.

"Was?"

"Now I run my own graphic-design business from home. But I used to work for *Faire du Charme* magazine." He held up one of the glossy publications fanned on his coffee table. Where on earth had she found it? He thought he'd gotten rid of them all.

Christie leafed through the pages. "Impressive. Why did you leave?"

"My ex-wife is the assistant to the editor-in-chief…as well as his current spouse."

"Oh. Sorry to hear that." She studied a large picture on the wall beside his TV. Its simple black frame set off rows of waving corn and a red tractor beneath a hazy purple sky. "Is that what you photograph now?"

He wished. Artistic photography was a financial gamble. To provide for Jacqueline's expensive lifestyle, he'd put aside his dream of showing his work in a gallery. Once his illness arrived, and she left, he'd lost interest in photography altogether. That was, until he'd seen Christie. Her mobile face made him itch to capture every expression.

"Haven't taken a picture in over two years. I took that one seventeen years ago, the day I graduated high school. Working that farm paid for my ticket to New York." He stood and walked toward the kitchen, his foot recovered. "Would you like something to drink?"

"That's okay," she replied. "I probably should get going."

Eli put up a hand to forestall her rise from the couch. "Please stay. The elevator's out and stairs are dangerous in the dark. Besides, I'm still too wired to sleep after what happened to John. I'd appreciate the company."

She considered him for a moment then put her purse back on the coffee table. "All right. Anything that's still cold would be great, then, thanks."

He grabbed a couple of glasses from the cabinet and noticed that she'd arranged the kids' artwork on the refrigerator door. Someone had drawn a picture of a blond-haired boy in a race car, and he guessed Tommy had put Christie to work on the sketch. With an effort, he swallowed down old resentments at Jacqueline's absence from the kids' lives.

"How does sweet tea sound?" he asked, trying to get his head back into their conversation.

"Perfect. Where was the picture taken? It reminds me of home—Kansas."

Back in the living room, he wiped the condensation from the glass before handing it to Christie.

"I've been to Kansas." He sat beside her and tried to ignore the electric sensation of her arm against his as she lifted her drink.

"Very good," she said after a long gulp. "What part of Kansas?"

"Hutchinson. My parents travel the state-fair circuit. They're in charge of the games on the fair's midway." He winced inside at the crazy sound of that. But it had been his life…well, theirs, really.

"And you?" She traced the rim of her glass and his eye was drawn to her slender fingers.

"I stayed with my grandparents in Kentucky and visited my parents during school vacations. My grandma's the one who taught me how to make sun tea."

"Do you use Luziannc tca bags?"

Eli lowered his glass and nodded. "They're the best. I put the pitcher on the windowsill every morning."

"Your grandma sounds great."

The familiar emptiness rose. "She was. But she passed the year after Becca was born, my grandfather six months later."

Her warm hand found his. "You miss them."

He jerked away, unnerved by the leap of his heart at her touch. "Every day." He stood. "Excuse me. I should check on Becca and Tommy."

In the hall, he pressed his burning forehead against Tommy's door, glad for the shadows. He was enjoying this time with Christie too much. As much as he wanted her to stay, he probably needed her to go before she got under his skin even more. The way she laughed, spoke, touched him…it made him forget the danger she posed. He had no business letting anyone into his life.

Tommy's door creaked as he eased it open. Scout raised his head, ears pricked forward.

"Hey, boy," he whispered. He tiptoed into the room, rubbed Scout's ears and pressed a light kiss to Tommy's forehead. The boy slept on his back, one arm flung across his eyes, the other dangling over the side of his bed. He tucked the loose arm under the covers before backing out and shutting the door.

At Becca's door, he ignored the Keep Out sign and peeked in. Funny how much younger she looked asleep, her face free of the scowls she gave him. He advanced to her bed, gently pulled out her earbuds and placed them with her iPod beside her bed. She turned over and muttered in her sleep. After a moment her quiet breathing resumed, and he returned to the hall, his equanimity restored.

Seeing his children firmed his resolve to separate Christie from their lives. She was charming. Too charming. It'd be easy for them to get attached.

Though Becca and Tommy rarely complained, he knew their mother's abandonment had crushed them. She rarely called and visited even less. He tried to keep up a pretense that Jacqueline cared, assuring them that her work took her to countries without reliable cell service. He even bought them Christmas and birthday presents and signed her name. But it wasn't enough. Not even close. And he'd never let anyone hurt them like that again.

When he returned, he found Christie pacing by the window, purse in hand.

"I should be going, Eli. I really don't mind navigating my way out."

"A marble staircase without lights? Never a good idea." His eyes searched hers, willing her to stay longer. He could keep a few boundaries without letting her go off just yet. "Won't you stay until the electricity's back?"

She nodded, the candlelight silhouetting her in gold. "If you want me to."

"I do." With a firm hand on her back, he guided her back to the couch. This time, he seated himself in a chair—it was safer that way.

"So tell me about Kansas."

Her expression stilled. Strange. He imagined her life filled with homecoming parades and town picnics.

"Do you have any brothers or sisters?" he probed.

"An older brother. William." She wrapped her

arms around herself and leaned forward. "He passed away when I turned eighteen."

He half rose then sat back down. "I'm sorry. You don't have to talk about it." He wanted to offer comfort, but how much closer could he afford to get? With an effort, he remained in his seat.

She rubbed her temples. "It's okay. He died of leukemia at the end of my senior year in high school. I moved in with Gran to attend nursing school at Columbia a few months later."

A lot about her suddenly made sense. "Is that why you became a grief counselor?"

Christie's head snapped up. "What? No. Maybe. It's not something I really think about."

"Oh," he said, understanding more than she knew. Strange that she talked about cancer with strangers but when it came to herself, she stayed mum. He wondered if she shared her experience with her support group. Then again, her story didn't have a happy ending—not the positive focus she wanted. Time to switch subjects.

"And your parents. Are they still in Kansas?"

"They died in a car crash during my first year in college."

Eli rose. This time he would go to her. How had he managed to ask such horrible questions? The lights blared on. He blinked away the spots in front of his eyes and saw Christie wipe her damp cheeks. After all she'd been through this evening, he'd made her cry. What an insensitive jerk.

As she walked to the door, he trailed in her wake. He hated to say goodbye after stirring up those painful memories. But with the power back, what excuse did he have for her to stay?

"I'm sorry I brought all of that up."

She rummaged in her purse. "Don't worry. I try not to dwell on it. It's better that way." She jabbed at an unlit cell phone.

Was it better that way? Her closed expression screamed "Drop the subject!" and with difficulty, he did.

"May I call and request a car for you? It's late and I wouldn't want you walking far for a cab."

"Thank you. I was planning to splurge and call for one given the hour, but my battery died."

He dialed the number of a nearby service and watched her withdraw a tissue. She blew her nose and straightened her narrow shoulders. When he hung up, she turned, eyes dry, lips curving upward once more.

Only now he wasn't fooled. That smile covered deep pain. He'd been determined to keep her at arm's length for his children's sake. But now he understood that he needed to stay away for her sake, too. She'd suffered too much loss to spend her days with a guy who might be living on borrowed time. Too bad knowing that didn't make it any easier to say goodbye.

"The driver will be here in five minutes." He recalled her claustrophobia and the unreliable elevator door. "May I see you downstairs?"

Christie nodded and preceded him. "Tell the children I said goodbye."

He pushed the elevator button. "I will. Thanks again for watching them. Oh. And I almost forgot to tell you. The doctor told me John's brain tumor has shrunk."

Her green eyes widened. Was there any color more beautiful? "That's wonderful news. He's had a tough time, but he's a fighter."

When the elevator dinged, he caught the flash of the rabbit's foot disappearing into her hand. What a superstitious little soul. He definitely liked Christie Bates.

They rode the elevator in silence. He glanced her way a few times, wondering at her silently moving lips.

A black car idled by the curb when they stepped into the foyer. So soon. If only they had a few more minutes.

"Goodbye, Eli." Her wistful voice produced an almost-physical ache in his heart. They'd been through a lot tonight. Having it end after her painful admission felt wrong.

Worse, he'd let her share that without ever admitting anything about his condition. Maybe it would be better if she knew. At least then she'd understand why this really needed to be goodbye.

"I have cancer," he blurted. "Had, I mean."

She touched his arm, the gentle sensation lingering long after she dropped her hand. "I'm so glad you're in remission. Tommy told me about your illness, but only because he knows I work with cancer patients. The children respect your wish not to talk about it."

Now, that he had not expected. Did she understand his reason for telling her? That he needed the reminder of why he shouldn't see her again?

The town-car driver honked and she opened the foyer door and walked out. He followed, pulling the car door wide for her.

"Goodbye, Christie." He would remember this night—remember her—for a long time. "Thanks again."

"Take care, Eli." Her voice sounded quiet. Tired.

He nodded, unable to say more as he watched her duck into the car. His feet stayed rooted to the stone stoop long after the taillights disappeared into the rain. If only he was the kind of man who could see her again. A man whose future didn't blur into a question mark.

But now, as he trudged back inside the building, he told himself to focus on his kids and what they needed. If they were confiding in her that he'd put a lockdown on all cancer discussion, maybe his health issues bothered them more than he realized.

And while he might not ever subscribe to the touchy-feely brand of positive thinking that Christie did, he would make sure his kids had someone to talk to. Someone a whole lot better versed in this stuff than him.

Even though an energetic, beautiful nurse and counselor came to mind, he vowed to find someone else.

For both their sakes.

CHAPTER FOUR

"MR. ROBERTS?"

Eli noted the time on his phone then glanced up at the Little Red School House's cardigan-clad secretary. Had forty-five minutes passed already? The emails and pictures he'd been viewing for his graphic-design business had been a welcome distraction from this unexpected meeting with Becca's principal. He powered down his device and stood. "Ready for me?" he asked, not feeling ready at all.

His cell vibrated. But after a quick check to make sure it wasn't a call about John, he shoved the phone back into his pocket. His kids were here at school, so they wouldn't need him. Anyone else would have to wait.

Although, he couldn't say with full certainty what he would have done if Christie Bates's number had come up on his phone.

Her expressive face came to mind along with her lilting voice. Why couldn't he stop thinking about her? It'd been a week since they'd seen each other. Time enough for him to forget a near stranger. But something about her felt familiar. Right.

"This way, sir," the school secretary prompted, jolting him from his thoughts. She peered at him over rimless eyeglasses then gestured into the suite behind her. A telephone shrilled on a chest-high counter.

He stopped behind her when she grabbed the old-fashioned receiver. "Little Red School House," she intoned and dragged the cord to her seat, her round eyes on him. "How may I help you?"

While he waited, he glanced around the bustling space. A copy machine whirred in the background, spitting out collated sheets of paper at regular intervals. File cabinets banged open and shut as a clerk filed paper work in overcrowded drawers. He inhaled the fresh smell of percolating coffee. Too bad he couldn't help himself to a cup. He could use the caffeine boost after pulling an all-nighter putting the finishing touches on the cover design for a novel.

What had Becca done to warrant the school's cryptic summons? Especially so close to the end of the school year? She'd acted normally at breakfast, relatively speaking. He still hadn't reconciled the quiet teen downing her Cheerios with the exuberant daughter he'd raised. That girl would have made Tommy a banana-skin hat and drummed on their heads with her spoon.

Before he could think further along that line, the secretary cleared her throat and pointed down the hallway. He rolled his tense shoulders and started down the short, dim hall. Which room was the principal's? After all these years, it was his first visit to the private office. Becca had never gotten in trouble and was a straight-A student. His eyes narrowed. At least he assumed so. When had he last seen her report card? Keeping up with Becca's and Tommy's lives was his priority. But somewhere, he'd let things slip.

"Welcome, Mr. Roberts," said a diminutive woman when he reached an open door. He recognized her cropped black curls and red, square-framed glasses from last fall's open house. Since he'd been too tired to wait out the eager parents surrounding the new principal, he'd left without saying hello. Now he wished they'd spoken, met under better circumstances. She strode around an imposing wooden desk and extended a hand. "I'm Principal Luce. It's very nice to meet you."

He suppressed a sneeze at her cloying perfume, shook her hand and nodded. "Likewise."

"Please have a seat." She was all business in her navy suit and heels.

He sat on the edge of an upholstered chair,

his fingers forming a steeple. He couldn't take his eyes off the open folder in the middle of her green blotter. Did the top sheet say "Becca Roberts. Disciplinary Referral"? Impossible. This must be a mistake. Leather squeaked and he glanced up to meet Mrs. Luce's steady brown eyes. He ignored the cell phone buzzing on his hip.

"Mr. Roberts, please accept my apologies for calling you in without notice." She inclined her head. "But the seriousness of the situation called for our immediate attention."

He shot to his feet. "Where's Becca? Is she okay?" So help him if anything had happened to his little girl—

"She's eating her lunch in the study room." The principal stood and paced to a water cooler beside her bank of windows. "How about something cool to drink?"

"Sounds good." Relief filled his head like helium. Maybe Becca had forgotten an assignment. It didn't sound critical enough to drag him here, but still, this was one of SoHo's best private schools. They took their students' academics seriously.

After taking the proffered foam cup, he sat. "Thank you." He drained the cold liquid. "If

I'd known she'd gotten behind on her work, I would have—"

"I'm afraid it's more than that," Mrs. Luce cut him off smoothly and returned to her seat. She pressed a button on a round black machine. The sound of calling birds and water tumbling over rocks filled the room, competing with the click-clack of two suspended silver balls knocking against each other.

Was the machine her attempt to soothe him? He thought of Christie and wondered if she tried this stuff with her patients.

"There's more?" Eli echoed.

"Take a look at this."

A jagged piece of paper appeared before him. Becca's right-tilted handwriting popped from the page.

"'Keep it up and you will—'" he read aloud then stopped, the last word too extreme, too improbable, to speak. Eli shoved the note back across the desktop. "That's not hers."

Mrs. Luce raised her eyebrows and lowered her square chin. "I think we both know that it is."

"Becca would never write that." His lips pressed into a firm line. Mrs. Luce needed to understand. She was new. Didn't know that Becca wasn't some troubled kid. "She's never had a disciplinary referral. Ever. If you look at her report card, you'll see she's a straight-A student."

Mrs. Luce's nostrils flared. "Have *you* seen her report card, lately?"

He swallowed back the rising guilt. "Not recently, but she had a 4.0 GPA last…last…" His mind skimmed back and stopped at Christmas. But that couldn't be right. Had it been that long? The distance between him and Becca yawned before him, a football field of sullen silences and monosyllabic answers.

"Semester. Yes. She was one of our top students. But she's currently incomplete in living science and health." She handed him the transcript. "And coupled with this recent threat on another student's life, I'm afraid we will not be able to recommend her for enrollment at our affiliate, Elisabeth Irwin High School."

The edges of the paper bent beneath his tense fingers. He perused her grades and double-checked the name at the top. This had to be a mistake. A misunderstanding. Becca would not flunk out of school. Not on his watch.

"Can we get Becca down here?" He dropped the paper as though it burned. "She'll clear this up."

Mrs. Luce chewed on her bottom lip then

picked up the phone. "Please escort Becca Roberts to my office, Cynthia."

Escort? He suppressed a snort. Was his daughter a criminal? What had happened to innocent until proven guilty? He and Mrs. Luce stared at each other, the silence stretching to its breaking point. Moments later, footsteps sounded in the hall. The door opened. Becca.

He strode to the door and opened his arms. Becca must be scared. Would need his assurance. But she took a far seat without acknowledging him, her eyes darting everywhere but in his direction. She couldn't have looked guiltier. He pulled out his chair and dropped into it. Was she responsible for the note? The incompletes? He rubbed his temples.

"Becca," Mrs. Luce began in a stern voice. "Please look at your father and tell him what you told us."

Her wide pupils turned her blue eyes black. "I wrote the note," she croaked. Her fingers fidgeted with the tulle band wrapped around her braid.

"What?" His mouth fell open. He pointed at the paper scrap. "That's yours?"

Becca nodded and studied her crisscrossed flip-flops.

"Why?" His voice came out hoarse and low.

He hated that it had taken a stranger to make him pay attention to his own daughter. "Why would you tell someone they were going to die? You…of all people…after what we've gone through."

Becca's ashen face jerked away. "Yeah. What would I know about death? We've never talked about it, right?"

His silence on the subject had been to protect her, not hurt her. The disposable cup bent in his hand. "That's no excuse to threaten to hurt someone."

"Is that what you think?" Becca stomped to the door. "That girl's a smoker. I was warning her about dying of cancer. You know—cancer? I think you might have heard of it, Dad. I didn't want her to end up with our sucky life." He flinched at her bitter tone.

The metal doorknob rattled in her hand. "May I be excused, Mrs. Luce?"

"Of course, dear. You may return to the study room."

"Thank you." Becca slipped through the door without a backward glance.

His hands gripped the chair's plush arms. This was worse than he'd imagined. Would Becca fail eighth grade? Leave her friends, change schools? He'd fought hard to keep his kids' lives as unchanged as possible, to maintain the life they'd had before his had fallen apart. Would this event bring everything tumbling down?

"Mr. Roberts, when we first questioned Becca, she simply confirmed that she'd written the note. In light of this…" Mrs. Luce cleared her throat "…clarification, we might need to reconsider our decision not to recommend her for promotion if she can make up her work."

"You think?" he asked rhetorically, furious with himself and sorry that Mrs. Luce had been put in the middle of this mess. He grabbed the annoying, clanking silver balls and stilled them, guilt heavy on his shoulders.

"Mr. Roberts," she began, pulling the apparatus out of his reach. "We see this every day. Children acting out in school when something is wrong at home."

"Everything's fine," insisted Eli, wishing he felt as sure as he sounded.

"Your family is facing a devastating crisis."

He shifted in his seat. Someone must have told her about his cancer. The guidance counselor. What was her name? The one who smiled a lot. Sort of like Christie without the charm.

"Mrs. Kevlar," he murmured and pulled out

his twitching phone. He powered it off without looking at the screen.

Mrs. Luce nodded. "Yes. Mrs. Kevlar told me of your health issues. And of your wife's… absence. Is there some chance that she might be of help?"

Absence? Was that the euphemism used for being dumped? He passed a hand over his eyes. "Let's leave her out of this. She won't want to be involved."

"But surely, as a mother, she'd—"

"She was never a mother to them." And it was true. He'd changed their diapers, read them to sleep, made their lunches, ordered their birthday cakes. As the eldest child of twelve, his ex had once told him she'd already done her share of parenting.

Mrs. Luce's face softened. Did she pity him? Now, that he couldn't stand. His family might be having a tough time, but they'd get through it. They always did.

"And have you been engaging Becca and Tommy? Talking to them about everything that's going on? Encouraging them to express their feelings?"

Now she sounded like Christie.

"We're going to counseling today," replied Eli, certain now, more than ever, that he'd been right to make that appointment. If only he'd done it sooner. Prevented Becca from digging herself this hole. He noticed a penny by his loafers. It was heads up. Christie would say that was good luck, though fate was hardly on his side today.

Mrs. Luce rested her head on the high brown back of her chair. The rain-forest sounds quieted, replaced by the muffled thrum of Manhattan traffic. After a long moment, she leveled her gaze on him.

"Given the extenuating circumstances, I believe we can work out a plan so that Becca still has a chance of attending Elisabeth Irwin this fall."

His heart sped as he leaned forward. "It would mean a lot." He would do whatever it took to get his family back on track. But for right now, he needed Mrs. Luce on his side.

The principal hit another button on her sound soother and set the metallic balls back in motion. "If you agree to attend family counseling until school starts in September, and Becca makes up her work over the summer, I will recommend her promotion to ninth grade."

Relief flooded him. "That's generous. Thank you."

She pointed a gold-tipped pen. "I'll need to

see signed documentation from your counselor along with Becca's completed assignments. You can pick them up tomorrow."

"Will do." He glanced down at the gleaming copper penny. He almost left it on the floor then discreetly pocketed it instead. Not that he believed in crazy superstitions. But it would remind him of how close he'd come to losing touch with his daughter.

"Would you excuse Becca and Tommy so they can leave with me? Our appointment is at Memorial Hospital in an hour." No way was he taking a chance they'd be late.

"Of course. And, Mr. Roberts?"

He stopped at the door and turned.

"Good luck."

CHRISTIE'S ACHING FEET carried her down the hallway of Memorial Sloan-Kettering Counseling Center. A pink-and-white-checkered dog leash drooped by her side, Sweet Pea trotting on the other end. Where did her pet's boundless energy come from? After working seven days straight, she couldn't wait to hang up her monkey-ears stethoscope and head home. Not that Sweet Pea worked every shift. As an Angel on a Leash therapy dog, the spaniel accompanied her two times a week and during their monthly Toward Tomorrow group forum.

"Paging Nurse Bates. Nurse Bates line 224," crackled the PA system.

She rubbed her forehead. Minutes from a clean getaway. She pressed a hand to her tender back and turned into a nearby nurses' station. She hooked Sweet Pea's leash on an unused IV pole and leaned over the gray countertop for the phone.

"Christie Bates," she said after punching the blinking red button.

"Christie!" exclaimed her friend and fellow grief counselor Joan. "Thank goodness you haven't left yet."

She twisted the cord around her finger. "Nope. Still here. What's up?" She leaned down and ruffled Sweet Pea's long ears.

"Look, I hate to ask a favor, but Michael is tied up in court and Haylee gets out of school in half an hour. Would you take my last client? We've been trying to cancel, but he hasn't answered his phone."

Her gaze bounced from the rushing nurses to the furiously scribbling doctors. An intercom buzzed while the receptionist drained her coffee and put a third call on hold. "No problem." She strove to keep the sigh out of her voice. They were all working on fumes.

"Yes! I knew you'd understand. Thanks so much, Christie. He's new and the file is outside my office."

She stepped aside to let a nurses' aide wheel a blood-pressure machine past her. On the other end of the phone a car honk sounded. "Where are you calling from?" She definitely heard someone shouting about roasted chestnuts in the background.

"I'm already outside. But I can come back in," her colleague finished in a rush.

"Don't give it another thought." Christie seated herself at the desk and pulled a pad from her pocket. "What do you know about the patient?"

"Father's in remis for osteosarcoma. His teenage daughter's been withdrawing. Straight-up family counseling. No surprises."

She pinched the bridge of her nose and squeezed her eyes shut. She'd suggested that Eli's kids needed someone to talk to. Could he be Joan's patient? Heaven help her if he was. "Joan, by any chance…is there a younger son?"

Joan's voice rose. "Taxi! What do I have to do, wear a fur coat and wave a ten-carat ring?"

Her voice lowered. "But yes. The boy's in second grade. Has a habit of running away."

The chattering nurses, ringing phones and beeping pagers receded, and a dull roar filled her pounding head. She was not ready for this today. Not when she hadn't thought about Eli in—she checked her watch—four hours.

"The name?" she whispered. A stack of charts skittered from beneath her elbow and onto the floor. She cradled the phone between her ear and shoulder and picked up the mess with unsteady hands.

"Yes! Finally," shouted Joan. "Look, I've got to get this cab. A lady with a wheelie walker's heading this way. But I owe you, okay? You're a doll." The line went dead.

She stared at the receiver before returning it to its holder. Her hands smoothed her pink scrubs, the puppy pattern matching Sweet Pea's therapy vest. This was not happening. If the name on the chart matched her suspicions, Joan was wrong. They were all in for a big surprise.

A minute later, she stopped outside Joan's office, her worst fear confirmed. If she'd known Eli's family waited behind that door, would she have said no? Despite her best intentions, he'd been on her mind all week, her thoughts replaying their conversation like a favorite song.

Her fingers tightened on his chart. She'd been careful all these years to guard herself from personal involvement in her clients' lives. Her childhood heartbreak was enough to last her a lifetime. But Eli's warmth, compassion and strength made her forget those rules and want something more. Something that could rip apart her patchwork heart. She sympathized with his situation, but that would have to be enough. Her shoulders squared. She'd be friendly and professional, the way she treated all of her patients.

She knocked and entered. "Hello, Tommy, Becca." She swallowed and risked a look at their father. Her stomach executed a triple somersault with a half twist. "Eli. I'll be filling in for Mrs. Osar today."

His good looks struck her with an almost-physical force. When he stood to his impressive height, she admired the pull of his fitted white dress shirt across his broad shoulders and the navy tie that set off his incredible eyes. His dark eyebrows rose as he stepped forward and extended a hand.

"Looks like you can't get away from us," he said with a wry twist of his lips. Her heart tumbled to a halt. Breathe, she reminded herself. Too much time around this gorgeous man and *she'd* need the AED machine.

His warm palm pressed firmly against hers. When she peered up at him, her cheeks flushed under his intense gaze.

"Sweet Pea!" squealed Tommy, breaking her trance. Eli blinked down at the wriggling dog but didn't let go.

She extricated herself with a small tug and stepped back, the sensation of his hand lingering. Why were her senses refusing to listen to reason? She needed to focus. Conduct herself properly. And hand holding with a patient was a huge step over the line.

Tommy launched himself at Sweet Pea. Her paws landed on either side of his neck, her pink tongue darting for his cheek. "She likes me!" Tommy laughed. He twisted his head, a token defense against the affectionate onslaught. Sweet Pea's excited snorts filled the room.

"And how could she not?" Her gaze flitted from the beaming boy to his stunned-looking father. Did he feel the same spark she did? And was he as determined as she to ignore it? "It's nice to see all of you again."

She smiled at Becca, who wore olive, knee-length shorts and a white T-shirt embellished with a glittering pink rose. "That's a lovely French braid. I wish I knew how to do that."

The girl knelt beside Tommy and stroked the

twisting tornado of canine love that was Sweet Pea. "I could teach you."

"That'd be great, Becca, thanks. My hair's always such a mess by the end of the workday." She lifted the heavy length from her shoulders and arched her stiff neck. Her eyes flitted to Eli and froze at his rapt attention. His gaze traveled over her like a physical caress.

"You said we weren't gonna see Christie." Tommy's fingers combed through Sweet Pea's curls.

"I didn't think we were." Eli's thumbs rubbed across his closed lids before meeting above his nose.

"I'm sorry about this," she said quietly to Eli. "And I certainly understand if you'd like to reschedule. Joan tried to call you but—"

"I know," he said shortly. "I ignored the call when I was in a meeting and then afterward…" He trailed off, distracted.

"This is the best thing that's happened all day." Becca gave Sweet Pea a belly rub then pointed to a jar of Hershey's Kisses on Joan's desk. "Can I have one? I'm—"

"Hungry," Tommy piped up. "You're always hungry." He picked up Sweet Pea and cradled her in his arms. She squirmed a bit but settled down. "Becca got in biiiiiig trouble today and had to go to jail."

"Did not," Becca gasped. She rocked back on her heels as if slapped.

Christie's gaze flew to Eli. He gave her a slight headshake, but his worried expression made her wonder.

Tommy jerked his chin. "Did too."

"It was detention." Becca stomped to the window and crossed her arms. A flock of pigeons winged by the glass like a storm cloud.

"Same thing. David said you're a juvie." Tommy turned big eyes Christie's way. "What's a juvie?"

She patted his round cheek and hid her dismay with a smile. "We don't use those kinds of words."

"Is it a bad one?" Tommy whispered in awed tones. He scrubbed a hand across his mouth.

"Mean enough. And if you can't say nice things then best to say nothing at all." She sent Eli a meaningful look. His mouth twitched, amusement softening his stern face. She felt as if she were glowing like a lightning bug on a Kansas summer night.

"Ever?" Tommy breathed, recapturing her attention. "That's hard."

"Not when you set your mind to it." She

chucked him gently under his soft chin, her touch making the ticklish boy giggle. When she glanced up, she caught Eli's unguarded stare, his face vulnerable for an instant. She quickly turned away, feeling as though she'd plundered a private thought. But not before she saw his expression harden once more.

He spun on his heel and gathered Tommy's book bag and Becca's tote. "Let's go, kids. We've taken up enough of Christie's time. We'll stop at the front desk to reschedule with Mrs. Osar for next week."

"Of course," she concurred, though she didn't agree at all now that she'd heard about Becca's problems. And was it her imagination or did a flash of disappointment cross Eli's set face at her words?

He seemed determined to go, but they needed help, stat. Waiting a week or more for Joan's schedule to clear might be too late to solve the Robertses' crisis. A sudden need to help this family seized her. To make whole what illness had torn apart. Perhaps she could step in, smooth things over until they got their next appointment? Surely she could trust her heart that far. She yanked off her stethoscope and pocketed it. They needed her. As a health professional, that was all that really mattered.

"Mrs. Luce wants a signed note from a counselor." Becca spoke up, her head bent while her thumbs flew across her cell phone. "We can't leave."

"Becca's gonna get spelled." Tommy put down Sweet Pea, who scrambled for the closed door and woofed. "Does she have to go potty? That's what Scout does."

Eli took Tommy's hand and gestured to Becca to join them. Becca dallied by the window, the late-afternoon sun burnishing the dark strands that matched her father's hair.

"I won't get expelled." She finished her text and pocketed her phone. "As long as we get a copy of a signed report today."

Christie scribbled on the progress report sheet in the chart and snapped it closed, a plan forming. She tossed it on Joan's desk and grabbed Sweet Pea's leash. Instantly, her pet whirled in yapping circles, knowing, before anyone else, what her master was about to propose.

"Here's an idea." She attached Sweet Pea's lead. Becca's wary expression turned hopeful. Tommy shouldered his backpack and bounded forward. Eli shoved his hands in his pockets and peered at her through his long, dark lashes. She wished she had a restraint to control her leaping heart.

"Let's stop by your condo," she said in a rush, getting out the words before she wished them back. "We'll get Scout and head to Washington Square Park. It's dog-park Thursday."

Eli blinked at her. "What?"

Oops. Had she really said that out loud? She retied her double-knotted shoes to hide her burning face.

Routines comforted her. To keep her life running on schedule she themed each day— manicure Mondays, home-shopping Tuesdays, baking Wednesdays…but only Gran and Laura, her roommate, knew her quirky secret. And now—of all people—Eli.

"I mean I take Sweet Pea for a walk there after work on Thursdays." She lifted her collar to cover the red splotches creeping up her neck. "We can meet the appointment time requirement I wrote in the chart and have some fun while we're at it."

Tommy's fist pumped like a New Jersey DJ as he stomped his feet, his sneakers blinking green and blue. "That's where we play soccer. The park is close!"

Eli remained still. Tense.

Becca slid her flip-flops back on and joined the group, her expression pleading. "Dad. We need that note. Please?"

His wary eyes met Christie's.

"I suppose. We wouldn't be going too far."

Christie released a pent-up breath and crossed her fingers behind her back, fearing they had gone too far already.

CHAPTER FIVE

ELI SNEAKED A sideways glance at the lithe woman seated on the park bench beside him. After haunting his thoughts and dreams, she was here. Real. And more beautiful than he'd let himself imagine. Even in puppy scrubs. Especially in puppy scrubs. Her appeal was natural. Organic. Different than the artificial, overgroomed world he'd inhabited as a photographer.

He inhaled Christie's wildflower scent, the delicate fragrance perfuming the city's exhaust-tainted air. The slanted afternoon sun gilded her auburn strands with fiery gold. She reminded him of a painting done by Parmigianino, a sixteenth-century Italian artist. Elegant, elongated lines and unstudied grace. If only he had his camera. He could capture her in color pixels, preserve this moment rather than let it, and her, slip away. But forever with Christie was an impossible wish.

"The dogs are getting along well," murmured Christie as she returned the waves of a group of smiling women seated on a nearby bench.

Scout woofed and, in a dog version of leapfrog, bounded over Sweet Pea. Her compact body stretched across the dog park's gray gravel, her white tail waving, her curved mouth meeting her tan ears. She was as eye-catching as her owner, her canine joy as infectious as Christie's high spirits. He twisted Scout's green leash and tried to rein in his awareness of the woman next to him. *Down, boy.*

Helicopters of maple keys spun down from the trees ringing the wrought-iron gated area. He plucked one of the green whirligigs from her hair, his fingers unsteady as they brushed her silken cheek. Despite the lingering heat, he felt her shiver.

"Are you cold?" Maybe she was coming down with something. Guilt churned his stomach. He shouldn't have dragged her into this session—or his life. Bright light illuminated shadows under her eyes, the hollows of her translucent temples where a blue vein throbbed and the bones of her cheeks. Why hadn't he noticed her exhaustion earlier? How selfish. It was kind of her to want to help. But he wouldn't take advantage. "Would you like to head home?"

She pierced him with faceted, emerald eyes. "Why don't you fill me in on what happened at school today?"

"Are you sure?" The news was eating him away inside, but just being here, doing something different with his kids, helped a little.

Why didn't he do stuff like this more often with Becca and Tommy? He could blame it on his demanding freelance graphic-design work, his need to sock away as much money as he could to ensure that his children were provided for, but that wasn't the whole story. Not the true one, anyway.

"Fire away." She smiled up at him. "Besides, Sweet Pea would stage a revolt if I dragged her home so soon. She really likes Scout."

As Tommy hopped over the yelping dogs and Becca stood a short distance away, her thumbs whizzing across her cell phone, he gave in and recounted the day's events. It was easier confiding in Christie than sharing with some unknown counselor. But then, they'd forged a bond during those terrifying moments working together to save John's life.

A minute later, his voice stumbled into silence, the brief squeeze of her hand on his knee scattering his wits. Every nerve in his body screamed to life.

He slid down the bench away from her. It was difficult not to trace his fingers over her knee, pull her nearer. She reminded him of the china dolls in his grandmother's hutch. As a boy, he'd wanted to take them out and create an intact, perfect family. Especially when his parents left for months on end.

But those dolls had been for looking, his grandmother had said, not touching. His eyes flitted to Christie. He needed to remember that lesson. He didn't have the hutch's thick glass to shut him out.

"So Becca still has a chance to pass eighth grade." She offered him a ghost of a smile and stood. She grabbed a water hose, squirting the dogs and Tommy to their barking, hooting delight.

Eli put a hand in the stream to splash some of the water on his flushed face. "As long as she completes an independent health research project and some living-science labs."

"And you continue to get counseling." She lowered the hose and pinned him with a look. "Correct?"

Drummers began beating their instruments near a huge fountain beyond the dog park. He caught sight of a few brightly clad musicians surrounded by a cheering crowd. Trees wearing their brightest green rustled, making him feel that he was in another world, the city noise nearly blotted out. Too bad his problems wouldn't disappear as easily. When he swallowed, his mouth felt as if it were coated with sand.

"Right. I'll call the center tomorrow to reschedule with Mrs. Osar. That'll take care of that part of the deal."

"Becca! Play with me!" hollered Tommy. But his sister ignored him, her dark hair obscuring her face as she continued texting. "Daddy, Becca won't play with me." Tommy jogged up to him, his eyes pleading.

"Will I do?" Eli replied, propelling himself to his feet and joining his son. Tommy's blond locks flopped at his vigorous nod. They'd brought a Frisbee from home, and Tommy tossed it to Eli, who chucked it far across the wide space for Sweet Pea and Scout.

Becca and Tommy had always been so tight, he mused. He patted a triumphant Scout, who'd returned with the saliva-coated toy, leaving a snorting Sweat Pea behind. He flicked it in the air again, giving Sweet Pea the advantage, and glanced at Becca. Why was she pulling away from Tommy, too?

An elderly man walking a Jack Russell terrier paused to greet Christie. Her megawatt smile made the man straighten his stooped posture and tip a plaid hat. He held out an elaborately carved cane for her to admire.

While she oohed and aahed, Eli glanced around the park. How many people did she know here? Quite a few were staring and nodding their way. If she came at the same time on the same day, it was possible they did, too. Had they formed some kind of clique, a family related by pets?

He followed her back to the bench, where a homeless man now lay, a scruffy mutt seated on the ground beside him. His leathery face creased when Christie passed him the loaf of bread they'd brought for the pigeons, along with some dog treats.

"There's clean water in the hose if you need to wash up," she said gently as she knelt beside him. Eli breathed through his mouth, the stench of unwashed flesh, cheap whiskey and garbage seeming to have no effect on Christie. "Would you like some help?"

His mouth dropped. He felt for the homeless as much as any. Donated lots to charity. But to see her interact with this guy suddenly made him think he'd never done much.

As she helped the staggering man to his feet, Eli grabbed for his thick coat, incongruous in the heat. The grimy fabric nearly slipped through his hands, but he held on. He wouldn't let her handle this alone. Not that he doubted she could. Her strength never ceased to amaze him. What a woman.

"Yo, hobo," called a slouching teenage boy in pants buckled at the tops of his thighs. "Crawl back to the trash can where you belong." Three similarly dressed youths fist bumped and laughed. All carried skateboards. What were these punks doing in a dog park? He stepped forward.

"Ahhhh!" They stumbled back when a spray of water hit them.

"Sorry," Christie gushed as she quickly tossed aside the hose and gave Eli a tiny sideways smile, which he returned. "Guess it must have slipped." Her mischievous eyes danced. She really was something.

"What are you doing?" demanded a scowling Becca. She marched over, stopping near the soaked teens. "Are you okay, Colton?"

One of the boys plucked at the shoulders of his soaked T-shirt and smirked Becca's way. "Hey. No worries, mama. How you like my new kicks?"

Mama? Kicks? And who the heck was Colton? Eli's simmering blood started to boil. Why was this sleazeball talking to his thirteen-year-old?

He looked older. Not out of high school. But close.

A soft hand gripped his rigid biceps. Christie's breath whispered against his earlobe, making him tense for a completely different reason. "Don't overreact. You'll drive Becca away. She's a big girl."

How much more distant could things get? He glanced from Becca's lovesick expression to the preening doofus with his boxers hanging out of his jeans. Then again, he didn't want to drive her into this jerk's arms. Maybe Christie had a point. She was the expert.

He forced himself to extend a hand. "I'm Becca's father, Mr. Roberts. And you are?"

"He's my boyfriend," Becca blurted. Her face turned red when the boys broke into loud guffaws. One shoved Colton, who shook his head and glared. The homeless man made a rude gesture to the boys and picked up the hose, dousing his pet. The mixed breed's black-spotted tongue lapped water from the air like a child catching snowflakes.

Eli felt the world recede and hit him in the face at the same time. Becca? Dating?

"What about Lindsay?" asked another boy wearing quarter-sized spacers in his earlobes.

When he flicked off Colton's hat, Scout snatched it and launched into a tug-of-war with Sweet Pea.

A third friend pointed at the growling dogs. "Or Alicia? She got curls like that dog."

"Thought you said your girl was Megan." A group member plucked Colton's cell from his oversized pocket and held it up. The display revealed a girl posed in a skimpy bikini. Colton grabbed the phone back and powered it down.

Becca turned on her heel, her eyes shining with unshed tears. Eli wanted to crush those quaking shoulders to his chest and tell her Daddy would fix it. Make everything right. But Christie's silent message—that Becca wasn't his little girl anymore—made him stay still. The idea that his daughter's problems were bigger than he could instantly repair made him pause.

"Jerks," Colton hissed. He ripped his hat from a snapping Scout, put it on sideways and chased after Becca. The rest of his friends headed out the gate, forgetting to shut it behind them.

"Sweet Pea!" Christie called when the little dog lunged at Colton's ankle. Scout growled, the gold hairs on the scruff of his neck standing up.

"Get him!" Tommy cheered. He ruffled Sweet Pea's frizzing curls before racing to the entranceway.

Eli's gaze jumped from Becca to Tommy.

Tommy was a wanderer. Would he bolt through the gate rather than shut it? Then again, Becca was in the midst of a tween life crisis. Would she and Colton fight? Just when he thought he had a handle on the single-dad thing, his hard-wired life short-circuited. He couldn't be everywhere at once. What he needed was a wingman. His eyes darted to Christie. Or wingwoman. With a last look at Becca, he caught up to his wayward son and marched him back.

When he returned, Christie held her wriggling dog. "What on earth got into you?" she asked in a stern voice. Sweet Pea's long ears lowered farther, her brown eyes bulging. "We never bite. Not even as a threat. Keep this up and it's no more play therapy for you." After a long stare, she lowered a subdued Sweet Pea. Her tiny paws nearly disappeared in the gray gravel.

"Now play nice," she said with a behind-the-ear scratch that got Sweet Pea's tail wagging once more. She turned back to the hose. "I'm sorry about those boys, sir—" Her voice trailed off. Eli followed her swiveling head but couldn't locate the homeless man or his mangy pet. "Darn," she muttered.

"Tell me about it." He nodded to an animated Becca and a sullen Colton. His fingernails dug into his palms as the creep touched Becca's braid. Touched her. The thought of that idiot anywhere near his daughter made him want to—

"Stop," said Christie as though reading his mind. "Give Becca a chance to handle this. She's stronger than you think and dealing with a lot."

He winced and forced himself to look away, sidestepping when Tommy rushed by, the yapping dogs on his heels. What else was going on in his daughter's life? Up until now, he'd thought school and dance were it. After today, he didn't know what to believe.

He blinked at Becca's now-smiling face. She should be furious with the two-timer. He sure was. She wouldn't fall for a phony like that... would she? Then again, hadn't he made that mistake once, too? At least he'd gotten Tommy and Becca from his train wreck of a marriage. And he'd do it all over again to have them in his life. No matter what, he wouldn't regret a moment that led to his amazing kids.

He took an involuntary step forward. A flock of birds rose, cawing, to some nearby trees. How could he make her see how wrong this guy was for her? Times like this made him wish Becca had a mother to turn to. Their father–daughter relationship was strained already. How much pressure could it take before it broke altogether?

"Laters," Colton called as he swaggered by Eli and joined his skateboarding friends on the cement path beyond the dog park. Like them, he left the gate open. But Becca dashed over to close it. She trailed after him along the metal fence like a lost puppy.

"Colton!" She waved her cell at him. The universal "call me" sign.

The kid gave her a noncommittal shrug and wandered away. A girl resembling the one on Colton's phone materialized and joined the group as they headed for the fountain. It made Eli ache to see Becca's stiff back and fisting hands. He straightened his shoulders. This joker was not dating his daughter, and that was the end of it.

He was charging forward to set Becca straight when a sanitation worker in a green uniform stepped in front of him to scoop up another dog's mess.

"Eli," Christie said. Something in her tone, the way she said his name, the rounding and softening of the vowels, made the tension inside lighten. She pulled at a delicate silver chain from which hung a single shamrock charm.

"May I speak to Becca? Woman to woman? Help her put things into perspective."

For a moment he bristled at the thought of another person assuming they knew better than he how to handle his daughter. But then again, hadn't today taught him that he'd lost touch? Perhaps she had the answers—even if they could double for Hallmark cards.

He stuffed his hands in his pockets and studied Becca. She leaned against a tree and frowned down at her cell, looking every bit as lost as he felt. His lungs deflated. He had to do what was best for his kid. And as painful as it was to admit…right now…that wasn't him.

"Sure. I'll hang out with Tommy," he forced himself to say. "Thanks, Christie. If you can help her, it would mean the world to me. To all of us."

CHAPTER SIX

No PRESSURE, CHRISTIE THOUGHT, as she headed Becca's way. Just the fate of the entire Roberts family resting on her shoulders.

The girl glanced up at her approach and shoved her phone into her pocket.

"Want to go to the Shake Shack with me?" Christie asked. The food vendor was on the southeast corner of the park, far enough away to let Becca feel safe about opening up without fearing her father might overhear. Speaking of whom…she narrowed her eyes at a staring Eli until he turned and whipped the Frisbee after Tommy and the dogs.

Becca's thin shoulders lifted and fell. "Sure. I'm not really hungry, though."

They closed the gate to the dog area behind them and headed down a treelined walkway toward the southern fountain. In-line-skating New Yorkers whooshed by them, outpaced by determined mothers jogging behind ergonomically designed strollers.

"What? You're not hungry?" She shook her

head and looked up at the blue sky. "Impossible. The world must be coming to an end." She gave an exaggerated sigh. "And I want to live."

Becca made a snuffling laughing-through-tears sound as they passed a man on a woven blanket strumming an acoustic guitar. "Sometimes it feels that way. Like the world ending."

"It can seem like that at times," Christie agreed, leaving it at that. "Patience, Not Pushing" was her motto and it usually paid off. She plucked a fragrant pink bloom from an almost-bare azalea bush and passed it to Becca.

After pulling off a few petals, the girl dropped the flower. "He loves me not," she said, her voice barely audible.

Christie tucked a loose strand into Becca's French braid. "How could he not?" She didn't pretend not to know whom Becca meant.

They stopped beside a midsized fountain enclosed by an iron railing. Tourists snapped pictures of the water sculpture on its brass base, posing beside urns bursting with flowers and greenery.

The steady stream of gushing water swallowed the city's cacophony. If only it would settle her chaotic nerves. Becca stared at the clear liquid as it dripped from the top urn to the middle before splashing to the large bottom tier.

Christie closed her eyes and leaned toward the faint, rising mist.

Without turning, Becca pulled out her cell phone and passed it to her.

"Are you sure?" Sometimes patients acted impulsively then withdrew if they felt they'd revealed too much. Better to let Becca set the pace.

"Yeah. It's a text from Colton. After he left the park."

"'Leave me alone, b—'" Christie read aloud then stopped. "Oh. I see what you mean." She handed back the phone. What a jerk. Now she felt like Eli. Ready to strangle the kid. But she kept her expression neutral.

"I know. Right?" Becca turned and leaned against the metal enclosure.

Christie joined her at the rail. "So how do you feel about that?"

A short burst of air escaped Becca. "Like I could strangle him."

Christie stayed mum and watched the swirling water, sensing that Becca needed to say more. But it had to be voluntary.

After a couple of minutes, Becca faced her. "I think he's cheating on me." Her anguished blue eyes met Christie's.

"Does it matter?"

Becca blinked, her lips parting in surprise. "You think it's okay for him to see someone else? He's my first."

Her heart began to pound. Oh, goodness. This was about to get major. She hid her growing dismay and said, "Firsts are important."

"Exactly." Becca began to pace, scattering pigeons with every footfall. "I thought my first kiss would be with someone who loved me. So, yeah. It matters."

Christie released a pent-up breath. Thank heavens. "I agree. What I meant is could there be an even larger issue? Something worse?"

Becca pulled out her vibrating phone. "What could be worse?"

"How does he make you feel?"

Becca's eyes slid from left to right as she scanned the screen. "Right now...terrible."

The man on the acoustic guitar had followed them and was now strumming a '60s folk tune under a towering elm tree.

She fished out a couple of dollar bills and dropped them in his empty case. "Just right now?" She caught Becca's eye. "Sometimes? Or most of the time?"

Becca bit her lip and stared at her flip-flops, her cheeks white. Finally, she said, "Most of the time."

Christie put an arm around her and guided her toward the Shake Shack. Sometimes the best way to deal with a breakthrough was not to make a fuss over it, let it settle into the patient's psyche until they felt comfortable with the revelation.

The smell of fried onions and greasy burgers permeated the air. Becca's stomach grumbled audibly.

"Still not hungry?" Christie teased. Thank goodness the line was short. Sometimes it wrapped around the table-filled area.

Becca laughed. "Maybe a little. But I don't have any money."

Christie patted her pocket. "It's on me. Order what you like."

"Okay. But next time's on me." When Becca stepped up to the counter, Christie chewed on the inside of her cheek. Had she encouraged Becca to think there would be a next time? Managing children's expectations had never cured her of her desire to see their every wish fulfilled, to hope that what they wanted, no matter how seemingly impossible, could happen. It was a matter of faith, something that, after her years as a grief counselor, had only strengthened.

"I'll have a Shack Burger, a peanut butter

shake, cheese fries and a Frisky Dog, hold the kraut." She pivoted toward Christie. "What would you like and can we get a Bag O' Bones for Scout and Sweet Pea?"

She nodded, feeling awed, as she always did, by the fearsome appetites of teenagers. She pulled out her wallet after the man behind the counter called back their order.

"Sorry I can't pay," Becca told her then sucked in a harsh breath. Christie followed her gaze to the couple mashed against each other at a far table. It was Colton and another girl. What bad luck.

"What should I do?" Becca hissed, her body rigid.

Christie slid money to the cashier and studied Becca. Poor girl. Detention and now this. Big problems for such a young teen. "What do you want to do?"

"Kill him." Becca turned her back on the couple.

"Is he worth twenty years to life of prison food?" She grabbed their food and drinks, leading Becca to a table far from Colton.

Becca squirted ketchup on her burger and looked up. Miserable. "Maybe."

"Do you mind?" Christie pointed at the fries. Becca's chin quivered. "I've lost my appetite."

"And waste all this good food?" She bit into a salty fry and pretended to savor it. "So you're going to get arrested and starve yourself? Colton must be really worth it."

Becca's bitter laugh ended in a snort. "Worth*less,* you mean. And useless. And pointless." She picked up a fry and took a savage bite. She downed a few more then wiped her shining hands on a napkin. "I'm so lame. Just another stupid girl chasing after a dumb boy." She tipped her head up and stared at the blue sky. "Way to represent for the ladies, Becca."

Christie covered Becca's hands with her own and squeezed. "I don't think that. We've all made mistakes when we thought we were in love. Never apologize or feel bad for going with your gut. And don't stop fighting for the one you love, as long as he loves and respects you back."

Becca peered at her and slurped her shake. She put it down and picked up her burger. "So what was your major dating disaster?"

An image of holding hands with her prom date before they glimpsed the ambulance's flashing lights in front of her childhood home made her wince. "Some other time, okay? Promise." As soon as she could relive that experience for herself, she added silently.

"Okay." Becca took another drink. "Do you have a boyfriend?"

The wind ruffled the orange-and-white-striped umbrella overhead and carried the smell of fresh popcorn their way. Christie chewed on another fry, stalling. Kids and their arrow-to-the-heart questions. How to admit her over-scheduled life didn't leave room for romance? Or was it her fear of loving someone, as her analytical roommate, Laura, asserted, that made her overschedule her life? Either way, it was too complicated for her to figure out, let alone articulate to a thirteen-year-old.

"I did once. But not in a while."

Becca stopped chewing her burger. A pickle slid from the bun and plopped to the mayo-smeared wrapper below. "Are you ever lonely?"

All the time, she thought. "Rarely," she fibbed and thought of something happy enough to make her smile. "How could I be lonely when I meet new friends like you?"

Becca's dim eyes brightened. "Thank you, Christie."

She waved at the food. "It was nothing. Have to feed starving children don't I?"

"No." Becca's braid whipped back and forth as she shook her head. "Thank you for everything. For helping me, helping my family and, I think, maybe helping Dad."

Warmth crept into her cheeks. Before she could resist, she asked, "You think I'm helping him?"

A loud sputter sounded when Becca polished off her shake. She pulled out the straw, sucked on it, then twirled it between her fingers, her expression faraway.

"He smiles when you're around. And that hasn't happened in a long time."

Happiness swelled inside Christie. Was she glad to help someone in need or did her feelings go deeper than that? As she looked into Becca's curious blue eyes, so like her father's, she realized the answer was staring her, literally, in the face. If Eli was only a client, she shouldn't be thinking about his eyes.

"I'm glad I can help," she said, once she could speak over the wild tango of her heart.

Becca leaned forward. "Is he still there?"

Christie glanced up at the now-standing couple, the girl yanking a reluctant-looking Colton.

"Becca!" he shouted as he ripped his arm free and strode to their table.

She tensed, hoping, just hoping, that their talk had made a difference. That Becca could handle this.

Becca stood. "Let's go. It stinks out here," she said to Christie, ignoring a scarlet-faced Colton. She sauntered past him without a glance, tossed their garbage and gestured to Christie.

"Ready?"

She shut her gaping mouth and followed Becca. Way. To. Go. Now that was representing for the ladies.

"Come back here." Colton followed them to the fountain. "Come back or we're through." His tone changed from a threat to a whine when Becca marched on. "I didn't mean what I said before, Becca. Please."

Becca halted and squared her shoulders. Christie gave her an encouraging wink. "'Bye, Colton. And don't bother texting." She whipped out her phone and tapped the pad. "You've just been blocked."

"You—" Colton hollered.

Luckily the guitar player, now surrounded by a small, clapping crowd, drowned out what was surely an offensive word.

"Good riddance to bad rubbish," Christie murmured as they wandered back to the dog park.

Becca gave her shoulder a little shove. "I like that. Thanks, Christie."

She dodged a man wheeling an Italian ice

cart. "Can't take the credit. It's my gran's saying."

"Wish I had a grandmother. Hope I get to meet yours someday."

Christie's heart squeezed. There wouldn't be any more meetings after today since Eli would be rescheduling with Joan. The problem was, she felt less and less convinced that it was the right thing for her and the family. They needed her. Was it possible she needed them, too?

Becca stopped her before they opened the dog-park gate. Scout and Sweet Pea rushed the entrance, their nails scratching on the metal. The distant hum of cars passing along Fourth Avenue filled the humid air.

"Thank you, Christie." Becca threw her arms around her. "Colton is a jerk. I should never have gone out with a guy like that."

Christie hugged her in return. "We all date a few frogs. It's the only way we can recognize the good ones when we find them." She caught Eli's eye over Becca's shoulder and stepped back. "And I'm just a phone call away if you need me. I could even help you with that research project. Maybe you could come into the hospital." Hopefully that would be okay with the more open-minded, now-smiling Eli.

Becca clapped her hands. "I would love that."

"Love what?" His deep bass vibrated through her. He and Tommy walked out with the dogs and shut the gate behind them.

Her pet turned in yapping circles until Christie picked her up. Resistance was futile when it came to cuteness of Sweet Pea's magnitude.

"Christie promised to help me do my health project." Becca passed a dog biscuit to a leaping Scout and a squirming Sweet Pea.

"That's very generous of her." Eli raked his hands over his short hair. "But I'm sure she's far too busy to—"

"Becca!" Colton yelled from a grove of trees to their left. He ducked his head out and gestured. "I need to talk to you."

Becca fed the rest of the biscuits to the dogs and tossed the Bag O' Bones into a wastebasket. "Good riddance to bad rubbish," she said in a raised voice. "Right, Christie?" She linked arms with her and pulled her toward the north gate.

Christie glanced over her shoulder and caught a glimpse of Eli, his head pivoting between his daughter and Colton. She couldn't take all the credit for Becca's turnaround, but the warmth of Eli Roberts's admiring stare felt awfully nice.

SHE'D REALLY DONE IT, Eli mused. In under an hour, Christie had gotten Becca on board with school and off track with her boyfriend. He tightened Scout's leash then hurried to catch up with Christie and his family.

The difference she made was undeniable. Impressive. Becca wasn't sulking and Tommy hadn't pulled a vanishing act. He smiled to himself as she steered them around some scaffolding. No crossing under ladders for his kids. She might have her superstitious quirks, but she cared. Most of all, she was good for them. He needed to rethink things with Christie.

As they neared Fifth Avenue, a group of huffing joggers raced by, numbers pasted to their chests. He overheard Tommy jabbering to her, catching words like *T. rex* and *brontosaurus,* although it sounded more like *brontothauruth.* But she bobbed her head as if she understood his tyke perfectly.

Although giving in to his attraction and growing feelings for her was out of the question, his kids benefited from having her in their lives. Just because he couldn't allow her into his heart didn't mean he had to shut her out of his world totally.

For all he knew, she wasn't interested in a relationship any more than he was. They'd stay in the friend zone. Hang out. He liked to think she'd enjoyed herself today as much as he had.

She had color in her cheeks now, as if the fresh air and the outing had agreed with her.

Pain shot up his leg, forcing him to stop. He rubbed his calf and dodged Christie's sharp, concerned look. Despite the twinge, he forced himself not to limp. No signs of weakness. It wasn't good for the children or her. He still thought about her losses, especially her brother's leukemia. If they were to continue spending time together, he needed to protect her feelings as much as his kids'.

The rat-tat-tat of a man running a jackhammer overwhelmed the honking, tire-squealing, break-hitting noise of the bustling intersection. They'd arrived at the crossroads. Christie glanced back at him, her deep green eyes propelling him closer.

"Are you ready to cross?"

He nodded, hit the crosswalk button and turned her way. The lowering sun backlit her pert nose and delicate chin.

"This was fun. I'm glad we came," she murmured, her voice pitched for his ears only.

He glanced from an iPod-scrolling Becca, earbuds in place, to Tommy, who'd turned his chatter on the dogs. He swallowed over the uncertainty clogging his throat. "Me, too," he said quietly. "Would you like to get together again?"

Her eyes widened and he spied a fleck of gold beside each iris. "With the children," he amended hastily. "You've been a great help to them today. Thank you."

She ducked her head, her gleaming mahogany locks sliding forward. "No trouble at all. And I'm happy to help." Her bowed lips curved upward. "Anytime."

"Great. We'll talk at the next support-group meeting." Scout lunged, preventing him from saying more, as a couple eating hot dogs strolled by.

He'd promised to bring John to the next one, now that he'd recuperated. There, he'd see if she was serious about working with Becca on her project and spending time with him and the kids. As long as they kept things within friendship boundaries, he was ready. Ready to take the next step.

Waiting for the walk signal, he had the strange sensation that more than a light was about to change.

CHAPTER SEVEN

"That Father Dolan, he's quite a looker. My head was spinning and it wasn't just the wine."

"Gran!" Christie shook her head at the White Horse Tavern's bartender, overriding her grandmother's signal for another round. Two pints of Guinness were enough for a Sunday afternoon. At least, it was for her. She felt a bit fuzzy around the edges. "Did you even listen to the sermon?"

Fluffing her short, white perm, Gran pursed coral lips. Sharp lines radiated from them like a sunburst. "Ach. Couldn't catch a word for looking at those blue eyes. You must have noticed, a *single* girl like you."

Christie sipped her stout and pictured another pair of blue eyes, deeper and more soulful. "Not really." She braced herself. An all-too-familiar lecture was brewing. She could feel it, recite every word before it was spoken.

"How old are you now?" Gran began, firing off her usual opening salvo. She waved to an older man as he seated himself on a stool at the tavern's room-length wooden bar.

In the background, a jukebox played a Bob Dylan song, "Forever Young." How ironic. She twisted her cloth napkin and surveyed the crowded pub filled with round wooden tables and walls covered in vintage black-and-white photos of the neighborhood through the decades. She inhaled the bar's sweet, yeasty smell. "Twenty-eight."

Gran nodded. "By your age I was—"

"Married with two babes and one on the way," she finished for her. The faster they got The Talk over with, the sooner they would get back to having fun. Her weekly tradition with Gran— church then the White Horse for lunch—was the highlight of her week. "Why would you want me to settle down so soon? Don't you always say you gave up your chance to be a Radio City Rockette?"

Gran crossed her calves beneath her lavender dress and angled her chair toward her staring male acquaintance. "Still have the legs for it, too. If it hadn't been for your sweet-talker of a grandfather, my name could have been up in lights." A lace-edged hankie appeared like a magic trick from her cardigan sleeve. She dabbed at her eyes. "God rest his soul."

A group of chattering, picture-happy tourists stopped beside their table. They angled their cameras at a white-painted chandelier, carved horse heads on its hexagonal points. She blinked as one snapped a shot of her and a posing Gran, who'd transformed herself from a bereaved widow to a glamour-puss in two seconds flat.

"Gran. Don't arch your back so." She tucked a wayward strand behind her ear and pulled up the strap of her light blue tank dress. "You'll put it out."

Two beer steins thunked on their table, an inch of foam topping their dark contents. Before she could protest, the florid bartender pointed a thick finger toward the elderly man Gran had greeted earlier. "Compliments of the gentleman at the bar."

Gran raised her glass to him and sipped, froth lacing her upper lip before she wiped it away. "My thanks to you, Elliot," she called over the now-thinning crowd. She signaled for him to stay put when he rose. An ornate mirror behind him reflected his distinguished head of white hair and wide shoulders. "I'll see you Tuesday."

Christie's mouth fell open when Elliot waggled bushy eyebrows and winked. Were they dating? Did Gran have a better love life than her granddaughter? She sighed. Then again, who didn't? Maybe she needed The Talk after all. Gran was an expert at living life, while Christie excelled at hiding from it.

Maybe that was part of the reason she enjoyed these visits so much. Her grandmother was the most vibrant person she knew. Some people shied away from their elders as reminders of their own aging. But they had it backward. Who better to hand you life's reality check than those who'd learned not to squander it? Gran was a survivor. A healthy, strong woman who'd aged with grace, dignity and a bit of mischief to spice things up. Many of Christie's patients would give anything to live Gran's charmed, colorful life. Even for a day.

"Hot date?" She traced a ridge in the scarred tabletop with her fingertip. A loud cheer rose from a group in front of a dart board, nearly drowning out her question. Money changed hands and men jockeyed into position once more.

Gran's penciled eyebrows arched over sparkling green eyes. "He's taking me to La Esquina," drawled Gran. "The enchiladas will be spicier. But it beats shopping from my couch...alone." She cleared her throat and shot Christie a meaningful look.

Christie fingered her favorite Home Shopping

Network necklace—a beaded four-leaf clover on a silver chain. Jewelry trumped a random date every time. The bling lasted forever, a rare quality in her life. Besides, her work and volunteer schedule didn't give her a chance to breathe, let alone wonder if she felt lonely. Yet she sensed a cold void at night, lying in bed, worries for her patients circling in her mind before she fell asleep.

Eli's surprise request to see her again—with the kids—had made her restless, keeping her awake for a different reason lately. Her next support group couldn't come soon enough. Her cheeks warmed when she thought about seeing him again and what he might propose.

"You're blushing." Gran's hand descended on hers, her blue veins bulging beneath paper-thin skin. "Who is he and when do I meet him?"

Christie gulped her Guinness, the smooth, toasted-grain flavor doing little to settle her jumpy nerves. How to describe her relationship with Eli? Or their nonrelationship relationship.

Two oversized Caesar salads appeared, delivered by Aiden, the tavern's young owner. He'd taken the reins of the family business ten years earlier and upheld the tradition of keeping a sharp eye on all of his customers and paying particular attention to his regulars. Patrons felt like family, part of the White Horse's homey charm.

"And how are the lovely Mrs. and Miss Bates today?" He twisted a Parmesan grater over Christie's bowl until she held up a hand. She inhaled the briny aroma of anchovies, her stomach rumbling.

Gran batted her eyelashes. "Grand now that we've seen you, Aiden. And how is your Margaret doing?"

A lock of dark hair fell across his eyes when he ducked his head. "Haven't spoken to her in a week. We're not together anymore."

"Oh. That's too bad." Gran's pearly whites shone. "She shouldn't have let a fine, strapping man such as yourself go." She nodded to Christie. "Isn't that right?"

"Perhaps love isn't in the cards for me after all," Aiden answered, missing the exchange when he turned to replace their vase of wilting flowers with a fresh one.

"You're too young to give up hope. A nice fellow like you. Why, who wouldn't be proud to step out on your arm?" Gran lifted her chin and squinted at Christie. "Don't you agree?"

She tried not to wince when her grandmother's foot connected with her shin. Gran had been trying to set them up for years and had yet to admit defeat. She nodded quickly and sent Aiden a sympathetic smile. "Thanks." She pointed to the bowl. "This looks great."

"Happy to hear it." His eyes lingered on her before he tipped his head. "Good day to you, then, ladies."

She watched his broad back disappear behind the swinging kitchen door. A lucky girl would have him someday, though it would never be her. She'd known him too long to see herself as anything more than a friend.

Gran waved her breadstick like a maestro. "I'd tell you to chat up Aiden now that he's available, but it looks like you've already found a fellow. What's his name?"

Christie squirmed in her high-backed chair. It figured. Gran *would* get right back to the point. Dating Aiden would be so much simpler than this complicating no-man's-land she'd entered with Eli. But the heart wanted what it wanted, or so she'd once read in a book of inspirational quotes. Did that mean her heart wanted Eli? Or to help his family?

"His name's Eli, and he's just a client." She shoved a large bite of tangy salad into her mouth before she gave away more than she intended. A crisp garlic crouton crunched between her teeth as she dodged her grandmother's omniscient stare. If the Rockettes hadn't worked out, she could have been an ace FBI agent, Christie mused.

"Just a client?" Gran smoothed a cloth napkin on her lap then cut the grilled chicken topping her bowl. "Since when do clients make you blush? You're not fooling me, Christine Abaigeal Bates. Now tell me all about your Eli."

Her heart sped as his warm smile came to mind, the caring way he treated his children, the firm feel of his arm around her. "He brought one of my cancer-support-group members to a meeting—you know, John Vaccaro? We've seen him here a few times."

"Yes." Gran shook some pepper on her meal. "Such a pleasant-looking man."

Uh-uh. Not happening. Christie sent Gran a stern look. "And off-limits to you. I don't mix my personal life with business."

"That's your rule, not mine." A dark green leaf dangled from Gran's fork. "Besides. Your whole life is business. When do you make time for the personal part? And don't say spending time with your dear old gran counts."

But it did, in her books. "I'm helping his family," she blurted then clamped a hand over her mouth. Now she'd done it. Why hadn't she muzzled herself with a mouthful of lettuce? Gran would pounce on this tidbit like Sweet Pea on a Greenies bone.

Gran pulled out a compact. "That's what Maria said in *The Sound of Music*. Very clever, my dear…getting in with the kids first."

Her fork clattered to the tabletop. "Gran! The children need me. It's for their sake, not mine or his."

Gran lowered her powder puff. Christie's nose felt a bit shiny, too, as did her damp forehead. Had the temperature risen or was Gran's inter-rogation getting to her? Hopefully there wasn't a lie detector in her grandparent's carry-on of a purse. She wasn't altogether sure she'd pass.

"The Julie Andrews character said that, too… before she married the count."

"He was a baron." She dipped her napkin in her water glass and rubbed it across her heated face. "Can we talk about something else? How's life at the seniors' center?"

"Fine. We'll drop it." Her grandmother nod-ded to a couple of regulars entering the bar. "For now. But I'll be wanting to meet your young man if this continues."

Christie nodded, though she'd never let her worlds collide that way. Strange that Becca had asked to meet Gran, too. She shook off the feel-ing of inevitability and dug into her lunch, nodding and commenting as Gran updated her on the latest seniors'-center news.

For the next half hour, she lost herself in the familiar rhythms of the pub while Gran hit the highlights on the over-sixty-five community. Nancy had maxed out her credit cards buying outfits for a salsa-dancing class, Trish had discovered Jack was two-timing her with the bingo lady, and Mary Beth had gotten engaged after twisting her ankle on a hike in the Adirondacks then met her fiancé in the E.R. "Which goes to show you," Gran concluded with a nod, "that life only happens when you live it."

Christie's empty glass paused in midair. Gran was right. She'd packed her world with so many obligations that she didn't have an inch to live it. A familiar voice inside whispered that she didn't deserve to. But it sounded fainter than usual. Could Eli be responsible for that?

Suddenly she wanted to shake things up in a dance class, too. Stand on top of a mountain and holler loud enough for everyone to hear. Zip-line over a rain forest, high-fiving monkeys as she zoomed by. With Eli—and his children, of course.

She drained her glass and signaled the bartender for the check.

Perhaps it was time to live her life after all.

CHRISTIE LOWERED HER head at the meditative close of her support group and contemplated her clasped hands. They looked pale against the black pencil skirt she'd borrowed from Laura. One of the perks of having a roommate her size—double the wardrobe. Such a bonus considering their practically nonexistent closet space.

Not that is was a fair exchange. Laura's fashion vocabulary included words like *Thakoon, Prada* and *Alexander Wang* whereas hers was comprised of *the Gap, vintage* and *Home Shopping Network.* But her tees and jeans were too comfy to exchange for designer duds that made her want to lose ten pounds. At least she wouldn't trade them for more than a few hours.

She smoothed her hand over the cloth-covered buttons of her—Laura's—silk lilac top. Vertical ruffles were falling like a waterfall across her fingers when she glanced up and caught Eli's eye again. She bit back a smile, her cheeks heating for the gazillionth time tonight. Even Elizabeth had asked her if she was getting a fever. Sheesh. Maybe the fitted look was a keeper after all.

She stood as best she could in her shrink-wrap of a skirt. "Thank you, everyone." She strode to the table in her borrowed heels and held up plastic bags. "Who'd like some dessert to take home?"

After handing out the last of her oatmeal bars, she hugged the departing bunch and turned Eli's way, heart in her mouth. He'd been quiet tonight with only a muffled snort when she'd read her daily quote: the more difficulties one encounters, the higher in inspiration life will be.

All things considered, it showed progress. He'd even shared that he and John were chemo-buddies. The last two survivors in their group. It was great that he'd spoken up. If only he hadn't quieted the group and made Elizabeth's tracheotomy hum. She could almost see her members looking around and wondering who would be the last one standing in their group. To smooth over the tense silence, Christie had offered to freshen up drinks and changed the topic.

The thought of losing any of these people, of losing Eli…

She watched him help John into his suit jacket and push the wheelchair her way. Her heartbeat sounded in her ears as they approached. She needed to get a grip. And hold on to her faith.

"You're quite the heartbreaker in that suit tonight, John." She leaned down to kiss his weathered cheek. What a relief to see him looking so well. After receiving a pacemaker to regulate his heartbeat, he was on the mend. Better yet, further tests confirmed his tumor shrinkage.

She closed her eyes to blot out the image of his limp, gray form on the floor just two weeks earlier. It'd been such a close call. She slipped a hand into her purse and ran her thumb over the soft down of her rabbit's foot. How lucky that Eli had been here to help.

As if reading her mind, his warm eyes met hers. John craned his neck, looking in Eli's direction then hers, noting their silent exchange.

He cleared his throat and rearranged a navy polka-dotted handkerchief in his left pocket. "Wish I could say I got dressed up for you, Christie. If I was forty years younger...well, now that'd be another story." John winked. "But I've got a date tonight."

"What?" she and Eli asked at once.

John's white dentures flashed. "So, you don't think the old man's still got it?" He lifted his lined, but firm chin.

Oh, he had it in spades, Christie thought, taking in the devilish twinkle in his brown eyes and inhaling his Old Spice cologne. Vinegar and spice made everything naughtily nice, her gran would say. "Who's the lucky lady?"

"And when is this date?" Eli added, the expression he sent her apologetic as he pivoted

John's chair toward the meeting-room door, pushed him through the threshold, then down the hallway. Did this mean they wouldn't have a chance to set a time for their next get-together? Her pulse sped as she walked beside them. No. She'd been nervous for days. The thought of delaying their plans filled her with anguish. And didn't that just pull her up short? She was kidding herself if she thought she didn't have feelings for Eli.

John held up a hand when they got to the front door of the YMCA. "Got to get this." Her mouth dropped as he pulled a smartphone from his pocket, yanked out his hearing aid and put it to his ear.

"I'm coming out right now. Sit tight, doll face."

Doll face? Eli sent her a sideways smile that made her clamp a hand over her mouth. She would not laugh at John. But what was up with the geriatric dating pool? They didn't let arthritis, wheelchairs, even cancer stop them. So what was stopping her?

"Sorry to leave you kids, but my lady's outside. At my age, there's no time to waste." John chuckled and pushed the door open. He waved over his shoulder and wheeled himself down the ramp toward an idling cab before Eli could react. She caught a flash of a shapely leg in the dim interior as the driver opened the door and helped John inside. The old man definitely still had it.

"You'll catch flies that way," Eli observed, his breath whispering across her temple as he came to stand beside her.

Her nerves tingled to life. She snapped her mouth shut and tracked John's cab as it wove into the bustling evening traffic. Well, good for him. Why let a chronic illness and a brush with death slow him down? If anything, it had sped him up.

"Christie!" Tommy's high-pitched voice sounded behind her. His damp head burrowed into her waist as he wrapped cold arms around her.

"Did you have a good swim lesson?" She patted his back and glanced up to see Becca and Mary approaching.

The gap in his teeth appeared in an impish grin. "We got to dive for pennies at the bottom of the pool and I found all these." He held out a fistful. "You can have them for cancer."

Touched by the gesture, she nodded solemnly and took the twenty cents. "This will be of great help. Thank you, Tommy." She smoothed the boy's cowlick.

"Hey, Christie," called Becca. She hiked up the strap of her dance bag. "Our dance recital's next week and—"

"Becca, have you finished your living-science make-up lab for tomorrow?" cut in Eli. Christie glanced from his stern face to his daughter's surprised expression.

"Most of it. But Mary said she'll work with me when we get home."

Mary smiled and waved hello to Christie. "Science was my favorite subject. Would have been a nurse if I hadn't met my Patrick."

Tommy raised his hand as if he was in school. "There's a Patrick on *SpongeBob*. Can we go home? It's on TV now."

"Will you be riding home with Mr. Vaccaro?" Mary glanced around. "Where did he go?"

"Apparently on a date." Eli's mouth lifted slightly. "But I need to speak with Christie for a moment, so I'll catch a separate ride in a couple of minutes, okay?"

Mary's eyebrows rose as she glanced at them, the assessing look making Christie blush. "Take all the time you need, Mr. Roberts. Patrick is working the night shift, so I'm happy to stay." She hustled the children outside and joined in their chorus of goodbyes.

The aroma of freshly baked pizza drifted

from a small restaurant across the street. Christie's stomach grumbled, reminding her that she'd been too anxious about tonight to eat the couscous Laura had offered. She pressed a hand to her gut. Did Eli hear that?

"Looks like it's just you and me, then." He cleared his throat. "Are you hungry?" He'd jammed his hands in his pockets and nodded toward the pizzeria.

He *had* heard her traitorous intestines. Not the most attractive quality in a date with— She chopped her thought in half and bit her lip, tasting the strawberry lip gloss she'd bought. No. This was absolutely *not* a date. She glanced down at her fancy outfit. So, then, why had she dressed up for one?

"I'll get my purse." She walked carefully across the wax floor, wishing she'd worn her Keds instead of these mile-high heels. Good thing she wasn't afraid of heights. One of the few phobias she'd managed to avoid.

When she emerged from the meeting room, her heart skipped a beat at Eli's sudden, rapt attention. He looked so handsome standing against the open door, the city backlighting him like a holiday tree, his smile a present she'd saved for last. Only she couldn't open it. He was Pandora's box. She could look but not touch, no matter how much she longed to press her finger to the cleft in his square chin, feel the hard planes of his rugged face, run her hands over his dark hair.

"Good night, Anne!" she called as she ducked under his arm and into the clamoring night, electric with illuminated signs, packed sidewalks and ribbons of lit traffic.

"Night, you two!" Anne yelled as Eli shut the door after a polite wave. "Have fun!"

She cringed. Anne couldn't possibly think this was a date, could she? She looked up at Eli. Did he?

CHAPTER EIGHT

ELI AND CHRISTIE strolled to the crosswalk in silence, their brushing hands making her unsteady ankles wobble. When the Walk sign flashed, she stepped off the curb and stumbled. The street was dotted with pools of water left over from an earlier rain, but his lightning reflexes saved her from a puddle dive.

Her heart pounded like a trip-hammer when he pulled her against his side, his arm encircling her waist. Neither of them made a move to separate until they arrived at the restaurant. When he released her and held the steam-covered glass door open, she let out a pent-up breath. A bell jingled as they crossed the threshold into the narrow, muggy space.

She inhaled the basil-and-tomato-scented air, her noisy stomach announcing itself again. Eli's mouth quirked, but who didn't love pizza? Her feet skidded across slippery, black-and-white diamond-shaped tiles to the counter. She pressed her hands against its warm glass and peered at the thin-crusted pizzas. How to choose? She wanted them all.

She fished out some cash, but Eli had already slid two twenties toward the gum-snapping cashier whose false eyelashes batted his way. Leaning forward to take the money, her low-cut tank gave quite a show. Christie frowned. Service came with more than a smile here, apparently.

Without a second glance, Eli turned from the now-pouting clerk. His eyes lit on Christie. "What would you like? It's my treat."

His treat? The evening felt more like a date, and as much as the notion of romance with him appealed, she couldn't think of him that way. He was the father of the children she'd agreed to help…and that was that. Curse his blue eyes.

"Thank you. But I'm happy to pay my share." She pointed to three slices and slid her money across the scratched, stainless-steel counter. "A Sprite, as well, please." The worker blew a large bubble then popped it. She inhaled the pink ooze, her expression speculative as she gave Christie a curt nod.

In the background a whistling man tossed dough into the air, catching it with his fingertips before giving it another swirl. The heavy clang of industrial-sized oven doors overpowered an a cappella version of "O Sole Mio" piped in from wall-mounted speakers.

"And a Coke with two cheese slices for me, thanks," added Eli. The worker's curls swung as she sprang to attention and sashayed to the soda machine. Eli shrugged and handed back Christie's money. "Can't teach an old dog new tricks—guess I'm old-fashioned."

And sweet. His chagrined expression disarmed her. She didn't protest when he insisted on settling her in a high-backed wooden booth before making a couple of trips to grab their warmed slices and cold drinks. Her eyes tracked his broad back as he waded through a crowd of teenagers swarming the front.

When he returned, his head brushed hers as he leaned over to place their paper plates on the table. She smelled cologne—lemongrass and musk—and the scent of his clean skin underneath. Her mouth watered, though from the pizza or the delicious man she couldn't tell.

Folding a slice in half, she bit off the end. Her eyes lowered in appreciation of the spice, cheese, tomato and onion flavors washing over her tongue. If there was a pizzeria heaven, this was it. Why hadn't she tried this place before?

Sweet Pea.

Her eyes flew open. She always went straight home after meetings to let her dog out. How had she forgotten? Feeling like a bad pet mom and an even worse roommate, she pulled out her iPhone.

"Sorry about this," she said. "I have to text Laura to ask her to take out Sweet Pea."

Looking as guilty as she, Eli punched some numbers on his cell. She heard him talking urgently to Mary as she tapped on her keyboard. He must be asking for a time extension. Funny that, even as adults, they still needed permission to stay out late.

She glanced down at her black screen. If Laura didn't text back within a minute, she'd leave, no matter how much she was enjoying the food and the company.

But her cell buzzed as Eli pocketed his phone, the line between his brows smoothed, his face relaxed once more. She forced herself to look at the green talk bubble.

Enjoy your hot date! Sweet Pea's covered.

She whipped the phone beneath the table, her thumbs firing back a response.

It's work, not a date!! Be home soon.

Her cell vibrated through the small purse against her hip before she could lower her glass.

Haha—is that what you call it these days?! Don't rush but you owe me a Pinkberry's. Love ya—L.

Chocolate and granola it is. And it's not a date!!

She replied then slipped her phone back into her purse. *Sheesh.*

"You must get along well with your roommate." Eli held a bottle of Parmesan out to her. She tried to ignore the way his biceps flexed as he passed the jar.

She shook the white flakes on her remaining two slices and passed it back, her fingers tingling where they touched his. "How can you tell?"

"You smile whenever you talk to her or about her."

Was it her imagination, or did he suddenly look a bit wistful? Living with his kids and rarely getting out except on business must be lonely. She had a friend at home. Whom did he have? Was there a way she could be that person for Eli without investing too much of her heart?

"I met Laura at Columbia. It was friendship at first sight." And it had been. Her future roommate had arrived late to class, stopped the lecture to beg everyone, including the professor, to search for her missing diamond earring, then offered to buy the group cappuccinos afterward. Only an intrigued Christie had taken her up on it and they'd been tight ever since. "How about you? Where did you study photography?"

He wiped his mouth with a napkin. "I earned a master's in Visual Arts at NYU." A closed expression shut down his face.

Touchy subject. Maybe it was where he'd met his wife? *Ex*-wife, she corrected herself. Either way, best to drop it. But despite her intentions, curiosity surged about his relationship history. She chomped on her second slice. Ham and pineapple. Sweet and salty. What was it about opposites making the best combinations? It hadn't worked for Eli and his ex, though. Their approach to parenting, at least, seemed to be at odds.

"How did you get into fashion photography?"

"My ex-wife, Jacqueline, was interning at *Faire du Charme* and convinced them to give me a shot when I graduated."

The magazine his ex-wife currently edited with her new husband, she recalled. It was the industry's go-to, must-have fashion authority. Impressive that they'd hired someone so fresh out of college. He must be very talented. No wonder he maintained a comfortable lifestyle with his graphic-design business.

"Laura's mother shares her copies with us every month. It's her bible." While her roommate had wealthy parents in the Hamptons, Christie had worked for every dime since middle school. Growing up with a chronically ill brother with hefty medical bills meant she paid her own way and pitched in when she could with babysitting savings. She blinked back the image of her parents huddled over a dining-room table littered with invoices, organizing them in piles: must pay, wait to pay, and wish we could, but can't pay.

Eli chewed on an ice cube and studied her. "How about you?" His eyes lingered on her outfit, making her flush. Thank goodness the blouse's high neckline hid her telltale splotches. "Do you follow fashion?"

She snorted through her nose, her mouth too full of pizza to allow the sudden laugh an escape route. "Only if it's on the Home Shopping Network or at a clearance sale," she mumbled.

His wide shoulders relaxed against the booth. He wore an apple-green polo shirt that brought out the blue of his eyes and hugged his defined chest. He looked like the guy in front of the camera instead of behind it.

"I don't know that channel."

What? Impossible. Her throat burned as her Sprite threatened to go down the wrong hole. Did he live in a cave? She pictured his chaotic apartment. Then again, maybe he did.

She pointed her straw his way. "You haven't lived until you've beaten out thousands for the last Marie Osmond Baby Olive doll. One time, I even made it on air."

His mouth parted, his pupils wide. "And you were excited about this?"

"Definitely. I actually spoke to Marie. Now I just need the Amaya Holiday Tiny Tot and my collection is complete." She smiled, picturing the porcelain doll's brown curly hair, blue satin dress and gold lamé slippers. "Trust me. They're incredible."

"I'll take your word for it." Amusement warmed his voice. He tossed a crust on his oil-soaked plate, looking shell-shocked but fascinated.

"Mary would like them. She sews, right? Makes Becca's dance costumes?" She started on the last slice, her sweet-banana-pepper-and-barbecue-chicken combo.

He lowered his glass, his fingers drawing lines in the condensation. "No. I do."

She tried summoning a vision of this tall, brooding guy hunched over a machine, stitching sequined hems. It was too improbable. Then again, he would do anything for his kids. Hadn't he proved that by inviting her into their lives?

"And the outfits…they come out—" Oh, dear. How to say this? She pictured poor Becca in puckered seams and crooked hems.

He put his elbows on the table, his dimples popping. Was it possible to be this nice, this handsome and this available in Manhattan? Yet here he was, the poster child for every Match.com advertisement. Only he wasn't looking for a date and neither was she.

"Haven't had any complaints. In fact, the other mothers ask me to make their daughters' costumes, too."

Other mothers? Jealousy seized her at the thought of other women clamoring for Eli's attention. She forced her tense fingers to release the daily-specials placard. She was being irrational. "How did you get started making costumes?"

His eyes wandered to a woman feeding her toddler bits of pizza. "Jacqueline left the day before Becca's recital without making her costume."

Her hand rose to her mouth. No wonder Eli had such a pessimistic view on life. "That's awful."

He looked at her, the blue depths of his eyes calm. "In some ways it was good. I was too busy teaching myself to sew to think about her."

Christie's breath hitched. She would have fallen apart, run away, but Eli...he hadn't missed a beat. Amazing. "How did you do it?" She meant that question on so many levels.

He shrugged. "I searched for 'hemstitch' using Google, pulled an all-nighter and the rest is history." His laced fingers stretched overhead as he shot her a smile. "I'm practically a legend at feather appliqué."

She laughed. If he could joke about that terrible time, then she'd follow his lead. "Another use for your arts degree, then."

"I have the battle wounds to prove it." He pointed to a small white line on the back of his hand. "Got that while cutting tulle. Do you have any idea how flimsy that fabric is?"

She nodded, smiling. "I made my own dance costumes, too, once I was old enough." She held up her palm and showed him a similar scar. "We match."

A strange look crossed his face. "Yes. We

do," he said, though it didn't sound as though he considered it a good thing.

Topic-shuffle time. "How's counseling going with Joan?"

Eli grimaced. "Pretty good. Tommy talks a blue streak but Becca barely says a word. You're the only one she opens up to."

There wasn't a formula to predict why a teenager related to one person over another. Joan was lovely. But Christie and Becca had a common past that the troubled girl must sense. She should try to see her more.

"I'd like to watch Becca dance sometime." She tidied up the table, stacking the empty plates and crumpled napkins.

His lips twisted upward in a crooked, adorable way, the left side followed by the right. "Actually, Becca wanted me to mention that to you. She invited her mother to her recital but she hasn't answered Becca's voice mail. It'd be good if you were there in case—" He stirred his drink with his straw, lids lowered, a tic appearing in his right cheekbone. "In case she doesn't show."

"But maybe she will." Christie offered him a hopeful smile. Perhaps she was away and would return in time to get the message. It seemed improbable that a mother wouldn't see her daughter dance. "Have you tried calling her office?"

Eli raised weary eyes. "A dozen times, but her assistant claims she's too busy to come to the phone."

Christie felt her smile slip and held it in place with a wish and a prayer. She needed to stay upbeat for Eli. "Then at least she knows about it."

"She's known about a lot of things," Eli said in a hollow voice. "It rarely makes a difference. Look. I know it's short notice, so I don't know if you…" his voice faltered "…if you have a date this Saturday?"

She could almost hear her gran laughing at this one. She hadn't had a date in, well, a really long time, even if last year's food-vendor visit with a male nurse counted. It was the closest she could imagine. Definitely a big fat N-O to her having any plans. Still, she didn't want to jump at the first suggestion of something…romantic? "May I get back to you on that?"

Something dark flashed in his eyes. "So, you have to check with someone? Like a boyfriend?"

A subarctic chill frosted his voice. Was he jealous?

She exchanged the salt for the pepper shaker against the plastic wine-list holder then changed them back. Why had she played coy? Honesty was always the best policy. And bottom line, she wanted to get to know him better.

Plus, she hadn't forgotten there were eager dance moms chasing after him with costume requests.

"No. I—I might have to work. Sometimes they stick us on longer shifts." Phew. At least that was true. An actual possibility. Her speeding pulse slowed. Hopefully it wouldn't happen on Saturday. Her eyes slid to Eli. She'd love to see the family again. All of them, now that she was being honest.

His shoulders lowered as he breathed out long and hard. "Oh. Good." He popped a red-and-white-striped mint into his mouth, his eyes suddenly crinkling in confusion. "I mean, that wouldn't be good, you having to work overtime. The kids enjoyed your company and we—" He looked over at the mother, who now held a sippy cup to her fussing baby. "I mean, *they* would like to see you. I still haven't thanked you for all you did with Becca. That boyfriend, I swear I could have—" His hands curled on the table.

She put her hand on top of his. She hated seeing him upset. "It wasn't me. Becca stood up to the creep. All I did was—"

She broke off when his hand turned under hers, their fingers suddenly entwined. The sensation of his palm against hers short-circuited her brain. Total system meltdown. What had she been talking about? And why was he holding her hand? Pleasure burst inside her chest like a bubble.

Eli squeezed her hand and pulled away, looking as confused as she felt. Did he feel the chemistry, too? She clasped her hands in her lap, wishing away the emptiness he'd left behind. She was glad he'd let go. Neither of them could afford to hold on. Not to each other. Could she fall for a guy with a bigger threat to her heart than Eli would be? A cancer survivor... She blinked fast to keep her emotions in check. He couldn't afford to get involved any more than she could. He'd lost too much already. He deserved someone who'd commit to him without reservation, without baggage heavy enough to bury her.

And still, that didn't stop her from wanting to use herself as a barrier between him and the dance moms. She was such a mess.

Hurrying to the receptacle to throw out their trash, she had a minute to calm her spinning senses. Hopefully, she'd be less affected by him when his kids acted as a buffer. This one-on-one thing was too much to handle. Exactly the reason why she avoided getting personally involved with her clients.

"Ready to go?" He held out her purse when he joined her.

Why was a manly guy holding a woman's purse one of the most endearing things ever?

With a nod, she followed him out onto the street. The air had cooled slightly and a small breeze blew back her hair. She jumped over a crack as they walked to the curb.

Eli flicked his eyes in her direction. "Whose back are you trying to save?"

Another break in the cement made her detour to the left. "My gran's. She had a hernia repaired last year."

They stopped under an overhead lamp, the light giving Eli's hair a soft glow. "You know this superstitious stuff doesn't work, right?"

She looked down at her pinched feet. Never again would she put fashion ahead of comfort. Even for Eli. She looked away from his gorgeous eyes. Especially for Eli.

"I've seen it work too many times."

"And fail, too, I'm guessing." His long arm shot up and caught the attention of a cab. "Want to share?"

She gulped. An intimate ride in the backseat of a cab with him was more than she could handle right now. "I'll get the next one. I have to stop at Pinkberry anyway."

His eyebrows rose, his eyes searching hers. "Then take this one. I'll have Becca call you about the recital."

Yes. Becca calling. Much, much safer. "Sounds good." She ducked into the taxi and he shut the door behind her. Pushing a button got the window down before he could turn away.

"Thanks, Eli. I'll see you soon."

His face brightened. "We'll look forward to it."

She watched him walk back to the street corner and stop beneath the pool of light. He looked like a movie star, one hand raised and waving down another cab.

After giving her driver directions, she leaned forward and watched Eli bend his large form inside a taxi that jutted into traffic ahead of hers. For a couple of blocks they followed, his solitary head outlined against the rear window.

Like millions of New Yorkers, he rode home alone. Would he feel lonely when he arrived? Or would he think of her and relive every moment of their time together tonight, the way she would?

A dangerous warmth curled through her, settling in her heart. She knew better than to daydream about him. Yet tonight, she would do just that, and thoughts of this complex, compelling man would fill that aching void inside her.

ELI PAID LITTLE attention to the buildings, cars and people flashing by his window. Instead he pictured Christie in that purple top, its silky material begging to be touched. Would it feel as smooth as her skin? Impossible. He'd never felt anything so soft except his newborn children.

He couldn't believe he'd actually held her hand tonight. Of all the dumb things to do. Yet when she'd reached for him, he'd acted on instinct. The desire to touch her was elemental. Basic. And far too strong to resist.

The driver honked to move jaywalkers out of the way as they swerved off Broadway onto Broome Street.

The feeling of her fingers wrapped around his lingered, the sense of rightness burning away the cold doubts plaguing him. With her hand in his, he'd felt lighter, more positive…her optimism seeping into his flesh. Her touch made him want to believe that everything could be all right.

He rubbed a hand across his face and watched a man and woman strolling down the street, their arms linked. It was the kind of simple, day-to-day companionship he'd always longed for. But life had dealt him a different hand of cards and he had to play the one he'd gotten. Believing anything else was dangerous.

Hope was a four-letter word he didn't dare

say, let alone think. His body had healed but his spirit would never be the same. When his chemo friends had succumbed to their illnesses he'd learned that it was better to keep his expectations low rather than getting his hopes up only to be crushed by despair. But he didn't want his kids to think that way.

Becca had spoken to him once this week— about Christie, but still…that was an improvement. And at Joan's urging, she'd also written an apology to the girl who smoked. Even better, she was playing with Tommy again and spending less time texting. To keep this trend going, he needed Christie. *They* needed her. If only his feelings didn't grow every minute they spent together. The bond they'd formed over John was strong, something they'd always share.

The cab jolted to a halt outside his building. He paid the driver then greeted a departing neighbor who held the door open. Inside, he raced up the stairs. Ever since the blackout, he'd been running them the way he had before cancer. And each day he felt faster, stronger. Maybe he could jog again. Even pick up his Nikon and add his own photography to the graphic-design business. Was there room in his life for second chances?

And was Christie one of them? Maybe he could share her optimism. Hold her hand again.

He didn't have to deny himself everything. The more he thought about it, the more right it felt. He was going to spend time with her anyway. He could take her to a movie sometime. Have a grown-up life away from his kids.

Besides, the loner inside him sensed that she felt alone in a crowd as often as he did. Together...

He stopped on the fifth floor and shook out his throbbing calf. What he was thinking was dangerous. But he knew he'd never get her out of his head.

Why was it so hard to start acting as if he had a future? As if he had the right to wish for tomorrow?

He resumed his climb, this time at a walk. He'd take things one step at a time, starting with including Christie in his kids' lives. Letting her go wasn't an option. The heck with Becca calling her about the recital. He'd call her himself. Make sure she wasn't going anywhere. It was something to hope for. To wish for, even.

He paused with his key in the lock. There. He'd said it. *Hope.* It wasn't so hard.

So why did such a small word feel more like a curse than a blessing?

LATER THAT NIGHT in her loft, Christie's phone rang. She tightened the string on her sleep shorts and grabbed her cell, trying to calm the fierce rush of her heartbeat. Could it be Eli?

"Hello?" She flopped onto her bed and curved an arm under her head, her pulse thudding in her ears.

"I hate him," sobbed a young girl's voice.

She sat up and crossed her legs yoga-style. "Becca? What's wrong?"

A bitter laugh sounded. "Everything. Dad won't talk to me about anything important and the one time I ask him to let me do something alone—go with my friends to hear them play at Washington Square Park Saturday afternoon—he says no. And I'm the only one who doesn't get to go. Now I look like a loser," she sobbed. "A loser who's failing eighth grade."

"First of all, you're not a loser. Probably only half the kids will show tomorrow, and secondly, you're going to ninth grade because we'll get that health project done together." Phew. She gulped some water from a glass on her nightstand. "What were his reasons for saying no?"

"Something lame...like there wouldn't be any adults around. But hello, I'm thirteen not ten. Not that he'd notice. He just wants me to be as miserable as he is."

"Maybe he's worried something will happen

to you. He's lost so much. I don't think he wants to risk you, too."

"Like he cares."

Christie traced the green-and-white pattern on the quilt she and her mother had stitched long ago. "He does. He just doesn't know how to communicate well."

Becca's sigh came through the phone. "Yeah. That's what our therapist, Mrs. Osar, says. But he's not getting better at it."

"Give him time, Becca. People don't change overnight. Maybe he needs another chance."

After a long silence, Becca said, "I'm over waiting for him to change. I just want to live my life without him stopping me."

"Please be patient, Becca. Think about it, okay?"

"Okay. Oops…got another call," Becca's voice rose, a tinge of guilt entering it. "You're coming to the recital, right?"

"Wouldn't miss it. I'll talk to you soon. Night."

"Night."

The line went dead and Christie fell back against her pillow. That was not the Roberts family member she'd expected, but she was pleased she'd been there just the same.

CHAPTER NINE

ELI TRIED NOT to stare at Christie on the way to Becca's dance recital Saturday night.

No easy feat when she looked so incredible. The Lincoln Town Car he'd rented was stuck in traffic, so he had plenty of time to watch her discreetly as she chatted with Becca about the school health project. He caught something about her volunteering to come in and work with Christie when school finished this week but couldn't follow much more when he was daydreaming half the time. With Tommy home sick this evening, there wasn't anything to distract him from the gorgeous woman sitting beside him. She drew his attention like a fireworks display. But just because he *could* drink in the sight of Christie in a modest black sheath dress didn't mean he should.

Funny how much he'd been thinking about her ever since he'd given himself permission to...explore all his options with her. Hope for something more.

He didn't have a plan. Wasn't ready to let

a woman into his life romantically. But he'd opened some kind of mental door to potential happiness, and thoughts of Christie had rushed in at the speed of light.

"Everything okay, Eli?" She turned to him suddenly, her green eyes missing nothing as her silver shawl fell off her shoulders.

The sight of her creamy skin and nicely toned arms nearly made him swallow his tongue. He wondered why such a conservative display affected him so much.

"Fine. Great." He told himself not to stare, but it took a lifetime to lift his gaze to meet her eyes. "Thanks for coming tonight."

She gave him more than just a feminine eyeful. She'd drawn Becca out and gotten his daughter talking, a feat he hadn't managed on the drive over to pick up Christie. Though Becca wasn't talking to him, he enjoyed hearing her animated and full of life. He'd missed that in the weeks of tension between them.

Horns honked in a traffic snarl up ahead as their driver inched forward. A car blasting heavy bass pulled up beside them, its occupants screaming louder than the beat. He raised his window, blocking the sound as well as the spicy curry smell spilling from a nearby food vendor.

"I'm looking forward to it." She shifted closer

on the seat, closing the gap between them. Her floral perfume flooded his senses.

Their proximity in the intimate, darkened space exhilarated him and his pulse raced. Amazing that he could form a coherent thought, let alone a sentence.

"Me, too." His voice hit a gravelly note as he contemplated how easy it was to be with her. How natural it would feel to slide even closer... He cleared his throat, knowing his daughter watched with the too-shrewd eyes of a teen. "That is, Becca and I will be interested in your expert opinion on the recital. I remembered you mentioned making your own dance costumes as a kid."

"You dance?" Becca leaned forward, engaged, her expression unguarded. How long had it been since he'd seen that kind of openness from her?

"Only a little." Christie smiled and shuffled a tap step along the carpet between the seats. "My gran says Irish blood is one-fourth superstition, one-fourth whiskey and one-fourth dance."

Becca took off her shoes and stretched her feet. "That's funny. What's the last part?"

"Blarney." Christie laughed. "It means stretching the truth," she amended at the girl's confused expression. "And no one does it better than Gran when she's telling a story."

Eli noted the way her cadence changed when she quoted her grandmother. Where Christie had the faintest lilt to her speech, her relative must have a heavier accent.

"Did you get nervous before performing?" Becca asked, craning her neck to peer out the window at a billboard. It featured a boy Eli recalled seeing on one of her posters. Too much teeth and bangs, he thought, rubbing his short hair. Did Christie share her tastes?

The car moved forward again and the familiar sight of Dos Caminos's outdoor area came into view. In another few feet they'd turn onto Sixth Avenue, just minutes from the Little Red School House.

"Always." Christie leaned across the seat to give Becca's arm a gentle squeeze and press a penny into her hand. "Put this in your tote bag. It was heads up when I found it before you picked me up. So it's good luck for tonight." At Becca's faint smile, she continued. "Imagine your nerves as something to wind you up and push you to do your best. Just breathe deep."

Becca nodded, her shoulders dropping as she relaxed a little. The car rolled to a stop and his daughter sprinted out the door before he could wish her good luck.

"Break a leg!" Christie called after her retreating form. Then she turned to Eli. "I think she's more nervous than she lets on."

"Dance means a lot to her." It was one of the few things he still understood about her. "She's been able to count on it through all of this upheaval." Their therapist, Joan, had commended him for keeping things as normal as possible for the kids' sakes.

And it was one of the few things they had in common. Sewing wasn't a hobby performed for the satisfaction of well-constructed fairy wings. He did it to be a part of Becca's life.

After they exited the town car, Eli guided them through the crowd of parents and milling, overexcited junior dancers whose colorful outfits made the scene resemble a tangled rainbow. Christie grinned, pointing out her favorite costumes or toward a preschool ballerina in a wrestling match with her brother. The whole place was barely controlled chaos.

"We're in here," he announced, glad for the opportunity to put his hand on her waist and steer her toward the auditorium.

He touched her lightly, but it was enough to make him close his eyes against a flood of longing. For a moment, he indulged in the fantasy of taking her home, slipping off her heels and pressing his lips to her bow-shaped mouth.

"There are some seats." She pointed to an empty row near the front. "We can save an extra for Jacqueline."

His ex?

He hated to crush her optimism, but there was no way Jacqueline would be putting in an appearance tonight. She'd shown far too little interest in her kids.

"Jacqueline's not coming," Eli whispered as the lights dimmed in warning for parents to take their seats.

Christie settled her shawl and purse on the chair beside her and then took out her program. "I'll save one just in case."

Seating himself beside her, he wondered what it would take to make her stop wishing for the impossible. Didn't she realize the cost of impractical dreams? The hole they left behind when they didn't come true?

Then again, would he want her to? His eyes flicked to her profile, its unique lines barely discernible in the gloom. Her unwavering positive outlook, frustrating at first, was starting to grow on him. Especially once he'd glimpsed the vulnerable cracks in her strong exterior. They only made her braver and more human.

"I'm not sure she'd sit with us even if she did show up," he muttered more to himself than her.

Not that his self-involved ex would necessarily see Christie as a threat.

"Sometimes, it's the gesture that counts," Christie whispered back, leaning close enough that he caught another hint of perfume.

He breathed deep. Focused on the moment. He was so grateful to be here with her. She settled him the same way she put Becca at ease. Made him feel less tense. More alive.

"This is fun," she murmured, pointing to the shadow of small feet behind the green velvet curtain on the stage. "Have you been to dozens of these over the years?"

He draped his arm along the back of her chair, telling himself he was just stretching out. Not touching.

"At least two a year. The first time I ever saw her dance she was only five." He pictured Becca, her head wreathed in sunflower pedals. "She turned in circles the entire dance while her classmates followed some kind of choreography. But they still earned a standing ovation."

"That's precious. And now she'll be a featured performer with a pas de deux as Clara."

She touched his forearm and pointed to Becca's name in the program. "Can you believe it, Eli?"

"I couldn't be prouder." He tried to ignore the electricity coursing up his arm at Christie's touch and the effect she had on him when she said his name, stretching and rounding the vowels.

Their fingers grazed as he held up an end of the drooping program. He peered down and smiled, thankful he was still around to see his little girl dance. Still here to spend an evening with Christie. "She's worked really hard for this," Eli added, knowing Becca hadn't had the kind of support other kids might. She'd achieved a lot in spite of her mother leaving and his absences to take care of his disease.

"You've got some great kids." There was a hitch to her voice that surprised him. "You're really lucky."

He didn't think about himself as Mr. Fortunate very often. But in this…Christie was one 100 correct.

His gaze lingered on hers when she looked up, her deep-set eyes a shade darker than usual. He wanted to know her thoughts, but just then, wild applause broke out as an older blonde woman dressed in a formal red evening gown strode across the stage to the microphone. He recognized the head of the dance school, a former ballerina herself. The woman tapped on the mike and then leaned down.

"Ladies and gentlemen, we are pleased to welcome you to tonight's show. As you know, the students have been working hard and we appreciate your strong support. For our first number, I hope you'll enjoy our newest—and youngest—students performing the teddy-bear dance."

"I did that dance," Christie whispered, her temple brushing his. His eyes closed at the sensation of her warm breath against the side of his face. When he opened them, a dozen girls stood in a line holding stuffed bears. The piano player banged out the opening notes and the girls shuffled and whirled, their toys clutched to their stomachs, pigtails bouncing.

"…because today's the day the teddy bears have their picnic." She sang along softly, her toe tapping the air, her voice never more musical.

"And it looks like you still know the steps," he teased, pointing toward her foot.

"When you're that age, the stage is magical." She nodded in time to the song, enjoying the show while he enjoyed her.

He imagined her onstage as a girl in her satin ruffled dress, green eyes shining as she held her stuffed animal overhead and turned. His heart contracted at the thought of the tragedies that loomed in that innocent child's future. Had her brother watched that performance, or had he been unwell even then? He couldn't imagine what it'd been like growing up with a terminally ill sibling. How had she survived losing her brother and her parents with her faith intact?

It was a question that gnawed at him every time he thought of his own children and his unpredictable future. A scuffle behind them distracted him from the unsettling idea.

"Sorry," barked a man seated in the next row, dropping camera gear and bumping into Eli's chair. "My daughter's up next and I promised to tape it since my wife's at home. Our son's got the flu."

Eli nodded. "My son's got the same bug." He stood and held out a hand to Christie, recognizing an opportunity to talk to her privately. Becca's number wouldn't be on for at least a half hour. "We'll get a drink so you have a better shot."

"Thanks, man." The doting father unfolded a mini-tripod.

Cheering broke out as the teddy-bear dancers scampered off the stage. One lingered, calling to her mother until the dance instructor hurried onstage and led her away.

Time for a quick escape. "Let's get that drink."

Christie's white teeth flashed and her hand folded into his. "Sounds good."

They shuffled past a few sets of knees then strode up the carpeted aisle to the exit doors. In the beige-tiled entry, several wooden benches lined the floor-to-ceiling windows. The glass reflected them as they strolled toward the concession stand, to all appearances a happy couple. To his eye, however, they were a possibility beyond imagining.

"A Coke and a Sprite, please." Her smile seemed to fluster the vendor, who blinked a few times before giving himself a shake, snatching her five-dollar bill and filling the cups.

She'd caught Eli off guard, too, paying for their drinks before he'd taken out his wallet. He shoved his billfold back down and held his tongue. Her curved mouth and the sideways look she sent him were too irresistible to ruin with some he-man, macho act. If it made her happy to treat, then so be it. But he'd definitely pay the next time.

He thanked her when she handed him the soda and nodded to a bench beyond an oversized ficus tree. "Let's sit over there." He couldn't wait to have her to himself. And the greenery would give them some privacy, blocking out the staring clerk.

With a hand on Christie's lithe back, he guided her away from her admirer. She was his, for tonight at least. Though even that wasn't technically true. Did she have someone in her life? She'd only half answered that question at the pizza parlor.

The tune of "Danny Boy" sounded as they sat. She pulled out her iPhone, read the message and fired off a response before he drained his cup.

"Was that your boyfriend? Danny?" He already hated the guy. Christie and Danny. The perfect Irish couple. How grand.

She snorted. "That was my very nosy gran." She crossed her ankles and lifted her soda. "Let's just say she's a bit excited about tonight."

Gran wasn't the only one. Eli forced himself to look away. "She knows about us? I mean, the recital?"

"Not from me. Laura told her." When she shook her head, a curled lock fell across her right shoulder.

Eli laced his fingers tight before he did something stupid, like run them through her hair. The feel of its softness was burned into his memory.

"Are you meeting up with her after? You said you didn't have a boyfriend, right?"

Could he be more obvious? If this quasi-dating game had umpires, he'd have fouled out for blatant fishing. But the penalty would be worth it to know her status. Any boyfriend, Danny or not, wasn't good enough for her.

Christie's small nose wrinkled. "Who has time for a boyfriend?" Her cheeks pinked as her eyes flitted to his. "And Laura's family drags her to fancy events with velvet ropes and ten-dollar drinks. Not my scene."

Relief that she wasn't in a relationship was tempered with a gut-clenching vision of Christie in a club, surrounded by men. Her roommate must lure her out sometimes. "What do you like to do on the weekends?"

"Sleep. Whenever my schedule lets me." Christie picked up a fallen teddy bear and strode after a giggling crew of dancers headed to the refreshment stand.

As a photographer, his job had been to capture angles. But never had he been more conscious of the importance of curves, of the places where Christie's body eased from one spot to another, from ankle to calf, calf to hip, waist to torso, neck to up-tilted nose, forehead to shoulders and down to the arch of her back. A long breath escaped him.

He looked away the instant she turned back.

What was a young, vibrant woman like Christie doing on a Saturday night with a single dad recovering from cancer? He wouldn't fool himself into thinking she was there for him. She'd come for the kids. Becca, in this case. Still. She could have turned him down. Told him she had weekend plans. And he would have understood. Not that he would have liked it one bit.

Another round of applause rang out from behind the set of closed double doors as she sat down beside him. "That must have been for the lollipop dance." Christie pointed at the program with her narrow fingers, her pink nails glowing under the fluorescent lights. "If we count the applause, we can sneak in just before Becca's number."

Was that a hint of mischief glinting in her eyes? He leaned closer, drawn by her devilish expression. "Are you suggesting we skip more of the performances? You'll miss seeing the different costumes I made."

"I have to admit, I'm curious about your skills if Becca's costume is any indication." She grinned. "Do you have any lollipops onstage now?"

Before he could answer, the exterior door opened behind them with a warm hiss of air. A woman teetering on gold heels clattered in, a wailing girl a year or two younger than Becca pulled behind her.

"You can eat after the show, so suck it up. Nobody wants to see a crybaby on the— Oh, Eli!" Her carefully plucked eyebrows smoothed and her white teeth flashed as she sashayed his way. Heather, the undisputed leader of the dance moms.

Christie's body tensed beside him. A quick glance showed her lips pressed in a firm line, her large eyes narrower than he'd ever seen them. He tucked a casual arm around her back and smiled at the surprised look that transformed her face. He turned to Heather, whose flirtatious expression faded.

"Nice to see you, Heather." Eli wrapped his fingers around Christie's shoulder. He nodded at Heather's daughter. "The costume looks great, Ashleigh."

And it did. Her fairy wings glittered and her tulle ranged from a bottom layer of fuchsia to gradually lighter shades. It might be one of his best yet.

"Thank you, Mr. Roberts. I love it." She twirled, her whining halted for the moment. The spinning showered the floor with sparkles. Perhaps he should have been less gun-shy with the glitter glue, though.

"I'm glad. Anytime." He pulled Christie closer when he felt her slide away. There was no chance he'd let Heather's autopilot flirting chase off Christie.

Heather kissed his cheek, her long fingernails digging into his biceps as she squeezed it. When she straightened, she tossed back her long blond waves. "Why don't you stop by sometime? I'd love to have you take a few photos of me. You know how to really capture a woman." Her hand slid down his arm. "You've certainly got me."

Christie jerked free and stood. "Aren't you late for a performance, Mrs.—"

Heather gave her trademark throaty laugh, ignored Christie and winked at him. Suddenly he was glad this was Becca's last dance year at the Y's community center. He was done with these predatory women.

"As Eli knows, I'm divorced." Heather's half-hearted attempt to smooth down her miniskirt only made it ride higher. "So I go by—"

"Ms. Tries-Too-Hard?" Christie stepped in front of him, her hands balled at her sides. "Why don't you let your daughter put on the show now?"

He stood, ready to intervene in case this

turned into one of those fight scenes from Mary's favorite show, *The Real Housewives of...* somewhere. Highly entertaining on TV, he had to admit. Not so much in real life. Especially where Christie was concerned. Her high color and stormy eyes, however, suggested she could more than hold her own.

Heather glanced between them, shrugged and lifted her eyebrows. "Eli. When you're ready to spend time with a real woman—" her eyes looked an unbowed Christie up and down "—you'll know where to find me."

Her heels beat a staccato rhythm as she traipsed around the auditorium to the backstage area, her daughter trailing behind her.

Christie paced in front of him. He'd never seen her so riled. Was it because of him? Hardly. Then again, he'd felt the same way about the soda guy. Maybe they were both nuts. His grin turned into a smile that became a chuckle before it turned into a full-on belly laugh.

"If she hadn't had a child with her, the things I would have said," Christie fumed then stopped and gawked at him. "And what exactly is so funny?"

He scrubbed a hand across his smiling mouth. "You, Miss Positive Energy and Light."

Her mouth opened and closed, her lips forming soundless words. For a moment he thought she'd be mad at him, but then he heard it, bell-like peals of laughter. She collapsed beside him.

"Ms. Tries-Too-Hard?" he managed to say. Where was optimistic, sweet, caring, scared-of-cracks-on-a-sidewalk Christie? And why did he like this spitfire side of her just as much... maybe even more?

Christie pulled a hankie from her purse and waved it in front of her flushed face. "She got my Irish up. Did you see that outfit? And the way she behaved in front of her daughter? What kind of example is she setting for her child?"

He nodded, glad he hadn't been on the receiving end of her ire. It was the first time he'd seen Heather back down, and she'd gotten into her fair share of scuffles with the other dance moms.

Applause broke out again. "Uh-oh. How many did we miss?" Christie blinked down at the program then up at him. He couldn't resist winding a loose curl around one finger. It had escaped her low side bun during her "fight." His fingers lingered on the silky skin of her neck and, unable to resist, brushed the shell-like earlobe that had fascinated him all evening.

Her quick, breathy intake stopped his heart. She

was so beautiful. Strong. Funny. Kind. And—he pulled his hand away—too good for him.

"Perhaps we should go in," she suggested, half rising, her voice rushed.

Eli tugged her back down. He couldn't let this chance go. He had a few minutes with this amazing woman and he'd rather spend them looking at her expressive face than at synchronized tappers.

Without releasing her hand, he blurted, "Are you having a good time?" He almost smacked his head. What a stupid question.

Christie's mouth quirked then grew serious again. "Actually, I am." Her eyes met his, their gazes locked as tightly as their hands.

"I'm glad," he heard himself say from some disembodied place that did not come from the land of reality and logic. "Happy you came." He pressed her hand, exhilaration shooting through him when she squeezed back.

"Me, too. It reminds me of my dancing years. I wish Tommy could have been here."

"Trust me. He's sorrier than all of us combined. Poor guy." He debated asking her the question that had been in the back of his mind. "Did your brother watch you dance?"

Christie's lids lowered for a moment. In the silence, he gave himself a swift mental kick. He wanted to know more about her but not cause her pain. And her pale, clammy palm proved he'd done just that. "You don't have to answer."

When she reopened her eyes, her lashes were wet and spiky, but her voice was steady. "He always made these insane signs to make me laugh. Like 'Christie the Great' or 'Christie Is the Best Sistie.' He did it to help me get over my stage fright, but the other girls made fun of it, so I begged him to stop."

He gathered her other, trembling hand.

"Now—" her voice dropped to a notch above a whisper "—I'd give anything to have one of those signs."

His heart expanded, wishing he could take away her pain. He'd gotten used to heartbreak. "You must have loved him very much."

"Not as much as he deserved," she said beneath her breath, more to herself, it seemed, than to him. "Excuse me." When she scooted off to the ladies' room, he berated himself. She'd done him a huge favor in joining him tonight— more than he'd guessed now that he knew about her brother. How brave of her to come to the recital for Becca, and him, when dance held such powerful memories.

He grabbed her shawl and purse and waited by the door into the auditorium. After a couple of minutes, she joined him, her cheeks damp but no longer ashen. When the crowd clapped inside the auditorium, they opened the door, tiptoed down the aisle and found their seats.

"I'm sorry Jacqueline didn't come," Christie breathed in his ear, sending shivers of awareness down his spine.

He looked into her earnest face and found himself unable to lie. "I'd rather have you here."

Christie bit her lower lip then studied her lap. "I'm glad, too," she surprised him by saying. Her shimmering eyes lifted to his.

His tight chest eased at her soft expression. They settled back in their seats and counted down the remaining routines, the silence between them as promising as the dancers who flitted gracefully across the stage.

CHRISTIE CLUTCHED HER shawl closer an hour later as she leaned back in the rented car beside Eli. Becca's performance had earned her a standing ovation and she glowed from the success as much as the reflected Broadway lights that flashed through the windows.

"So where would you like to go to celebrate? Pinkberry?" Eli handed his daughter a small bouquet of fire-and-ice roses that he'd stowed under the front seat.

Thoughtful. But then, wasn't he always? She glanced at Becca and was disappointed when she dropped the tissue-wrapped flowers on the leather seat and pulled her buzzing cell phone from her dance tote. She turned around and buried her head in the corner, her voice urgent and low. A sudden stop sent the bouquet tumbling to the floor.

She wished there was a magic eraser for emotions. She'd use it to wipe the hurt from Eli's face. He looked crushed as he picked up the flowers and stowed them in the door's side pocket. It might be something he did every year, but still…to have his efforts preempted by a phone call? Thwarted by a recent argument? Becca owed him more than that, no matter how much she resented him. Eli had made his share of mistakes. But Becca needed to own up to hers, too.

"Driver, would you turn up the radio?" Becca called then went back to her whispered conversation. The classical music blared, a symphony with enough bass to drown out her murmuring.

Who was Becca speaking to? Christie leaned forward. "Actually, would you mind turning that off?" She touched her temple. "A bit of a headache now. Thanks."

Eli shot her a grateful look while Becca twisted around in the sudden quiet.

"Got to go. Call you later?" Becca's eyebrows came together as she listened to the response. "Why not? Where will you be? Oh. Fine. Whatever. Later." She punched off the phone, shoved it in her bag and flopped back in the seat.

"That didn't sound like a friendly call," Christie tested, hoping Becca would open up. She had a sneaking suspicion she'd been talking with Colton...though how that lowlife had sneaked his way back into Becca's good graces was beyond her. Then again, young girls were easy to manipulate if they didn't have close relationships with their fathers. And Becca and her dad had fought recently.

Getting rid of Colton wouldn't right the wrongs in Becca's life. Resolving her issues with Eli would. Until then, she was a target for every Colton in the world.

Becca refused to meet her eye. "Did anyone see Mom?"

"She must be away." Eli reached out to pat her knee but she jerked it beyond his reach. "Sorry, honey. I'm sure she would have been as proud as we were."

"Is she out of town or out to dinner? She never called me back. Did you check with her secretary?" She crossed her thin arms and shot her father an accusatory look.

"Why wouldn't I?"

Becca pulled at a loose string on the seat's seam. "You're not exactly big on communicating."

Eli inhaled long and deep, his lips parting for a slow exhale. Those words had to hurt. But he showed impressive control…maybe too much when it came to emotional honesty with his children.

"So how about Pinkberry? It isn't too far and we can bring some home for Tommy." His measured words sounded mild, belying the throbbing vein at his temple.

"There are Popsicles in the freezer." Becca waved a dismissive hand. She wore her resentment like a bitter second skin. "And I'm really tired."

Eli raised a slanted eyebrow. "But we always go for a treat." A horn blared to their right as a driver narrowly missed a jaywalker.

"Things change, Dad. Not that you'd notice."

His face froze, blue eyes darkening, before he leaned forward to give the driver instructions.

"You did a wonderful job up there, Becca," Christie said, using a bright tone. The air was heavy with unspoken feelings and thoughts. It was either force a cab-ride therapy session or switch topics. "You looked like a professional ballet dancer."

Becca's face relaxed into its first real smile of the night. "Thanks, Christie. How long did you dance?"

"Until I was thirteen."

"So, why'd you quit?"

"We couldn't afford it after my brother got leukemia." She made it a point not to lie to kids, especially teenagers. It was the surest way to ruin any chance of making a connection. "I worked odd jobs to help pay the medical bills instead."

Two pairs of blue eyes stared at her. Eli's probing. Becca's intent. She straightened her slouch. "You never told me your brother had cancer."

Christie glanced out the window and tracked a bicycle messenger weaving in and out of traffic. What she would give to zip away from this conversation. "It was a long time ago."

"Still. You must have hated quitting dance. Hated him." Becca shot her father a guilty look.

Her heart sped at the thought. Had she hated her terminally ill brother? It was a terrible possibility...one she'd considered but wouldn't believe about herself. It wasn't his fault he'd gotten leukemia…or his fault that her parents had been too preoccupied to notice her, let alone raise her. She'd loved him, despite how she'd behaved toward the end. Her mind reburied the memory as deep as it would go.

"Christie wouldn't hate anyone, especially her brother." Eli's eyes met hers, his expression confident and more trusting than she deserved. Thankfully he switched the subject. "Becca is starting ballet classes at the Joffrey in the fall." He pointed to Becca's unclipped seat belt and mimed her closing it.

She put on her seat belt and pulled her hair loose from its tight bun. "Actually, I'm not."

A rush of air exploded from Eli. "Not what?"

Becca's face was obscured as she finger-combed her stiff locks. "Not going to the Joffrey."

Christie's heart sank as she wondered why these revelations weren't coming up in their family counseling with Joan—then again, the sessions were more formal, a format that resistant kids like Becca sometimes rebelled against.

She glanced over at Eli's tense face, her chest constricting. So many bombs were detonating in his life. Why would Becca turn down such an opportunity…unless it was to spite her father? Get back at him for curtailing her fun? It was an all-too-familiar motivation and one she'd never stop regretting herself.

"That must have been a difficult decision." She turned up the air conditioning. The cramped space felt stifling.

Becca shrugged. "I guess. But dance doesn't make me happy anymore."

"And what does?" She pinned Becca with a long look. "Colton?"

Surprise registered on Becca's face. "No. Yes. I don't know. Maybe." She pulled off a shoe and rubbed her toes. "Can we talk about this another time, Christie? Alone?"

She looked to Eli, who nodded stiffly. How awful to have your child not trust you with their feelings. But she'd seen it enough times to know that it happened to even the best of parents. She'd try to reassure Eli the next time they were on their own.

"But you're a good dancer." Eli spoke to Becca's averted profile. "Why give up? Don't be a quitter."

Christie winced. Family Counseling 101. Never turn questions into accusations.

Becca turned, every inch the cornered teenager. "Why not? You did it, Dad. Mr. Photographer, Iron Man, marathon winner. Whatever happened to those? Have you taken any pictures lately? Cleared off your weight bench? Gone on one of your old six-o'clock runs?"

Six-o'clock runs? She glanced at Eli. That was her routine. She'd never seen him while she'd been out. Then again, with her earbuds in and Laura's German shepherd, Angel, by her side, she was usually oblivious.

"What happened?" Eli's voice sounded strangled. "I got bone cancer." His fingernails dug grooves in the leather armrest.

"But you're over that, right?" Becca stretched out on the seat across from them and put in her earbuds. "Not that I've ever been allowed to know anything about your illness. If I hadn't eavesdropped on your phone calls, I wouldn't even know you were in remission." She turned over on her side, her back to the adults.

Ouch. Could the car be filled with any more pain? Becca's suffering flared hot on one end of the vehicle while Eli's grim hurt chilled her cold on the other.

The automobile pulled to a stop in front of her redbrick building.

"I'm sorry, Christie," Eli began, but she stopped him.

"This is what I'm here for. The good. The bad. And the ugly." She nodded to a head-bobbing, oblivious Becca. "I'm not going anywhere."

The relief on Eli's face nearly split her heart in two. He'd had a lot of people cut and run in his life. His fair-circuit parents had let his grandmother raise him, and his wife had walked out when he'd needed her most. Why would he trust now? Yet somehow he was. And if he had faith in her, there was hope for this family yet.

"In fact," she continued, a plan forming, "we'll be going somewhere tomorrow. Just the two of us." Healing Eli would help the children and now she knew where to start.

"Is that so?" His shoulders relaxed. "What are we doing?"

Christie opened the door and stepped onto the curb.

"How early can Mary come over in the morning?"

"Her husband drops her off at six before he starts his day shift. Why?"

Christie smiled. "Then meet me in front of your apartment tomorrow at six. And bring your running gear. 'Bye, Becca." She slammed the door on Eli's shocked face and flipped a wave over her shoulder as she jogged up the stairs.

Holistic healing. Mind, body and spirit. She unlocked the door, smiling to herself. Eli was in for Christie's version of all three.

CHAPTER TEN

WAKING FROM THE nightmare the next morning was like clawing her way out of a grave. The clumped dirt of it seemed to cling to Christie as she struggled to pull free.

"Christie!" A gentle hand tapped her cheek, making her eyes flutter open. Her roommate's refined features swam into view. "You're having a nightmare."

She sat up, her lungs burning. It'd felt so real. The suffocation, the crushing pressure, the sheer terror of being buried alive.

"Have a drink." Laura handed Christie a napkin-wrapped glass of water and perched on the edge of her double bed. Laura's streaked blond waves were arranged in a messy knot above her head, her contrasting dark eyebrows winged over her aquiline nose.

"Thanks," Christie choked out, the liquid spilling a bit as she brought it to her trembling mouth.

Cool morning air poured through an open window, making her shiver but clearing away the last clinging tendrils of the dream. She stared down at her hands, wondering why they looked spotless when the grimy sensation of fresh dirt lingered.

"Are you okay?" Laura stood and cinched the red satin robe her parents had bought her for Christmas.

Christie nodded and moved to sit in the rocking chair beneath her doll shelf. "Yeah. I just need a minute. Sorry for waking you."

"That's what friends are for, right? Ruining your beauty sleep?" Laura gave her a long, considering look, before her generous mouth quirked, displaying small dimples that everyone, including their besotted landlord, found irresistible.

Laura dodged the small pillow Christie halfheartedly chucked her way and moved past the screens that separated the sleep space from the rest of the loft. "I'll start the coffee," she called.

Christie gulped more water and glanced at her bed. It was a rumpled mess, the sheets and blanket a tangled ball from her tossing and turning. On a nightstand, a box that contained pictures of her family remained where she'd left it before falling sleep.

Sweat cooled on her body, her sleep shirt clinging to her. Why had this nightmare returned after a seven-year hiatus? She'd thought she left it behind in Kansas. But it looked as though she'd run out of escape routes.

"Hazelnut okay?" called her roommate from the kitchen area.

She stood and began rummaging through their joint clean-clothes pile for a running outfit. "Perfect."

"Better get a move on for your hot date!" Laura's laughter floated over the partition. "And don't wear your usual. Borrow one of my yoga outfits. Way cuter."

Christie bent to pick up a top but spotted a snapshot lying on the wooden floor. Staring back at her was her brother's Huck Finn face, his gap-toothed smile wide as he held up a catfish he'd caught at Rattlesnake Creek. Had she been looking at it when she'd drifted off?

The picture was taken on his tenth birthday, she recalled with a faint smile, her shaking fingers smoothing the cowlick that sprang from his freckled forehead. Her father had declared his fish the catch of the day by almost ten ounces, handily beating her entry in the ongoing competition that had been their childhood. Since they were only eighteen months apart, it had been a fierce, closely matched battle.

She laid the picture on top of a chess piece

inside the carved wooden box passed down from her mother. After placing the box inside her drawer, her hand hovered, unable to shut it away.

"Hey! Sleeping Beauty. Chop-chop."

The gurgling sound of their coffee maker echoed in the narrow, vaulted space. The brew's sweet, nutty scent spurred Christie into yanking on one of Laura's coordinated, yet clinging, outfits. She glanced at the clock—5:30. If she hurried, she'd have enough time to get her caffeine fix and dash to Eli's for their 6:00 a.m. run.

"You realize you're going to get more construction-worker attention in that outfit than a mouse in a snake pit," Laura warned as Christie wandered into their galley kitchen and poured herself a cup of coffee. She cast a glance at herself in the freestanding oval mirror across the room and gasped. Her lean legs stretched on forever in black spandex, an inch of flat stomach exposed by the short, pink tank.

Laura snatched her back as she hurried to change.

"Uh-uh. You'll be late. And since this is the first real date you've had in, like, forever, I'm not letting you mess this up. Besides, you look gorgeous."

Christie tugged at the top and gave in. "Fine.

But I feel ridiculous in this." She stepped past her friend's slender form and did her best to avoid treading on her electric-blue-painted toenails.

"Hey. That's my favorite outfit you're insulting." Laura handed Christie the half-and-half and some packets of sweetener. "And it's my lucky one at that."

Christie added the cream and sweetener then stirred, the spoon clanging against the sides of the cup. She wiped the container with a hand wipe for her compulsive roommate's sake…a quirk she accepted and loved about Laura just as her friend helped her through her anxieties.

Raising her mug, she quirked an eyebrow. "Didn't the gym owner ask you out the day you wore it?"

Laura leaned her elbow on their taupe countertop and cupped her chin, a faraway look in her hazel eyes. "Yep. That's why my membership's free." She pointed to the outfit. "See. It's lucky."

Christie gulped the warm drink, energy coursing through her with every swallow. "Sorry again about waking you." In a space a smidgen below seven-hundred-and-fifty square feet, every squeak, crack and bang was easily overheard, let alone a girl in the throes of a nightmare. Too bad the whirring window fan set in their faded brick wall hadn't masked the noise and let Laura sleep. She'd been out late last night at a cousin's cotillion.

"Are you kidding? I was so determined that you'd make your date I was already up." She rubbed her temples. "Plus, the champagne toast gave me a headache."

Christie eyed her sympathetically as Laura pulled open the fridge then came back with a frown. "We're out again."

"It's not a date." She pulled her hair into a high ponytail then pointed her spoon at Laura. "And what are we out of? And don't say pickles. I'm cutting you off."

Laura made a face at her. "Everything."

The girls sighed, their usual sound for all things blamed on their relentless lack of funds at the end of every month.

"How about I get some bagels on the way back?"

Laura peered into an empty cupboard and drained her coffee. "Murray's?" She rinsed out the chipped porcelain mug handed down from her eccentric aunt…the relative also responsible for their pink, diamond-patterned settee, elephant table lamps and the cherub-encrusted, gilt oval mirror. *Eclectic chic* was how Laura described it to their friends, although she wasn't nearly so kind when privately complaining about their clashing decor.

Christie nodded. Murray's was on the route. "An everything bagel with veggie cream cheese?"

"Sure." Laura rubbed her eyes, smudging leftover periwinkle eye makeup. "I wish you'd come with me last night. I could have used the support. All I heard from my uptown cousins was, 'So, when are you going to get a real job?'" She straightened a crooked potholder above their oven. "Can you imagine? Guess working as a public-school psychologist isn't good enough."

Christie gave her a hug. Not wanting to carry anything extra, she left her giant key ring behind and grabbed their spare key from the smallest in a set of Russian-nesting-doll counter jars—compliments of Laura's aunt. Then she headed to the door, leash in hand. "I'll go next time."

"I'll hold you to that." Laura looked up at their vaulted, exposed-beam ceiling. "Fingers crossed that my next family event isn't on a home-shopping night. Wouldn't want you to lose out on some limited collection thing they've only made a million of. Lord knows we could always use another doll around here."

"Hey, at least I pay the rent." Their laughter rang in the echoing, open space. Laura was notorious for running behind on the payment due to her insistence on splitting the bill for her weekly Four Seasons mother–daughter lunches and treating her students to surprise presents at work. She called them behavior incentives. Christie called them rent blockers, but she understood her roommate's big heart and wouldn't have her any other way.

"And don't bring Marie Osmond into this," Christie warned. "It's sacrilegious."

The force of Laura's eye roll loosened a false eyelash, making it droop from the corner of her eye like a black teardrop. Yet despite the smeared makeup and mussed bed head, Christie had to admit her roommate still looked beautiful. She knew Laura's colleagues wondered, even to her face, why she hadn't gone into modeling. Only Christie, who witnessed her roommate's razor-sharp wit the most, knew that her intellect easily eclipsed her appearance.

"Whatev." Laura yawned and placed the cup beside a matching one in the drying rack. "I think I'll go back to bed."

"Were you ever in it?" Christie cupped her hands around her mouth. "Angel! Here, girl!"

A scrambling, scratching sound erupted from

the rear of their apartment. In seconds, a waist-high German shepherd bounded toward her, a trotting Sweet Pea hot on her heels. Both skidded to a halt at the door, Sweet Pea's little tail sweeping the floor while Angel's beat the crisp morning air.

Christie clicked the metal clasp on Angel's collar and gave Sweet Pea a neck rub.

"Sorry, little one. But you know you can't keep up."

"Here, Sweet Pea," Laura called. "Treat!"

At the magic word, her dog scampered away. Good thing Laura kept a bedside stash.

"Come on, girl." Christie unlocked the three dead bolts and swept open the chain. In the hallway, her arms strained to keep Angel from pulling her off her feet as she turned the key in a lock before stuffing it back in her wristband's pocket and heading downstairs.

Fifteen minutes into her run, she yanked Angel back from a hand-holding couple. Her heart swelled, imagining Eli by her side that way.

A long breath poured from her mouth, a sigh more than an exhale. Like it or not, her gran was right. She was lonely. Running with Eli would be a low-pressure way to get to know him, to discover her real feelings for him without risking too much of her heart. A few more minutes and they'd reach Eli's home. Her heart jumped. Would he be waiting?

Funny, as thoughts of Eli crowded her head, the day didn't feel low-pressure at all....

AND HE *WAS* WAITING. Her speeding pulse pounded at the sight of his tall, muscular form atop his landing. She'd seen plenty of fit men in her life, yet never before had she fully appreciated ripped lines, sharp angles and powerful ridges. As he faced the opposite direction, she let herself drink in his toned, masculine beauty, the sight leaving her more breathless than the run. He wore black jogging shorts that exposed heavily corded thighs and calves and a long pink scar visible on one leg that made him look more warrior-like. A fitted gray sleeveless shirt left his broad shoulders bare, his biceps flexing as he stretched his arms overhead.

Angel chose that moment to sniff a fire hydrant, nearly yanking her off her feet.

"Christie!" she heard him shout. So much for a smooth *Baywatch* slo-mo approach. Then again, this was far more typical. She had to laugh.

"Guilty." She returned his smile as Angel and Scout bumped noses, sniffed personal areas and otherwise seemed to become fast friends, their circling bringing Eli alarmingly close. Her hands rested on his hard chest as she attempted to free herself. It didn't help that his clean, soapy smell and tangy cologne turned her fingers into thumbs.

"You two lovebirds getting out of the way or what?" grumped an old man carrying a sack of what smelled like cinnamon buns.

Eli smoothly sidestepped the snarled leashes and pulled her aside.

"Lovebirds," she repeated with a forced laugh, hyperaware of the large hand spanning her waist. When she looked up at Eli, his face was serious, considering and intent. His eyes were the cloudless blue of a bright, sunny day.

"It's been a while since I've done this," said Eli, his voice husky enough to make her wonder if he meant more than the run. He brought Scout to heel.

"Don't worry." She wrestled with Angel and got her into a sitting position. If only Laura had let her take the dog to obedience school. She reminded herself to work with the dog at home. "It'll come back to you."

His piercing eyes left her breathless when he said, "I hope so."

And with that, they were off, jogging block

after block, their pace easy enough to allow for conversation about therapy with Joan, Tommy's cold, and Becca's mysterious caller and her decision not to dance. More and more shops opened as they whizzed by, the dogs competing for the alpha spot. Thirty minutes in, Eli pulled up beside a bakery. Murray's. Christie blinked at him in surprise. Had she mentioned she needed to stop here?

"They make the best bagels. Would you like some? It's my treat." His impish grin made him resemble the young farm boy she imagined riding on the red tractor in his living-room picture.

Belatedly, she remembered the money she'd left on the kitchen counter.

"That would be great. Except I promised my roommate one. Would you mind getting her one, too? I'll pay you back."

When Eli smiled a bit too smugly for her taste, she gave him her order and hooked the dogs to a pole holding up the shop's awning. She sat at a small, white plastic table and contemplated the brown stain at its center. Laura would freak if she saw it and proclaim it swimming in E. coli.

A minute later, Eli's shadow fell across her. "One salt bagel with strawberry cream cheese and an everything with veggie cream cheese to go." He handed her the bag with a flourish and sat down, passing her a bottle of water, as well.

She sighed. Eli was always considerate. She chewed her salty-sweet breakfast and watched him as he fed bits of his egg sandwich to the begging dogs. In fact, he was so much more than considerate.

He was everything—and she couldn't deny it any longer. She'd seen the way his gait hitched the last fifteen minutes of their run, how he'd shaken his head when she'd asked if he'd like to stop and had run faster instead. No wonder he'd won marathons. He was no quitter.

"Good thing I bought two." Eli looked up at her, his eyes dancing as he bent over and divided the last piece between the dogs. He settled back in his seat, pulled another bagel from his bag and took a large bite.

She marveled at his exuberance. When she'd first met him he'd seemed so negative. Later, she'd come to appreciate his protective, caring way with his family and the lengths to which he would go to help them.

Now she saw Eli for himself. Free to spend time with her without any agenda. And it was heady stuff. His wolfish grin as he chomped away at his meal was more intoxicating than a Sunday afternoon with her gran.

Speaking of which…how would she keep this from her information hound of a grandparent? It'd been hard enough to convince her that Christie was only helping with Eli's children. Yet here she was on a second mini-date with Eli, no children in sight.

"You've hardly touched your bagel. Do you want something else?" His low bass snapped her out of her trance. She looked away. Had she been staring at him the entire time? How humiliating. Here he was, willing to go along with her suggestions for the betterment of his family, and she was indulging in girlish, romantic fantasies. She could practically feel her degree going up in flames.

"It's fine, thank you. I was just thinking—" Thinking? Thinking what? Her mind searched for an answer but hit a blank wall instead. "How long has it been since you went running?"

She grabbed her water bottle but knocked it over instead, her mind distracted by her pushy question and Eli's sudden quiet. "The only reason I ask is that Becca mentioned it has been a long time for you," she continued in a rush. His large hands joined hers in mopping up the mess.

"A year and a half," he said, breaking the awkward hush and forestalling her from more humiliating babble.

She watched him unconsciously rub his scarred calf. "Are you feeling okay?" she asked then winced. Curse that ingrained nursing training. Was this a date or checkup? Then again, maybe it was a little bit of both.

His handsome face, flushed from the run, looked thoughtful for a moment then relaxed into a small smile. "Better than I've felt in a long time. Joan suggested I take it up but I didn't follow through. I forgot how much I enjoyed it."

As he said the last part, his intense eyes found hers, the heat in them making her face warm once more. She'd enjoyed their time together, too. Their proximity had been as exhilarating as their conversation.

"How long was your rehabilitation?" Christie pointed to his marked calf.

"About six months after my titanium-rod insert." He stretched out his leg. "I've spent so much time increasing my design-business client base that I neglected building up my stamina. I've been running up my stairs instead of taking the elevator lately."

He sent her a significant look, one she couldn't decipher. "Thank you," she said when he passed her his unopened water bottle and unscrewed the cap. When she slid it back, she could feel his eyes on her like a warm glow. Being looked at by Eli was like standing in the sun.

Since he seemed fine with her inquisition, she indulged her curiosity. This was all about getting to know him, right? No pressure. "So tell me more about your business. You said you design book covers and things."

His seat creaked as he shifted his weight. "After my surgery, I wanted to keep my savings intact in case…" He crossed his arms and turned to watch a cruising police car. He cleared his throat. "So now I do freelance design work for book covers, logos, marketing campaigns, internet and websites…things like that. The business grew quickly through word of mouth and referrals from my former *Faire du Charme* magazine contacts." He swigged some water and lowered the plastic bottle.

"That must have been difficult, starting a business while recuperating." He could have lived off his savings for a while, at least.

"No choice." She followed his stare to a young father jogging with a baby stroller and suddenly understood what had driven him so—his children. He was providing for them—not just for now, but for a future he didn't count on.

Her chest constricted at the thought. No wonder he'd holed up in his apartment, withdrawn from the world and from his children. It wasn't that he didn't want to live his life; he didn't trust in it. And after his experiences, she couldn't blame him.

Despite her epiphany, she held her tongue. Those were big realizations to face. Her training told her this wasn't the right time or place for him to make them.

"So how's Tommy?" She watched the dogs lunge toward pigeons strutting just out of reach.

"Better, thanks." He bent over to tighten his shoelaces, though she noticed that he gave his leg a quick rub before straightening. It was bothering him more than he let on. "He was out of bed when I left this morning. Wanted to come with us. Cried when I told him no."

"Poor guy. He must have hated being stuck in bed." She nudged Angel's nose from her knee. Honestly. Next time she'd double wrap their leashes around the pole.

"He's bored. That's why I told him I'd take him to Washington Square Park to play chess."

"I love chess." She'd grown up playing with her brother, a tradition that had fallen by the wayside with his failing health. They used to play for hours, the competition fierce.

"Then why don't you come? Unless you have to work…"

Her head shook, supplying an answer before she was ready to give it…to consider how fast all of this seemed to be going. Her insides lurched as if she were at the start of a rollercoaster ride—the up, up, up sensation filled with the terrifying thought of how far and how fast they were about to fall.

"Great. Though I should warn you." He stood, an eyebrow raised, sharp and full of attitude. "I take no prisoners."

And didn't she love a challenge? "I don't plan on becoming one of them."

A short laugh burst from him as he unhooked the dogs and passed her Angel's leash. "So it's like that, then."

Their walk turned into a slow, steady jog home.

"Better bring your A game," she huffed, the heavy bagel she'd eaten weighing her down. "Wouldn't want to shame you in front of Tommy." The waxy bag she carried for Laura started to slip.

Eli grabbed it in midair. "Losing is never an option."

"Then you've never met your match," she shot back. The expression on Eli's face was priceless. She loved catching him off guard.

"Maybe I haven't," he said, his sideways look long and considering. "Until now."

Her mouth dropped. Checkmate.

CHAPTER ELEVEN

"THERE IT IS!" shouted Tommy. He surged ahead as they neared West Fourth Street and the south entrance to Washington Square Park.

Eli lunged for his son, his arm already extended the moment the wrought-iron fence loomed into view, the wind hissing through the leaves of the flanking oak trees. He'd been preparing for this possibility since they'd crossed Third Street. Good thing he had. A second too late and Tommy would have darted into the speeding traffic, single-minded, as always, to the point of recklessness. Thankfully, he hadn't gotten lost lately.

His hand connected with his son's collar. "Hold up. Wait until the light changes," he admonished, glancing over his shoulder at Christie and Becca. They'd trailed behind for most of the walk, their heads nearly touching as they conversed in low, urgent tones.

Tommy had tried getting Becca's attention a few times, but Eli had distracted the little guy by playing I Spy. When she'd heard Christie would be joining them at the park, Becca had offered to go—a first in months. More than ever, it became clear to him that his daughter needed a woman in her life. Specifically, Christie.

Something tugged at him when he drank in the sight of her in a white sundress, a summer breeze blowing back the gauzy material and her bright hair. Becca wasn't the only one who needed her. She completed this family outing. Made them—and him—feel whole again. He couldn't deny his growing feelings any more. But did he dare admit them? If he told her how he felt, would he scare her away? Given her past hurts, she might want to steer clear of a guy who'd had cancer. Was it better to play it safe and keep her in their lives as a family friend or take the risk to make her so much more?

"Do you see the park, Becca?" Tommy's sneaker heels flickered green and blue every time he bounced on the pavement. He turned to Eli. "Can I press it?" His stubby finger was already reaching for the walk button.

"*May* I—and, yes, you may." He sent Christie an amused look that she returned, smiling over Becca's head as they arrived at the curb. Warmth spread through his chest. Their private exchanges felt intimate, close. They banished the loneliness that sometimes went with being a single dad.

"Now hold your father's hand, Tommy," he heard her say when the light changed. "He feels safer if he knows you're near."

The afternoon sun reflected off Tommy's blond hair as he peered up at Eli, his blue eyes round. "I don't want Daddy to be scared." A small hand slipped into his and tugged him across the street. "Is that why you're mad when I run away?"

Eli was speechless, his eyes flying to Christie's. She raised her brows and gave him a subtle nod, urging on the conversation. She was so good at this stuff, so comfortable knowing what to say to kids.

"Yes." He brushed back his son's overgrown bangs as they neared the opposite sidewalk, the signal now blinking. It didn't feel manly to admit fear to his son…but he was a better man, an honest one, for doing so.

Tommy patted Eli's hand. "It's okay, Daddy. I promise not to run away again. Pinkie swear. I'll even tell our terrorpist, Mrs. Osar."

He smothered a laugh at the innocent word mistake and hooked his finger around his son's. Christie's effect on the children was incredible. What changes would she work on him if he let her? Perhaps he'd suggest they jog every day. Make it a routine and test the waters.

They followed the treelined pavement to an area separated from the park by a wall of multicolored pebbles set in concrete. A reggae version of "Here Comes the Sun" filled the air as players perched on green, metal-sided wooden benches, hovering over chess tables abutting the partition. Observers cheered and groaned when gamers made moves before hitting black double-sided chess clocks.

Eli eyed the regulators, wishing he had one of those clocks to keep his life on track. How much time had he wasted, since his cancer, withdrawing from his friends and family? Coming here today would help him stop thinking about his problems and help Becca with hers. He could get to know Christie better, figure out his feelings for her and, like the players at the tables, decide on his next move.

"Ten bucks says that girl's in check within a minute," said a man beside him wearing a straw bowler hat and a thin, black mustache. Tattoos inked his forearms into sleeves. Eli turned. Russian Paul. One of the park's infamous chess players.

A diamond pinkie ring flashed as the local celebrity pointed at a dark-skinned girl frowning down at a board. Her high ponytail and shoulder-length hoop earrings made her appear Becca's age. Her competitor, however, was older and wore a dress shirt and tie. A Wall Street type testing his prowess against the best in the city. Not that he appeared impressed with his current opponent. His arms trailed at his sides as he rolled his thick neck back and forth, waiting for her move.

Eli crossed his arms and shook his head. No deal. He knew better than to throw his money away on a bad bet. Russian Paul grunted in what could have been approval, disappointment or both and started to turn.

But a bill waving before his face stopped him. Christie. "You're on, mister," she said. Eli blinked at her. What on earth was she doing?

Christie's earnest face glowed in the bright afternoon sun. He should have thought to bring his camera. Did he even know where it was anymore? The need to locate it seized him in a way he hadn't felt in a long time.

"He's one move away from being in checkmate," she said, confidence ringing in her voice.

Russian Paul's mouth quirked. "You want to wager that the game is already won, young lady?" He pulled out a wad of cash. "Then let's double it."

Eli leaned in to warn her, inhaling her unique smell that drove him senseless. "It's Russian Paul. Save your money," he said, close to her ear. He wondered what she'd taste like if he kissed her soft skin—sunshine and spun sugar maybe.

Despite her sudden shiver, her delicate chin squared below glittering, deep-set green eyes. "Yeah? And I'm Irish Christie. So?"

"He's a legend around here."

"And I'm feeling lucky." She pulled another bill from her cloth purse. "You're on, Paul."

He smiled to see her spitfire side again, the one he'd enjoyed so much at Becca's dance recital.

The chess champion waved an elegant hand. "Considering I just won it, I'm not terribly concerned. Though you should be." His black eyes, the dark shade engulfing his irises, peered down at Christie. A smile played on his thin lips. Clearly he was enjoying the exchange, as were the few that stopped watching the game to observe them. Becca came up behind Christie and rested her chin on Christie's shoulder. The natural affection of the pose made Eli's throat swell. This was the last time he'd leave the house without his Nikon.

Christie rose on her tiptoes, peered around a

passerby then turned. "The banker guy is done. Stick a fork in him, as Gran would say. Look!" She nodded to the players.

The girl slid her rook across the board, bypassing a pawn until she hit the edge of the board. Her hand hovered for a dramatic moment as the gathered crowd held their collective breaths. With a triumphant smile that revealed a mouthful of rainbow-banded braces, she angled the rook in the opposite direction until it stopped before the man's king.

"Checkmate."

After a moment of stunned silence, raucous applause broke out. "Yes!" Christie whooped then held out the flat of her palm, fingers crooked. "Pay the piper."

How had she spotted a move that had eluded the best chess mastermind in the city? She said she felt lucky, but it was more than that.

"My brother pulled that move on me once." She rose on the balls of her feet and whispered in his ear. "Lost my favorite *Power Rangers* action figure over it. I memorized the strategy in case he tried it again."

Russian Paul doffed his hat, revealing a close-shaven head. "Let's make this more interesting." He gestured toward the now-empty chess table, a move that sent would-be gamers scurrying. "Play with me."

A collective gasp rose from the dissipating onlookers. Eli put his arm around Christie. She could more than hold her own, but he still had her back.

Surprising everyone, she took Russian Paul's twenty, passed it to an excited-looking Becca and sat on the bench with Tommy.

"Sorry, but we came here to play against each other." Her smile at Eli made his heart beat like a sixteen-year-old on a prom date. "Maybe another time?"

Russian Paul tipped his head and angled his brim. "Indeed. You have a lovely family. I wish you the best."

An unfamiliar look crossed Christie's expressive face as she watched the park celebrity amble away, hands stuffed in his linen trousers. Did she like the man's assumption that they were a unit? He hoped so. More and more, he couldn't imagine their lives without her, especially his.

Tommy arranged the chess pieces with Becca's help. "Dad, come on! What are you waiting for?"

A good question, he thought, taking a mental snapshot of Christie and his children, appreciating the thoughtful way she switched misplaced pieces whenever they weren't looking. He wanted to keep this image always. It would help him get through tough times. A lace of shadow and sun spilled across the giggling trio, their carefree smiles filling him with longing. If he had a wish for tomorrow, they would be it. And after today, he realized he wanted to share their happiness, take the risks he needed to in order to have it. Now he understood that, like chess, life required taking chances, regardless of the outcome.

Tommy was right.

What was he waiting for?

SEVERAL DAYS LATER, four feet and four paws trekked down the blue-tiled hall of Memorial Sloan-Kettering's Claire Tow Pediatric Pavilion. Christie maneuvered Sweet Pea through the shifting maze of equipment, linen carts and medicine trays, careful not to get in the way of children racing remote-control cars. Their giggles echoed off walls plastered in colorful finger-painted artwork and wooden animal cutouts. When her first scheduled stop neared—a pink door beside a window hung with zebra-print curtains—she passed Becca the leash.

Just this morning, she and Eli had talked over how his daughter would handle her first visit to the hospital. It felt great that he'd trusted her opinion. In fact, with every jog, he seemed to grow more open with her, willing to share his thoughts and feelings. Sometimes, he seemed on the brink of saying something about their relationship. They felt closer than ever. Were they about to commit to something bigger?

"Come in!" a young girl called at her knock.

"Hey, Vanessa!" Christie automatically picked up the bedside chart and glanced at her vitals. "Looking good. Your white-blood-cell count's up and you had a recent PET scan." The positron-emission tomography test meant they were still searching out treatment options for her medulloblastoma, a virulent brain cancer. Good news. Becca would make some tough visits today as part of her independent health project. She'd hoped the first round wouldn't be one of them.

"Sweet Pea!" Vanessa called, her arms outstretched. In her excitement, her knit cap slipped off, exposing her smooth head. Without the hat, she looked both younger and older than her fourteen years.

Becca hung back, a wriggling Sweet Pea clutched to her chest. Her ashen face froze while her eyes darted from the gray IV drip to the steadily beeping monitor that tracked Vanessa's heart rate and rhythm.

"So how do you like my crib?" Vanessa joked. The ability of pediatric patients to stay positive and kid around about their situation never failed to uplift and amaze Christie. One of the many unexpected gifts of working in a challenging field.

Color returned to Becca's cheeks followed by a tentative smile. "Very techno?" She stepped to the bed, passed over the small dog then backed away. Poor thing. If her father shielded her from this, it must be a shocking eye-opener. Was Becca imagining her dad when he was ill?

Sweet Pea lavished kisses on Vanessa, her paws on either side of the girl's neck. Between licks, the teenager managed to say, "Yeah. That was kind of what I was going for, with a little help from the oncology department."

"I like your curtains," Becca ventured. She strolled to the wild print and stopped beside a poster of a lanky boy crooning into a microphone. "And I have this poster in my room, too." Her voice rose. Christie released pent-up breath. Finally. A connection. Cancer kids only looked different. The rest was the same. The parts that mattered.

Becca's visit today to learn about cancer for

her health project was teaching her valuable life lessons, as well. How great that Christie was able to help open Becca's eyes to this world and facilitate a deeper understanding of what her father had gone through. In the long run, it might lead to their reconciliation. She discreetly crossed her fingers at the thought.

Vanessa put Sweet Pea down on her fuzzy yellow blanket and pointed at another poster, this one featuring several swishy-haired boys. "Love them, too."

Becca settled her hip on the bed. "They're totally awesome. I'm Becca, by the way. Haven't seen that poster. Wait. Is it signed?"

Vanessa nodded proudly and repositioned her cap. "Nick stopped in last week. It was my Make-A-Wish."

High-pitched squeals got Sweet Pea yapping and Christie wishing she had her earbuds. But since she'd been jogging with Eli for almost a week now without them, their whereabouts eluded her.

She wandered around the room, leaving the girls to their rapid-fire debate over which boy was the cutest, best singer, best dancer or had the most style. Sometimes in therapy the most effective treatment was to back off when something else worked. And Becca and Sweet Pea were more than brightening Vanessa's day.

The city skyline loomed outside the window, dark clouds hanging over it. That might mean rain tomorrow. Would her now-expected run with Eli be canceled? Disappointment wrung her stomach like a wet dishrag. This past week together had meant so much. It was still hard to process that he'd asked to make their exercise a routine. She never stopped feeling excited when she rounded the corner to Broome Street and found Eli waiting.

They saved most of their conversation for Murray's and she'd learned lots about him— his solitary childhood, where he'd picked up his love of reading, especially spy novels. How he got interested in photography by taking pictures of farm animals for sale. And why he'd moved to New York—to be with his high-school sweetheart and later wife, as well as pursue his dream of showing his pictures in a gallery.

"Christie? I think Sweet Pea's thirsty."

She glanced up and spotted her pet's pink tongue darting into a disposable foam cup beside Vanessa's bed.

"Oops. Sorry about that. Be right back with fresh cups and water." Out in the hall, she searched for the nearest utility room, grabbed some cups and held a pitcher under the water dispenser.

As the ice dropped into the nearly full container, her thoughts returned to Eli. Although she now knew his favorite sports teams, music, movies, hobbies and activities, the facts felt superficial. She wanted to know deeper information, such as how he'd felt when his wife left him, if he still had feelings for her, how he'd coped with his cancer, if he missed his parents...wished they'd made more of an effort to be a part of their grandchildren's lives or his.

Icy water splashed on her baby-blue scrubs, shaking her from her thoughts. She replaced the plastic lid on the water pitcher and headed back to the room. On the way, she waved to some of her littlest patients who whizzed down halls, riding on the lower bars of IV poles pushed by their brave, cheerful parents. A smile was a precious commodity to have in the pediatric oncology unit.

Once inside, she poured Vanessa another glass of water, shooed Sweet Pea away and sat in a rocking chair across the room. She watched Becca's animated blue eyes as she chatted with her new friend then slid back into her own thoughts.

Was she silly to imagine Eli would share so

much with her? Those were the kinds of personal details shared with a girlfriend, not a running buddy and family friend. If she wanted more, she needed to *be* more. Her rocking stopped and she leaned forward, body tense. Was she willing to take that next step? Become more deeply involved with both him and his family? Her resistance crumbled a bit every minute they spent together. She felt on the brink of giving in to those feelings, of throwing her cautious nature to the wind and letting it take her where it would—hopefully into Eli's arms.

"May I give Sweet Pea a treat?" Vanessa asked. "The nurses brought me some when they heard you were coming."

She nodded at the pretty girl, imagining her as she was in a bedside picture, all flowing blond locks and bronzed skin. A beach picture. Probably taken a couple of years before the cancer took hold. "Just two, okay?" Sweet Pea would be getting lots of treats today and, if she wasn't careful, a stomachache.

"Sounds good." Vanessa held up her hand. "Sweet Pea, sit."

The miniature spaniel's hindquarters plopped to the blanket. She raised her short muzzle and opened wide.

"You're so cute," cooed Vanessa before handing over a soft piece of spicy-smelling beef jerky. Her hands, bedecked with matching IV locks, stroked the munching canine's head. "I wish I was pretty like you. If I could have my Make-A-Wish over again, it would be to look like a model. Have my picture plastered on walls so no one would forget me."

Becca blinked hard and looked away. It took all of Christie's training to keep her smile in place, to hide the pain those words inflicted. It was an occupational hazard she never got used to. But Vanessa didn't need to deal with anyone else's emotions. It pleased her that Becca must have realized that, as well.

After a silent moment, Becca asked, "What's a Make-A-Wish?"

"That's my last wish before I…you know… I…" The brave girl's voice faltered.

"They're wishes given to reward strong cancer warriors like Vanessa," Christie broke in, her words steadying her patient's quivering mouth. And it was the truth. The foundation encouraged kids battling cancer, lifted their spirits. It wasn't a harbinger of doom. Far from it.

Becca handed the cup of water to Vanessa. "My dad never got to make a wish."

"Your dad had cancer?" The youngster's eyes

grew intent. She sat up straighter. "What kind? Did he— I mean, is he still—"

A rush of air escaped Becca. "Yeah. He's in remission. It was osteosar-something."

"Osteosarcoma. Jonah has that." Vanessa held up a *Teen Vogue* magazine. "He gave me this after his sister visited. He's in 16B. But you won't see him since he's allergic to dogs."

Paper swished, then Vanessa turned the magazine toward Becca, pointing at a page. "I wish I looked like that. Those eyes are awesome." She plucked at her hat. "One of the worst parts about being sick is looking sick."

Becca rummaged through her purse. "Maybe there's something I can do about that." She pulled out a small makeup pack and unfurled it like a sleeping bag. "Do you mind if I...you know. Give you the star treatment?"

Christie blinked, surprised to learn a new skill of Becca's. Not just the makeup, but her willingness to share talents most likely acquired in the dance world with someone she'd just met. Someone who really needed her. Christie felt a surge of pride that felt very near...maternal.

Heaven help her, Eli's kids were settling deeper into her heart every day.

At Vanessa's nod, Becca moved into action. With swift dexterity, she transformed Vanessa into a *Twilight* movie extra, her eyes as smoky and mysterious as the *Teen Vogue* model. Becca held up her cell phone, took a picture then handed it to Vanessa. As long as they weren't transmitting signals it wouldn't mess with the medical-equipment data.

"I love it!" Vanessa screamed. Her bouncing nearly toppled Sweet Pea from the bed. "How did you do it? I look amazing." After a few more squeals and photos, Vanessa grew quiet. Still. Suddenly gray-black tears trailed down her cheeks. "Thank you, Becca. It's been a long time since I looked good. I always wondered what I'd be like as a real teenager."

Christie's heart squeezed. What girl her age wouldn't want to look nice, to feel normal? Thank goodness for Becca and her hidden talents.

Sweet Pea gave a short bark, commandeering the attention she'd lost. Her fringed tail whipped the stale hospital air.

Vanessa laughed through her tears and fed the dog her last treat. "Sorry!" She looked down at Becca's phone and sighed. "I wish Jonah could see this."

"I'll go show him—16B, right?" Becca called over her shoulder as she raced from the room, her tissue-encased shoes sliding on the slippery tiles.

"Wait!" Vanessa called but it was too late. "Oh, no. How embarrassing."

"Be careful what you wish for." Christie grinned and sat on the bed. "You doing okay, Vanessa?"

"Hanging in there." Vanessa offered her a box of thin mints, Christie's favorite. How sweet that the girl always had them on hand for her. "What do you think Jonah is thinking?"

"That you look gorgeous."

Vanessa groaned and buried her head in her hands but Christie pulled them away as the door swung open.

"He totally freaked," squealed Becca as she rushed inside, her cell phone held aloft.

"No way!" Vanessa clutched Sweet Pea to her chest.

Becca dropped on the bed beside them. "He said, and I quote, 'Awesome.'"

Vanessa and Becca collapsed into giggles. For a moment, Christie imagined Eli "freaking" over a glamour shot of her and smiled. Lately he'd seen her at her worst after their morning run. Yet she'd caught his unguarded stare more than once. Often enough to make her wonder...

"And he wrote something on a piece of paper

then asked me to take a picture of it and bring it to you without peeking. If you thumb to the next picture you should see it."

Vanessa snatched the phone, eyes scanning the screen, her cheeks going up in flames.

"What's he say?" Becca pleaded, angling for a view.

"He says—this is embarrassing—he says that I look hot and he wants a picture for his room." Vanessa's rosy glow made her look more pleased than self-conscious.

Young love. Christie stopped her sigh, not wanting to minimize the importance of the moment. It was precious and poignant. Especially between teens with Stage III cancer. If anyone knew the importance of seizing the moment, appreciating a good day, especially after a bad one, it was kids like Vanessa and Jonah.

If only Eli would stop worrying about the future and enjoy his present. His remission was a gift, no matter its length. Christie checked her watch then froze. Something about the thought bothered her, reminded her in a weird way of herself. Was she equally guilty of not enjoying her day-to-day life? Did her past hold her back the way Eli's pessimistic outlook stymied him? She'd thought those hurts were long buried, but spending time with Eli and his family had shifted her perspective, making her uncomfortable with herself and the decisions she'd made.

She stood. "Sorry, Vanessa," she said, breaking into their post-Jonah analysis. "But Becca and I have to leave. See you next week?"

Becca put the final dabs on Vanessa's makeup-repair job, erasing any sign of her earlier tears, and rolled up her kit. "It was nice meeting you."

"Will you come again?" Vanessa picked up Becca's phone and viewed herself in it one last time. "And could you do cat eyes, like from the sixties?"

"Definitely. I've got big plans for you," Becca said then picked up Sweet Pea. "You know that other wish of yours? I'm going to make it come true."

Vanessa cocked her head. "What do you mean? Having my picture on walls?" Her short laugh ended in a snort. "Thanks, Becca, but besides Jonah, I don't think anyone would want that."

Becca flicked Vanessa's nose with a fan brush before stowing it away. "I do. Trust me."

The teenager's uncertain face lightened, small creases appearing at the corners of her eyes as she smiled. "Supermodel, here I come." She flung her arms as wide as her IV allowed.

Christie sent Becca a concerned look that did

little to dampen the confidence radiating from her expression. How would she make good on her promise? Vanessa had gone through enough disappointments without adding onto them. Then again, wasn't that exactly what Eli would think? No. She'd be optimistic and help Becca with whatever plan she'd formed. In times like this, faith, not doubt, was needed.

"Can we get you anything before we leave?" Christie pulled open the door, the hallway noise spilling into the room.

Vanessa smiled. "No. But could we try some lip gloss next time, too?"

Becca put down Sweet Pea and walked toward the exit. "We're going to do it all. Trust me. See you soon."

A few feet down the hall, Christie halted and looked at Becca. "So what's the plan and how can I assist?"

Becca inhaled deeply, the air leaking from her long and slow. "I know what my health project is now."

Christie straightened Sweet Pea's Angel on a Leash jacket and glanced up. "That's great. So why the long face?"

"Because Dad's the only one who can help."

CHAPTER TWELVE

ELI WATCHED CHRISTIE finish the last of her strawberry smoothie and stand, sweeping salt bagel crumbs from her navy shorts. The sky was gray as concrete behind her, the air breathless and warm. Rain was imminent. He could almost smell it.

"Early shift?" He looked at his watch. Usually they stayed longer, their talks lengthening every day. Amazing how quickly he'd taken their time together for granted. Counted on it. He'd planned on feeling her out about a possible date. But now this...an abrupt halt.

"Sorry to rush, Eli." Scout and Angel barked when she unwound their leashes from the iron grate separating the sidewalk from Murray's outdoor eating area. "I've got a standing appointment on Tuesdays and I get charged if I miss it."

He shot to his feet, fear lodging under his rib cage. Was she ill? She looked flushed from their run and as beautiful as ever in that natural, unstudied way of hers. Still. Appearances could be deceiving.

"Are you okay? Feeling well?" When he took Scout's lead, he held her hand, as well, more conscious than ever of her delicate bone structure. She looked capable of handling anything, but a fragile spirit lurked beneath that strong facade. It brought out his protective side.

"No. Nothing that dire. I always get a pedicure today and it's impossible to rebook Manika if I don't show."

He let go of her hand and turned, hiding his disappointment at their curtailed visit as he gathered their trash.

"How about I go with you?" he blurted then wanted to smack his head with the water bottle he'd lofted into the recycle bin. That was a ten on the lameness scale. As if she wanted a guy along while she got her toenails painted.

"Have you ever had a pedicure?" Her lips twitched in a way that made him want to kiss them, to taste the sassy amusement lurking in their corners.

"Maybe."

Her eyebrows rose.

"Okay. No." He shoved his hands in his pockets. "But I've heard of them."

"Are you sure you want to come?" She touched

her toes in a warm-up stretch, her auburn pony-tail swinging.

Eli shot the guys walking behind her a warning look that wiped the leers off their faces. He unclenched his hands, his eyes tracking the men's scuttle up the street. "Yeah. Let's go."

Pain in his knee flared when he sprinted for home.

"Eli!"

He jerked to a halt and turned, surprised that Christie stood where he'd left her. Wasn't she in a hurry?

"It's right over there." She pointed to a shop with a neon sign that read Toe-Da! "They have a place in the back for dogs."

He pulled Scout to his side and walked her way. "That's convenient."

"And good business." Angel barked as Scout returned. "They also do dog nails."

"Excuse me?" Now she was flat-out making fun of him.

"Seriously. You'll see when we get inside." She wrapped Angel's leash around her wrist and flicked a look at him. "Unless you've changed your mind."

Not if it meant more time with Christie. Tommy and Becca had spent the night at friends' houses to celebrate the start of summer vacation. He could stay as late as he wanted—the reason why he'd planned to approach Christie today....

"How long are we going to debate this?" He folded his arms and grinned at her.

"Until I miss my appointment?"

"Exactly." He lifted an eyebrow and angled his head to the left. "Let's cross up there."

A few minutes later, the dogs stowed in a room filled with chew toys and sheepskin beds, Eli found himself sitting beside Christie in a leather chair. His bare feet were sunk in a pool of swirling, flower-scented water. If John saw him now, he'd never hear the end of it. Though he had to admit, the warm liquid felt good, as did the vibrating automatic massager churning along his spine.

"Grand, isn't it? Aren't you lucky Dolores had a cancellation?"

"Uh-huh," he mumbled, closing his eyes when the kneading pressure hit his lower back. Aah. That was the spot. This was the most relaxed he'd been in a long time. Between the piped-in music, the hushed voices of the workers and the pristine white decor, he felt as if he'd stepped out of the city and onto another planet. If that planet belonged to women, then he was man enough to handle it. He came in peace.

His eyes closed when deft hands plied lotion on his tense calves, working the knots out of them. Even his titanium leg felt good. A sigh escaped him. Why hadn't he discovered this before? Then again, how could he? Before Christie, he'd rarely made time for anything besides his work and family.

"Red today?"

His eyes snapped open. Okay. There was only so far he'd venture into the land of femininity.

But the speaker was Manika rather than Dolores. He followed the direction of her impossibly long fingernail to a display case that contained a dizzying number of shades nearly the same color. Insanity. Who could choose one over the other?

"I'll take the I'm So Not a Waitress, thanks," said Christie, certainty ringing in her voice. Manika's asymmetrical black bob swung as she headed to the wall.

Christie turned, her cheeks flushed. "Not that anyone gets to see them when I'm walking around all day in my sneakers. But still. I like knowing my nails look great, especially when the rest of me is a hot mess."

"You always look fantastic," he said, unable to help himself.

"Oh." Her face matched the shade Manika skillfully applied to her slender toes.

He shrugged and backpedaled. "I just mean you don't need any of this."

He had to admit he enjoyed surprising her silent if only for a few moments. He liked watching her eyes close during the pedicure, her face relaxed and happy. And twenty minutes later, he agreed it was a shame to cover up her delicate, red-tipped toes. He'd never really thought much about feet until now. But seeing her high arches curving into soft rounded heels made him itch to hold one like a Disney prince. Try on the glass slippers to see if they fit. Him and her.

His generous tip earned him a mumbled thanks from Dolores while he waited for Christie's toes to dry. At the front window, he pulled on his socks and sneakers, peering at the heavy, dark sky. It didn't look much worse than it had earlier, but there was an oppressive stillness to the air that seeped in whenever a new customer rushed inside.

Twenty minutes later, Christie joined him by the glass. The top of her soft ponytail brushed against his arm, sending shivers of awareness through him. "Should we chance it?"

"We can race."

"My pedicure might smudge, but this looks

bad. I'll get the dogs." She dashed to the back as the city rumbled with thunder, soft at first, then growing louder. It was a thirty-minute run back to his place. Without lightning in sight, they might make it. Just.

"Thanks, Manika!" Christie called as she bounded his way, the dogs scrambling for the door. She tossed him a leash and they flew outside.

"Wow, did it get hot," she breathed beside him. A metallic rattle sounded as their feet pounded over a grille.

"It's definitely more humid." He eyed the clouds, their underbellies more purple now than gray.

They ran between people carrying umbrellas, dodging workers scurrying to their offices. Street vendors called to one another as they stashed their gear and stowed their products. Grateful riders flung open cab doors then slammed them shut, spared from the impending storm. Inevitability hung thick in the heavy air. Something flickered on the edge of his peripheral vision. Lightning?

"Let's push it." His breath came harder now, the pain in his knee a steady burn.

"You got it," Christie huffed, her legs pumping faster.

The dogs, excited by the storm and the faster run, were more unruly than ever. When Angel nearly yanked Christie off her feet, he held out a hand.

"I'll take her."

Christie shook her head, her small chin set. "Heel, Angel," she commanded, her tone as ominous as the thunder rolling through the city. The German shepherd wheeled back and matched her gait to Christie's.

Street numbers flashed by, the growing numbers suggesting they were closing in on his building. They would make it. Then Christie called a warning over her shoulder just as he felt a drop of rain slide down his nose.

They quickened their pace to a sprint, the turn to Broome Street in sight. Umbrellas snapped open around them, the sound as sharp as the lightning crackling overhead. Within seconds, rain fell, first in fat splatters, then finer, harder. The slick sidewalk grew treacherous and he automatically put a hand behind Christie's elbow, close enough where he could help, far enough away that she wouldn't know.

Another moment and they'd be home. But it was a minute too late. By the time they'd reached his stairs, their clothes were dark and dripping. He swiped at his smeared vision.

"Come inside," he called as a clap of thunder sounded overhead. She looked up the street then back at him, her hair plastered to her skull. A bolt of lightning made her jump.

"Hold the door!"

And with a final boom that could only have been heaven-sent, he had exactly what he'd hoped for. Christie. All to himself.

"AH-CHOOO." CHRISTIE PULLED another tissue from the box Eli had placed on the coffee table and rubbed her nose. What was it about rain that made her feel that a cold was coming on?

"Soup's almost done," Eli called from the kitchen.

"Great, though I don't think I've ever eaten chicken noodle at ten in the morning." It was sweet the way Eli had fussed since he'd pulled her close on that terrifying elevator ride, not seeming to mind or notice her clammy skin. If only she'd had room in her wrist pocket for her rabbit's foot.

"Did you dry your hair yet?"

She rubbed at the strands with the towel again. "I'm trying. There's a lot of it"

Cabinets banged open and closed. "Where is the ladle?" she heard him mutter. Then louder, "Use Becca's blow-dryer."

"I think I've borrowed enough of her things." She looked down at the rolled-up sweatpants and the T-shirt that she'd pilfered from Becca's closet. "Try the lazy Susan if you haven't checked there."

"Got it, thanks. Mary's been organizing everything lately, and I haven't learned her system yet." Something metallic-sounding crashed to the floor. "Lost the ladle."

Honestly. Men. Christie pushed off the plush blanket he'd wrapped around her and rose.

"Uh-uh. Stay put, Christie." Eli held out a hand. "I've got this. I'll use one of the serving spoons."

"Avoid the one with the holes in it," she called and bit back a smile.

"Huh. Hadn't thought of that." Eli laughed.

She burrowed into her fluffy covering. Yep. He had it under control. A part of her couldn't deny how good it felt to be the one taken care of.

"Ouch!" Eli's exclamation made her wince and glance into the open cooking space. He shook his hand and glared at the steaming pot he'd dropped to the granite countertop.

"Potholders are—"

"On the hooks above the stove. I see them now. With all of this reordering, it's hard to keep track."

"You're sure you don't want any—"

"Nope." With his hands encased in puffy red gloves, he poured thick, yellow soup into each bowl.

She wiggled her foot free of Tommy's oversized green claw slippers, a surprising fit, and admired her slightly smudged, but still glowing-red manicure. She was so not a waitress…a thought that made her smile. Luckily she'd gotten hold of Laura, who'd agreed to take care of Sweet Pea before heading to her office. She could linger as long as she wanted since she had the day off.

"It's hot." Two bowls thunked on the glass coffee table, and Eli laid a cloth napkin across her lap.

Unable to resist the chicken broth's aroma, she leaned forward and inhaled deeply, feeling warmed to her toes without taking a sip. This was the life. Eli beside her with a shared meal and a comfortable silence between them.

While she waited for the soup to cool, she gazed at the framed tractor photograph. He really was talented. His picture perfectly captured the beauty of everyday American life.

"Tell me more about growing up in Kentucky." She took a cautious sip of soup and sighed at the delicious flavor exploding on her tongue.

His spoon clanked against the side of the

bowl. When he turned toward her the cushion space between them sank, drawing them closer.

"I told you about living with my grandmother, and that my parents work the fair circuit?"

Christie nodded. "Where are they now?"

Eli's blue eyes clouded over. "My best guess is Kalamazoo. We haven't spoken in a few years."

Her hand rose to her throat. "Oh." More ghosts in Eli's life, their presence felt but never seen. "So, how do you know they're in Michigan?"

He downed another spoonful. "Mom posts her schedule online so carnival fans can follow."

Soup sloshed from her spoon onto the table and their hands brushed as they each reached for a napkin. She dabbed up the spill then asked, "How long has this been going on?"

"Since I moved to New York. They call every once in a while—when the kids were born, to wish me well on my wedding day, birthdays sometimes." His spoon stabbed into his bowl again and fished out another bite of noodles.

"And you never told them you had cancer," she said, thinking out loud. Then she took another mouthful. Eli had practically shut out the whole world. Why, then, had he let her in? The kids were one thing...but their jogs, the intimate moments alone…this had to mean something. It did to her, as scared as she was to admit it.

"No. They wouldn't have come anyway unless they booked the state fair in Syracuse." He polished off his meal and leaned back, arms crossed behind his head, an elbow resting lightly on her shoulder.

"But how do you know? If they knew how sick you were—"

"They would have pitched in to help, like Jacqueline?"

She tried to keep the pity out of her eyes.

"I couldn't have any more people coming in and out of my children's lives," he continued in a low, even voice. "They'd done it enough to me as a kid."

Her heart ached for the boy who'd been abandoned by his parents. The wound of their leaving had never fully healed. Suddenly his initial unwillingness to include her made sense. He'd thought she'd walk away, too, raising his children's hopes only to disappoint them. Amazing that he'd taken such a risk with her. She wanted to reassure him that she'd live up to his expectations, but her past rose up and mocked the words before she could say them.

"That must have been rough for you." When

his arm stretched out behind her, she rested her head against it. It was as close to being in his arms as she dared, every atom in her body aware of the muscular form against her side.

They turned their heads at the same moment and touched noses. His eyelashes brushed her brow when he blinked in surprise. She drew back and grabbed for another tissue, feeling a sneeze coming on. Perfect timing. For a moment she'd thought he'd been about to...

"Bless you," he said, his fingers brushing back the damp tendrils clinging to her forehead.

The gentle pressure of his hand lingered against the side of her face, his fingers cupping her chin so tenderly that it made her heart ache. Why did he touch her like this when they were alone, with the soft, gray light streaming through the windows and the rain drumming a low beat? Everything felt intimate, close...possible. Her heart rolled itself up into a thumping ball and lodged in her throat. Would she ever learn to accept that friendship was all there'd be for her and Eli?

She stacked their empty bowls and headed for the kitchen. Space. It would clear her head of impossible notions. But Eli followed, hot on her heels. He'd showered when they'd returned home and the clean smell of him made her nose twitch, her senses shift into overdrive.

"Tell me more about your treatment. You said you had rehab for six months." She turned on the water and ran her hands under the cold. *Snap out of it. He's just a friend.*

"Chemo and radiation for eight months, then surgery, recovery and rehab lasted another eight." He grabbed a towel and dried the cutlery and bowls when she'd finished washing them, his hands brushing hers, it seemed, at every opportunity. Was he doing this on purpose? Could he be pursuing her?

"And who took care of you? Jacqueline?"

He snorted. "When she heard about my diagnosis, she left. Said she'd spent too many years caring for her mother's ten kids and was done."

Christie wiped her hands dry on the towel Eli handed her, understanding Jacqueline's harsh decisions a bit more now. "But Tommy and Becca. She'd cared for them."

Eli shrugged and got out a pitcher of tea. At her nod he grabbed a couple of glasses and poured. "She never wanted kids, either. She told me that before we got married but I thought I could change her mind. Believed that once she saw her own, it'd be different."

That sounded like something she would have thought. Her heart took a sweeping dive in her chest. Poor Eli. He'd endured more than his fair share of disappointments, yet he also owned up to his role in them.

She took the drink he passed her and followed him back to the living room. When she tucked her heels beneath her, he gently tugged them loose and held them on his lap instead. The feel of his warm hands on her sensitive feet was overwhelming, but she was powerless to resist. Instead, she turned so that her back rested against the couch's side. It gave her a better view of his rugged, handsome profile.

"You weren't wrong to hope for that."

He tapped his empty left ring finger. "I should have listened."

"If you had, you wouldn't have Becca or Tommy." She shifted her weight and his hands gripped her slipping feet.

"Which is why I wouldn't change a thing."

Here was the chance to ask the million-dollar question. She couldn't pass it up. "Even her walking out?"

"Especially that." He leaned closer, their

noses touching once more. "Because then I wouldn't have met you."

Her lips parted in surprise. Her heart beat a rapid dance in her chest as she breathed in the moment and the man.

Time felt suspended as she thought about crossing the friendship line. There was no denying her feelings for him. But did she dare risk the chance that he might get sick again? That she'd end up hurting him somehow? He'd barely survived Jacqueline. She cared too much for him now to put his heart in jeopardy again.

"Eli, I don't know."

He pulled back and her whole body seemed to protest. *No!* She wanted that moment back again, even if she knew she'd made the right choice. The right choice hurt.

"I don't want to rush you." His deep voice rumbled through her, drawing her closer in spite of herself.

She wanted to lean into his arms. His warmth.

"You're not." She shook her head. Confused. "I'm just not sure. I don't want to—"

"It's okay." He nodded, his shoulders stiff. Tense. "I'm not going anywhere."

Yet.

Had she thought it or had he? The word hung

between them, a scary, dark possibility she couldn't face. She swallowed hard, scooting a little farther away from him before she gave in to this crazy swell of emotions.

"Christie, wait." His words made her realize she was still backing up, little by little.

She forced herself to stop.

"Mary is helping me… We're having a party here in a few days. For my birthday."

She was already nodding, absurdly grateful he wasn't shutting her out of his life because she hadn't kissed him. She wanted…so much. His friendship had become important in such a short span of time.

"I'm glad you're having a party, Eli." Her voice sounded funny in her ears, but then her heart still did little flips in her chest.

"No matter what the future holds for us, Christie, I'd like you to be there." He cleared his throat. "At the party."

"Okay." She would call for the time later. She was already collecting her things before she made an idiot of herself and kissed him. Backing away again. "Um. Yes. Thank you. I'll be there."

Of course she'd be there. Because even though she hadn't kissed him today, she couldn't imagine her world without him in it. And if he wanted more from her? She needed to get her head on straight and figure out what that meant for her future.

CHAPTER THIRTEEN

"Hush, Gran. Please. You're not an invited guest." Christie hefted a birthday present in her arms—an Ansel Adams anthology of America's national parks—and raised her hand to knock. She'd seen a book by the same photographer at Eli's apartment, but not this one. Hopefully, he'd like it. She'd been thinking about him every moment since the day of the storm....

"I *am* the party, so who needs an invitation?" huffed Gran. She held up a bottle of Jameson whiskey in one hand and tinfoil-wrapped Irish soda bread in the other. "Besides, it was a simple question. Is Eli your boyfriend?"

Her knuckles paused on the black-varnished door without rapping. It wasn't an easy question. He would be if she'd kissed him that day when they'd been so close. But she'd been scared and unsure. Now wanting more with him was a message her heart kept sending, a love song stuck on replay.

"Please don't embarrass me, Gran. We're just friends."

Lines burst around her elder's pursed lips. "Ach. As if I could embarrass anyone. I speak the truth, is all. Can we go inside now, instead of standing on the stoop like beggars?"

Christie looked down at the Persian rug before Eli's double doors and smiled. A far cry from her grandmother's old immigrant neighborhood. Gran's struggles in life had taught the woman to speak her mind. It wasn't in Christie's power to change that now.

The door swung open a moment after she knocked, revealing a smiling Mary on the other side. She looked lovely in a rose-colored blouse and a black skirt, making Christie glad she'd worn Laura's blue shift dress and open-toed heels. She tugged at the flared hemline, knowing its abbreviated length would drive her crazy all night. But that was what she got for ceding outfit control to her fashion-maven roommate.

"Hello, Christie. And this must be Rosaline. Welcome." Mary gestured into the lofty space and waited for them to cross the threshold. "May I take your things?"

"Only if you promise not to keep them for yourself," said Gran with a wink, handing over her bottle and the soda bread. Christie winced but Mary only smiled.

Mary lifted the package and sniffed, her eyes

closing as she sighed. "Can't make that vow with my husband around." She pointed to her uniformed spouse, who must have stopped in for a quick visit. "He's partial to Irish soda bread and this smells like a fine batch." With that, she bustled into the kitchen.

"Jaaaapers. Would you look at this," Gran whispered, elbowing her as she craned her neck, taking in the expansive space. "You've caught yourself a fine feller."

"Gran!" she hissed then plastered on a smile as a beaming Eli came forward, his eyes never bluer against a crisp white dress shirt and an emerald tie, his black dress slacks accentuating his narrow hips and long legs.

Just seeing him did funny things to Christie's insides.

"And what a looker," added Gran, her eyes sparkling as she extended a hand.

"You're cutting a fine figure yourself, Mrs. Bates." Eli raised her hand to his twitching lips. "May I return the compliment?"

"How could you not?" Gran turned in a slow circle, her yellow chiffon pleats swirling above her knees.

While they shared a laugh, Christie wriggled her toe in her narrow shoe, feeling oddly unsure of herself after the way she and Eli had last parted.

His eyes brightened as they turned her way. "Hello, Christie." His husky voice and direct look sent a shiver over her skin.

"Happy birthday." Why did she sound out of breath? Now she was the one making a spectacle of herself. "I brought you a present," she added inanely then wished she could smack herself in the head with it, put herself out of this awkward misery. After all the time they'd spent together, why did she feel so unsure and shy? Then again, Eli's piercing gaze and her gran's raised eyebrows weren't helping. Now, more than ever, she realized they might not be able to go back to being just friends.

He held her hands and angled them out from her sides, eyeing her minidress. "It's perfect," he breathed then winked at her. "I mean, I'm sure the present is perfect. Thanks. May I get you anything to drink?"

The question was asked of both of them, but his eyes lingered on her, making her heart beat faster. He definitely hadn't pulled away since she'd rebuffed his earlier advance. Was it wrong of her to feel oddly glad about that?

"Sweet tea?" she asked in a soft voice, unable to look away from this gorgeous man. She inhaled his lemon-scented musk, the clean fragrance of his skin, and resisted the urge to close the narrow space between them with a birthday hug.

"Jameson for me," said Gran. "Hey, you got anything more jazzy than this classical stuff? Sounds like a funeral dirge, and at my age, I don't need a reminder. Let's liven up the party."

Heaven help her, Christie thought, hoping Gran didn't scare everyone off before the clock struck nine.

But Eli simply pointed at the CD tower beside an elaborate sound system set in custom-built shelves. "Help yourself. Be right back." With a last, long look at Christie, his expression unreadable, he headed off. Why was he behaving so differently tonight? If she didn't know better, she'd swear he was flirting.

"I'm with you, doll," said a voice behind them.

Christie turned. "John!" After a quick hug and a discreet bow-tie straightening she gestured to her grandmother. "Gran, you remember John?"

John's spotted hand held the elderly woman's fingers. "Someone as good-looking and young as you should never be called Gran." Like Eli, he lifted her grandmother's fingers to his mouth. Unlike Eli, he didn't let go.

Gran preened, tossing back her soft white waves and fluttering her long eyelashes. "It's Rosaline, remember? But call me Rose."

A sense of inevitability built inside of Christie. Wasn't this what she'd imagined if these larger-than-life personalities got to spend any time together? One of the many reasons she'd kept the personal and private sides of her life apart? She glanced across the apartment at Tommy, who scampered around being chased by Jeremiah, Eli's neighbor's son, at Becca texting in a corner, a scowl marring her pretty face, and Eli, busy in the kitchen slicing lemons and placing them in a glass for her. Here she was, as far over that line as she could get, no matter that she'd pulled away from Eli the other day. It'd be hypocritical of her to keep these two away from each other.

"How about some Cole Porter?" John wheeled himself after a hip-swinging Gran.

Her flirty elder looked over her shoulder, Betty Grable style. "I'd get a *kick* out of it." They laughed uproariously at some private joke she couldn't fathom. Besides, she was more concerned about Becca's isolation. And she suspected Colton had everything to do with it.

As she crossed the room, she smiled politely at a few people then stopped in front of Becca. Unlike the rest of the partygoers, she wore ripped jeans and a black T-shirt that read Dear Life, You Suck.

"Nice outfit," Christie said, joining her.

Becca looked up from her text then pocketed the phone. "It fit the mood."

An upbeat tempo sounded as the music switched. She glanced over to see Eli join her gran and John, drinks in hand. She and Becca had only a minute alone before he came over.

"Don't let Colton bring you down, Becca."

Becca ducked her head, long brown hair obscuring her face. "How do you always know?"

"A lucky guess. Okay. Not so lucky. I mean, who else would make you look that unhappy?"

A half laugh, half snort sounded behind Becca's curtain of hair before she brushed it back. "So true."

"Then why take his calls?" Christie winced as Tommy nearly toppled a lamp lunging after Jeremiah. Mary caught him and escorted both youngsters to a train table set up with tracks and docking systems. She left them with a stern look.

"Because he's the only one who cares."

"Is he? What about me? Mary? Tommy?

Your father?" She nodded toward Eli, who stood apart, holding her drink, looking uncertain about approaching. "Don't we count? We're card-carrying members of the Becca Roberts fan club." She made a show of looking in her bag. "I know I've got mine somewhere."

A grudging laugh erupted from Becca. "I get it. It's just, well, why is it that the people you want to like you don't, and the people that you aren't worried about—no offense, Christie— do?"

She reshouldered her bag and said, "Maybe you're choosing to like the wrong people."

"Ha. Like I can control that."

"Can't you?"

For the first time, Becca looked uncertain. "I don't know how."

She put an arm around Becca's thin waist and steered her into a quieter area by one of the windows. Rivers of headlights and crowds of weekend celebrators flowed below. "Focus on the reasons why Colton is wrong for you. Every time a good thing comes to mind, replace it with one of the bad. That way you can control those feelings until they stop."

"Is that what you do when you think of my dad?"

Surprise burst inside like the spray of colored

balloons bumping along the tin ceiling. "What do you mean?"

Becca lowered her square chin and pinned her with a stare. "Hello. You like him. It's obvie."

She felt the heat of red splotches blossoming across her upper chest. Why, oh why, had she let Laura pick out the lower-cut dress? There was no hiding her real feelings now, not that she would mislead Becca. She opened her mouth then shut it. What to say? Her patchwork skin proclaimed the truth. Did Eli know, too? She glanced over her shoulder but he'd stopped to talk to Mary's husband, a napkin now wrapped around the drink he'd been holding for her. He caught her eye before she dropped her gaze and turned back to Becca.

"Don't worry," Becca said nonchalantly. "He's into you, too. So what's the holdup? He's single. You're single. Unless… Is it because of his cancer? He's better now, as in not going to get sick again. And it's not like there's a better guy out there."

"Wow. That's a compliment," a deep voice said from behind them. "What did I do to earn that?"

Christie froze. How much of that had Eli heard?

"Nothing," Becca answered then stopped, midexit, when Eli held up a hand.

"What's on your phone? Or should I say, *who* was on your phone?"

Christie winced. His concern was understandable given the earlier Colton incident. But why ruin his evening by getting upset? Hadn't Joan taught him in therapy to pick and choose his battles? Timing was everything, as was consistency.

"Check it out for yourself," Becca grumped before handing him the phone and joining her brother at his train table.

"She's still talking to Colton," he said, his voice flat as he scanned her texts. "But, oh wait, she says she won't ditch my party to meet him. What a punk that kid is."

Leaning closer let her view the screen and imagine the feel of being tucked against him, his muscular arms around her.

"And what a nice girl you have as a daughter," she reminded him. Christie looked up and pointed to Becca. She supervised the boys, joining them as they played with the trains. "See?"

Eli scratched his head. "That's why I don't get this. Why is she letting that creep hang out with her?"

"Because you're not."

He took a step back as if struck. "We've been doing more together lately."

"True." Christie put a hand on his tense arm. He looked ready to bolt. "But what have you done that's special? Just the two of you?"

"I… Well…now that I'm not making her costumes and she's doing her project with you, not much."

A cheer rose from a crowd gathered by Eli's baby grand, Gran at its center. "To Eli!" she called, raising her amber-filled glass. The lean curve of his back as he stepped forward, the swell of muscles under his shirt, was worth another toast in her books.

"To Eli," everyone echoed, clinking stemware.

Christie raised her sweet tea, took a drink to Eli's health then lowered it. It was bad luck not to. "You need to find something in common, something other than dance."

"Like what?" He sipped his whiskey, pushed on him by Gran no doubt, then coughed.

She waited for him to get his air back. What she was about to suggest needed his full attention. "How about taking another look at her phone? Check under pictures."

"Photos?" Eli's voice lowered. "Is there something I'm not going to want to see there?" He looked sharply at Becca, who was building Tommy a loop track.

"Just check, Eli." Christie sighed.

Eli's thumb scrolled through screen after screen. After a minute, his eyes lifted to hers, wetness lurking in their corners.

"These are great."

"Didn't expect that, did you?" Christie couldn't keep the smile out of her voice or off her face.

He lowered the camera. "Why is she taking pictures of kids at the oncology unit?"

"Why don't you ask her? Becca!"

Becca pushed a green train over a bridge then trudged over, her feet dragging. "May I have my phone back?"

Eli held up her phone. "Not until you explain what's on it."

Becca stared at her hands. "I'm not going to meet him, Dad. In fact—" she stared at Christie "—we might be breaking up."

Eli made an impatient noise and turned the phone around. The screen showed a picture of an upside-down Vanessa, her limbs holding her in place as they pressed against the inside of a yellow activity-lounge tube. Her eyes seemed to leap out of the snapshot, their dancing expression conveying a desperate happiness. The angles of her body communicated both her struggle and her triumph.

"Oh. That." Becca crossed her arms and bit her lower lip.

"When did you become a photographer?"

Becca's eyes widened. "I'm not."

Eli nodded firmly. "You are. Some have it and some don't. You, Becca-Bell, have talent."

"I do?" she breathed, forgetting—for once—to scold him about the childhood nickname.

"Yes. Do you see how you—"

With a satisfied glance, Christie wandered away, leaving the two standing a little closer, heads together. Becca might be the best gift Eli received tonight. Would their shared creative passion repair the damage years of distance had inflicted? Only time would tell. But it was a start—especially if Becca overcame her resentment and asked for help in completing the ambitious project.

Preoccupied, she nearly trod on Mary's gray heels.

"Christie, I'd like you to meet my husband, Patrick."

The florid, heavyset man swallowed his bite of buttered soda bread and extended a hand.

"Heard so much about you. It's a pleasure to meet the woman who's changed Eli's life."

Christie battled down another flush. "That might be a bit of a stretch. Mary's done so much."

The family helper shook her head, sending her pearl-drop earrings swinging. "I've tried. But it wasn't until you came that Mr. Roberts perked up. He even got out his Nikon yesterday."

A burned smell made Mary's nose wrinkle. "Oh, and if I haven't gone and forgotten the artichoke dip." She leaned in and kissed her husband before hurrying away. "See you after your shift."

The sergeant's walkie-talkie crackled. He cocked his head, listened to the static then replaced his hat. "Got to go, too," he said with a wave. "Nice to meet you, ma'am."

Christie nodded then wandered toward the boisterous piano group. They'd formed some kind of kick line, Gran at its center, as John banged out "New York, New York." Gran was right. She was the party, whereas Christie felt like the ghost who haunted it.

"Join us," hollered Gran, but Christie veered away. A fan kick was a no-go in a dress this short. She followed Mary instead and helped her in the kitchen by dumping pita chips into a bowl, scraping off the dip's blackened top and arranging chilled shrimp on a bed of lettuce.

She set the dishes beside platters of cheese, fruit and veggies. Christie appreciated that, despite Eli's wealth, Mary hadn't hired a caterer. The homey touch made it more personal.

Scout crowded against her legs, begging for scraps, as she carried the last tray to the counter.

"Scout, shoo." She pointed to his dog bed. "Good boy," she added when he turned twice and settled down.

"Food's out," called Mary. When the singers continued warbling, she shrugged and passed around napkins and plates to the rest of the attendees. "Guess they'll stop when they're hungry."

"Or out of Jameson." Christie nodded toward the nearly empty bottle perched beside the sheet music. Did Eli play? She'd love to hear it if he did.

Speaking of whom...her eyes took their fill of Eli's rugged profile. He was still scrutinizing the cell-phone pictures and speaking animatedly with a smiling Becca. The sight melted her heart. Finally. A bond that might take. A connection stronger than all of the Coltons in the world.

"Christie!" Becca called, waving her closer. "Dad's going to help with the photo shoot."

She made a plate for each of them and hurried over. "That's wonderful." She handed them the snacks. "So you like the idea of a calendar with pictures and wishes?"

He put an arm around Becca and pulled her close. "It's great. And if I call in a few favors, we can make it happen."

Becca looked up at her father. "I emailed Ms. Consalati and she said as long as I wrote a research paper, too, she would take away my incomplete. I'm going to high school!"

Eli rested his head atop his daughter's. "Yes, you are. And you figured it out on your own."

What a perfect thing to say. Eli was getting a handle on this father–daughter thing.

Becca's phone buzzed and she looked at the screen. "It's Vanessa. I so have to get this." Her cell was already at her ear as she walked away.

Eli turned toward her. "So Becca meant what she said about me earlier?"

Oh. Right. The conversation where Becca accused Christie of liking Eli. Her pulse sped. She waved a napkin in front of her face.

"How much of that did you hear?" Christie studied her bright red toenails.

"Only Becca saying I'm the best." Eli watched Becca disappear into the back of the apartment. "Where did that come from? And are you feeling okay? You look flushed."

Her lungs let go of the air they'd been hoarding. "More tea will help. Thanks." Christie picked up the glass she'd left on the table earlier and took a long gulp of its cool, sweet contents. Much better.

"So, why were you two talking about me?" Eli probed, shifting in his shining black Oxfords. In the background, the piano keys banged out the song "Let's Do It," an off-key chorus accompanying it.

Gran's husky contralto rose above the rest, belting out the lyrics "Let's fall in love…" as she gazed down at an eyebrow-waggling John. Why was life so uncomplicated for them? They were enjoying each other's company, plain and simple. So why, when it came to her and Eli, did their distance seem insurmountable?

"Something about her thinking we like each other." Christie's voice came out unevenly—he was standing very close to her, near enough that she could feel the warmth of him.

"Hmm. Guess she knows how to read her dad, at least." He ran a hand through his hair, the intensity in his eyes making her flinch and turn away.

Her chest rose and fell, colored dots appearing on the edge of her vision.

"Christie. Talk to me."

She shook her head mutely, unable to meet his gaze. There were too many secrets her eyes might tell.

He cupped her elbow and steered her farther from the party guests until they stood alone in a far corner. A sign outside the window cast red light on his pale face.

"Am I really alone in this?" His voice sounded as tattered as a retired flag. "I didn't want to press you after our run in the rain because you looked so…surprised by my admission that I want more. But can you really tell me you're not feeling something for me, too? Because I'm losing my mind, losing sleep. Every waking moment is me thinking about you…about us."

His urgent tone made her look up into his pleading eyes, the surge of hope in their depths making her heart leap.

She nodded and felt his hand tighten, his hold draw her close. Her eyes shut, and she shivered at the caress of his breath against her temple. This was it. All this time, imagining what it would be like to have Eli's arms around her, to feel him against her, their hearts beating together… It was close to coming true and she wasn't going to deny it any longer…even though she knew she didn't deserve any of it. And Eli needed to know why.

She wanted to admit what was in her heart before things went further, but she became suddenly conscious of the quiet crowd and the dimmed lights.

"Time to sing, everyone," Mary said. She carried a chocolate sheet cake with loopy writing and a blaze of candles. Luckily everyone was looking her way and not theirs.

John pounded out the opening notes to "Happy Birthday." Christie avoided Gran's speculative gaze as she and Eli stepped from the shadows and joined the assembly. Her voice blended with the rest, her body relaxing against the warm arm encircling her waist. Time to tuck away her rational self and live in this perfect, happy moment. There'd be time enough for doubts later.

"Make a wish, Eli," John called. "You'll need a big breath to blow out all those candles."

The group laughed then hushed as he closed his eyes and inhaled long and deep. Christie stepped aside to join Becca, Tommy and a tail-wagging Scout. Eli's breath exploded from him, obliterating every pinpoint of light and smearing some of the candle wax on the frosting. Wow. Whatever he'd wished for, he meant it.

"What happened to Mister I-don't-believe-in-wishes?" John wheeled closer and ruffled Scout's ears.

Eli shrugged. He picked off the candles and dropped them on a paper plate. "Guess I've seen the light."

"So, what'd you wish for, Dad?" Becca asked, grabbing hold of Tommy's finger as it inched toward the cake.

When the lights came back up, his eyes leveled on Christie.

"Something I can't live without."

CHAPTER FOURTEEN

THE NEXT MORNING, Eli rested his ankle on a waist-high step and touched his toes, stretching his hamstring. He switched legs and felt the now-familiar twinge in his knee. It had been bothering him for a week and seemed to be worsening. But he was getting older. Thirty-five. His body was bound to have its aches and pains, especially now that he was running again.

Straightening, he pulled a heel toward his tailbone but skipped the other, sore leg. No sense in pushing it. He didn't want anything to stop his jog with Christie. A thrill shot through him as he pictured her rounding the corner of the Korean market. He peered into the fog lifting from the black pavement, knowing it was too early but wishing she was here just the same.

Last night she'd come so close to opening up. Admitting her feelings. He wished they'd had more time to talk, but the party hadn't been the right time. Besides, they needed to think things through. It was one thing to own up to their emotions and another to decide what to do with them, especially given his circumstances and her past.

The low wail of an ambulance sounded in the distance. A reminder, if there ever was one, to proceed with caution.

If he could guarantee his future, he'd be relentless in his pursuit. She was everything he'd ever wanted. His old self would have pulled out all the stops to woo her, sweep her off her feet and turn her life into a fairy tale.

But they'd lived through too much darkness to easily find that light together. They'd have to go slow.

The ambulance pulled onto his street and shocked him by coming to a halt before his building. The driver cut the siren but left on the rotating blue, red and white lights. Had there been an accident? His heart thudded. He knew all the tenants and had seen most of them at his party. Everyone had looked well and was in good health. All except—

"John!" he yelled, bolting up the stairs. His knee buckled, and the rough stone cut into his tender knee when he went down.

"Eli!" Christie emerged from the fog, her eyes wide. She dashed to his side as he stumbled to his feet.

"What apartment do you need?" he asked the

medics as they hefted a mobile gurney to the door. Not 3B. Not 3B. Please don't say 3B.

"3B. But there's no rush."

Air whooshed from his lungs. No rush. That must be good, relatively. Maybe John had slipped, hurt a hip. Bad enough. But still. It could be a lot worse. Eli turned the key and held open the door. The sight of Christie's frozen, pale form halted his move to follow them.

"Don't you want to see John? Make sure he's all right?"

She shook her head, her green eyes awash in tears.

Eli cupped her shoulders. "John's okay, isn't he? They said there wasn't any rush." He glanced inside and watched the medics lug the stretcher across the foyer. His gaze darted back to Christie.

Her nostrils flared as her chest rose and fell. "There's only one reason techs don't hurry. And it's not a good one."

His head, angled forward to catch her soft words, snapped back. No. No freaking way. She wasn't suggesting that John might be—

His gut sank.

A hole opened in his chest as he plunged through the door, Christie following.

Beside the elevator, the techs leaned on the

portable bed and spoke about last night's Yankees game, how well they'd played, what the season's prospects were. But they said nothing… absolutely nothing…about a medical emergency. His world tilted, its polarity reversed. He leaned a hand against the wall to steady himself. Christie was right.

John was dead.

The elevator opened and the men maneuvered the stretcher vertically into the cramped interior. The metal cage grated shut and the gold-colored doors closed behind them.

A sob so quiet it could have been the wind sounded to his right. Christie. He'd been so focused on himself he'd lost track of her. In two steps he closed the space between them and pulled her into his arms. She pillowed her head between his shoulder and neck and he stroked her trembling back.

They stood in silence, arms wrapped around each other, hearts beating fast. What had happened? Last night John seemed great. He'd played piano, told jokes, asked out Rosaline. And hadn't his last medical report been good?

Eli jerked away and paced, every second feeling like a minute and every minute an eternity. Why were they taking so long? He knew in his gut Christie was right, but he needed to see John himself. He swallowed hard. Hadn't he promised John he'd be there with him at the end? They'd made a pact and he'd let his buddy down.

Voices sounded from above as the men bore a stretcher down the stairs. A black, zippered bag that looked improbably small for what it contained was strapped to its surface. He rubbed his pounding temples. So this was it. How it ended. At least he knew what to expect.

The elevator sounded and John's daughter-in-law stepped out. He'd forgotten she'd been caring for him since his stroke.

"Do I ride with you to the hospital and finish the paper work there?" she asked the men, holding the door open.

"Yes. But we'll need a minute to settle him in, okay?" replied one of the EMTs as they passed outside.

"Hannah?" Eli called as she bent to pick up her dropped bag.

"Hailey. Oh, and you're John's friend Eli, right?"

"Right. I'm so sorry for your loss. John seemed fine last night. I don't know if he told you, but I had a party and—"

She shouldered her purse, her long face somber. "Yes. He called to tell us how much fun it was and to remind me to pick him up early for his appointment." Her eyes drifted to the men lifting John into the ambulance. "When I got here, I couldn't wake him. They think he had another stroke."

Guilt swamped him. "I'm sorry. If I'd known he wasn't feeling well, I wouldn't have invited him."

A watery smile cracked Hailey's tense face. "Now, that would have killed him. John always loved a good time. And you've been such a great friend to him."

The hole in Eli's chest burned deeper with regret. "I wish I'd been a better one."

She squeezed Eli's hand. "No. You've been—" She shook her head and swallowed hard. "His whole family appreciated your being there for him. We'll call you with the arrangements."

The door shut behind her, the stillness turning the foyer into a tomb.

Christie came back into his arms and he held her close.

After a moment she sniffed and stepped back. "He's in a better place," she said at last. "At least, he's at peace."

He nodded automatically, nails digging into his palms. He wished, suddenly, that he was alone. Back in his apartment. Away from all the hope and faith stuff she'd made him believe in again. Why had he let down his guard and started to trust in the world? Today the darkness was so bleak it threatened to swallow him whole.

"ELEVEN O'CLOCK AT TRINITY. Got it. Again, my condolences." Eli hung up the phone and turned to watch Christie and the children snuggled on the sofa.

They'd woken the kids an hour ago, Christie taking the lead on breaking the news of John's death. Amazing how they'd gone from tears to watching a giant sponge with a high-pitched giggle. But it must make sense in kid world. Christie's domain. As for him, he couldn't make heads or tails of any of this.

His every movement felt wooden.

Tommy yawned. "I'm glad Mr. Vaccaro is in a better place. His apartment smelled like cheese. Now he'll have flowers, right, Christie?"

Eli watched, stunned, when Christie nodded and embellished the story. "Whatever his favorite ones are—they'll pick them every day."

Tommy's mouth stretched wide again. "I like that. Mine are dandelions but someone told me they're weeds so they don't count."

Christie pulled his head to her shoulder. "Of

course they count. They're the most important flower of all."

Becca turned to Christie, her attention as rapt as Tommy's. "Why is that?"

"Because they're the only flower that grants wishes. If you blow off all of the white fluff, you'll get your heart's desire."

Eli pressed his lips together, fighting the urge not to interject, to save his kids from this… this…nonsense. It might work for people with terminal illnesses, those who needed all the faith and hope she could throw their way. But his kids? He wanted them to be realists.

He paced to the refrigerator and pulled out a pitcher of sweet tea. John's death today had been one stone-cold bucket of reality, making him wonder…what if it had been him? How would Christie have handled it?

A quick gulp did little to soothe him. He glanced into the living room and saw that Tommy was now curled on Christie's lap, one hand twined in her hair, the other at his mouth, his thumb-sucking habit back again. They were cuddled so close, it was hard to tell where one ended and the other began.

Had he been right to drag Christie into his family after all? While she'd known John only on a professional level, she was now practically a member of their unit. How would his loss affect her? Would she be as self-possessed as she was now, or would it bring back painful memories of losing her own family? Crush the optimism she clung to? It seemed to be her only coping skill and he hated to put her in a position to lose that.

But right now? Optimism wasn't working for him. At all.

"Would you like me to take you back to bed?" Christie asked when Tommy yawned again. It was still early, only seven-thirty. Luckily they didn't have school and could relax, watch cartoons, play video games or any of the other things Christie had listed for him when they'd trodden upstairs.

Becca crouched in front of her brother and let him clamber onto her back. "I'll take him. I'm tired, too." She smiled at Christie then tugged at Tommy's stranglehold. "Thanks for talking to us. It really helped."

Becca shot Eli a narrow-eyed look as she disappeared down the hall to the bedrooms. When he heard both doors close, Eli released his pent-up breath. So now he was the bad guy for not joining in Christie's fantasy of the afterlife? Maybe it was time to end this before things went any further.

"Shh," she said when he must have made some kind of noise. "He's in a better—"

"Place?" He stepped back and rubbed his eyes to clear his blurred vision. "You think they serve whiskey where he is? Tell off-color jokes? Flirt with women?" He swallowed the last of his tea and set the cup in the sink with a hard rattle. "Because if not, he'd much rather be here. Trust me."

"Eli, are you okay?" She joined him in the kitchen. When she grabbed his hand, he pulled free. Her platitudes weren't working. He didn't feel soothed. He was furious, letdown and demoralized. Most of all, he needed to be on his own. To think things through.

"John's the one who's not okay. Me? I'm fine. Or I think I'm fine. But who knows? Because that's the beauty of it all. We just don't have a clue. Life is a cosmic joke and it always has the last laugh."

"I see," said Christie, her voice so quiet he instantly wished back those harsh words.

"I just don't—" The side of his curled hand connected with the counter, a dull thud when he wouldn't have minded a more satisfying crash. "I'm having a tough time seeing a bright side in anything right now."

Christie nodded. "You were right to say how

you feel. I don't blame you for that. And who knows. Maybe I'm the one who's wrong about all this faith and hope stuff." She backed away, her shoulders tense. "I just don't know how else to deal, okay? Ironic, right? The grief counselor who doesn't know what to say at a time like this?"

She shook her head, visibly upset. He wanted to reach out to her. To help her as much as she'd helped his kids.

Then again, maybe it was time they both realized he didn't have a clue how.

THREE DAYS LATER, Christie stood on the spongy grass of Trinity Church's Washington Heights Cemetery, holding Becca's and Tommy's hands. Her black heels sank into the soft ground, making her shift uneasily. It felt too close to her nightmare—this sensation of being pulled into the earth, the dirt closing in around her, the darkness.

"Ouch!" Tommy said then pulled his hand free.

"Sorry. Didn't know I was squeezing so hard."

His hand slipped back into hers. "It's okay. Look. There's Daddy!"

Eli limped toward the head of a casket raised

above a dark hole. In the expectant silence, a bird called from a towering elm, its leaves shading one of the last reserved burial spots in Manhattan. Christie forced herself to focus on him rather than the black rectangle. And to breathe. Those were Laura's last words of advice before she'd forced her out the door.

Since most of Christie's departed clients held services outside the city, she'd avoided cemeteries since her brother's funeral nearly ten years ago. Her parents had died in a car crash, their remains cremated and held in an urn on Gran's mantel. Deciding to come here had meant sleepless nights and panic attacks coupled with the determination not to let down Tommy and Becca. They'd called to ask her to ride with them, never questioning her attendance.

"Ladies and gentlemen," Eli's voice rang out. "I've been asked to say a few words about my good buddy John Vaccaro. We were neighbors for eight years and did chemotherapy together for one."

The crowd murmured for a moment then hushed. The whir of a mower sounded in the distance, and when the breeze shifted, flowers from nearby arrangements perfumed the air. Her eyes wandered to other graves then pressed closed, images of what lay underground exploding behind her lids. She inhaled slowly through her nose and exhaled through her mouth. Nice and easy. Just a few more minutes. She had this.

Eli cleared his throat, his somber eyes passing over the gathering then stopping, for a heartbreaking moment, on her. "He called our cancer fight 'chemical warfare' and in a way he was right. It was a battle. One he fought harder than anyone. Sure, he took the pills, kept his appointments and followed the rules the doctors gave us...but that's not how he won. He beat his cancer by refusing to give in to it. By living his life, full stop—even if that meant frequenting the White Horse Tavern, hanging out at Off Track Betting and chasing women." A titter rose from a trio of attractive older ladies standing beside the grave. "Even in the hospital, after his first stroke, he asked me for an IV tap of whiskey."

Laughter rippled through the group, many nodding and smiling. Christie wanted to join in but her breaths were coming faster now, the panicky feeling rising despite her best efforts to contain it.

"John knew how to enjoy himself," Eli continued, his dark suit contrasting with the azure sky. "He didn't waste a moment in self-pity. In fact, he once gave me some good advice that I wish I'd followed. He told me that life doesn't give you do-overs. If you waste today, you never get it back."

Eli looked down at his feet. When his blue eyes rose, they shimmered like the surface of a tropical ocean. How kind of him to say things he didn't believe for others' comfort. It quieted her racing heart, giving her the courage she needed not to bolt.

"I've done a lot of thinking since John left us. Went over the things he said, his life, and I realized I've been a fool not to take his advice. I can't get back the days I lost, but I won't miss any more. That's John's legacy to me."

Their gazes locked, the promise in his expression making Christie's pulse speed and bump. He'd apologized when they'd last spoken. But now she sensed a real change of heart. Did he actually mean what he said?

Eli took in the assembly once more. The late-morning sun backlit the rugged angles of his face and the breadth of his shoulders. "So in his honor, let's follow John's example and enjoy this day. Celebrate his life while we mourn his passing. Would everyone please raise your glass?"

A funeral-service worker pressed a plastic cup into her hand. The amber liquid and its spicy, woodsy scent was instantly recognizable. Whiskey. Of course. She raised it overhead.

"To John!" everyone shouted.

She downed the drink, its tart wash crossing her tongue before burning its way down her throat. Eli handed the microphone to a woman in a long, navy dress. She crooned "Moon River" as he joined them.

Christie shook in her shoes by now, her knees knocking together from too many emotions and too much…everything. The death, the funeral. Memories of her brother's passing. Eli's call to seize the day when she felt as though her whole world was imploding…

"That was the wedding song when John married his wife, Annabeth," Eli whispered in her ear, the warm rush of breath against her neck making her shiver in awareness.

Her chest tightened into a fist so fast she couldn't breathe. A sob caught in her throat, a painful wheeze she tried to quiet.

"What you said was beautiful." She cast an anxious look at the casket. "But I have to go." Any minute now and they'd lower it, undoing the slippery grip she had on her self-control and sending her emotions careening into a dark territory she wasn't ready to handle. She'd feel like that guilt-ridden teen standing beside her parents ten years ago, watching her brother disappear from her life and return to the earth forever.

A man in a tux and a top hat stepped forward and pressed a button on the metal apparatus holding up John's mahogany casket.

Oh, no. It was happening. She whirled, but Eli's hand halted her headlong flight.

"Please stay." His eyes were urgent. Tender. "We need to talk. I need to apologize."

She wanted more with him, wanted to believe in a future together. But right now she couldn't think past this moment.

Panic had her breath coming in short, hard gasps. "I. Have. To. Go. Sorry." She tugged her hand loose and sprinted for the redbrick sidewalk that would lead her to the cemetery's gates. She'd catch a cab. Put her head under a pillow. Rebury the memories today had brought to the surface. This was why she never came to her clients' funerals. It was her shameful secret. But a reaction like this was exactly what she'd been protecting herself from all these years.

"Daddy, Christie's scared," she heard Tommy lisp behind her as she angled past the family.

"Yeah, Dad. Mary will take us home." Becca's voice registered, the concern in her words evident.

Her chest tightened even more.

"We'll get to ride in her cop car!"

"It's her husband's, Tommy."

The voices faded as Christie dashed through the crowd away from them. Footsteps pounded behind her. Beyond embarrassment, she picked up speed while a somber tune wailed. Salty tears streaked down her cheeks, her red blotches in full bloom. Eli couldn't see her like this. And the rest of John's support group couldn't see her like this, either. She was the upbeat one. The optimist. The keeper of the faith who held everyone else together, for crying out loud. The believer in miracles. No one could ever know how she was scared to death inside. That those views were a mask used to cover childhood scars. She hated feeling like a fake, but right now...

If the shoe fits, she heard Gran's voice say in her head.

"Christie, wait!" Eli called once she'd clattered onto the walkway. *Don't turn back,* she told herself.

But she looked.

Eli's face was pinched with pain as he jogged in a jerky gait that favored his right leg. Odd. She'd noticed him favoring it after jogging. Now it looked worse. Her heart lurched. How could she run from him when he was in pain? His determination washed away the lingering anger she'd felt at his harsh words.

"I'm sorry for what I said. For the comfort I wasn't able to give you the day John died. I was mad but not at you. When I wrote his eulogy, I also meant it for you, for us. You see, I—I— God I suck at this."

She put a finger to his lips. "I can't talk here."

"But why?" He slid a hand down her bare arm. "You're shaking." Understanding flashed in his eyes. "Is it your brother?"

She nodded mutely and swallowed over the lump in her throat.

He put an arm around her and steered her to the car he'd rented, the one they'd picked her up in earlier. They slipped inside the cool dimness, the tinted windows obliterating the sun.

"Driver, would you give us a few moments?" Eli asked the man sitting at the wheel.

"Sure thing." The gray-haired man in uniform slipped out of the car, the door closing behind him with a soft click.

The smell of new leather filled the small space. She leaned against the buttery-smooth seat, grateful to be away from that haunting scene. Not so glad to have Eli here to witness her imminent meltdown. She'd held it together for the sake of the kids, but now that she was alone, her emotions rose with a vengeance.

She sobbed and gasped, snuffled and cried. Every feeling she'd bottled inside exploded, flowing from her with the force of a woken volcano. Eli held her hand and blotted her chin with a tissue but otherwise made no move to stop her outpouring.

Finally, when her well of misery ran dry, strong hands cupped her cheeks, lifting her face. His eyes were dark with concern.

"You've never told me much about him. Your brother."

"Bill," she whispered, the smell of ozone from the firecrackers he'd adored floating in on memory's wings.

"How old was he when he died?" Eli shifted so that she was cradled against his body, her back resting against his broad chest. The steady rise and fall of it soothed her.

"He was eighteen months older than me, so nineteen and a half."

"That's young. You were both young."

Christie nodded then swiped at another wash of tears.

"You once told me you didn't love him as much as he deserved. What did you mean by that?"

Her chest squeezed so hard she thought her ribs would crack. "That I wasn't very nice to him. Toward the end."

His arms only banded around her tighter. Was it her imagination, or did she feel his lips against her hair?

"Tell me," he urged in a low voice.

"It's hard." She buried her face in her hands. This wasn't something she let herself think about, let alone discuss.

"Be brave, sweetheart."

An endearment? Didn't he understand just how disgusting a person she was?

She twisted in his arms. His face was so familiar she could have traced its lines in her sleep. Maybe, before he made the mistake of starting to care about her, he should know the truth. Know her. It was exactly why she'd avoided serious dating. But Eli had slipped in behind her defenses and now she had no choice but to show her true colors, as ugly as they were.

"Do you want to know where I was the night he died?"

Eli's gaze didn't waver. "Yes."

"Bill's condition deteriorated in my senior year. He'd had leukemia for over three years, and most of my high-school experience had been spent working odd jobs to pay his bills, watching him when my parents took extra shifts and caring for him when his condition worsened."

A rough hand smoothed back the damp hair at her temples. "That sounds very unselfish of you."

Her hands clenched the hem of her black dress. "Not really. I loved Bill. He was my best friend." Her chest heaved before she continued. "But in my senior year I started to resent him. Everyone was excited about ending their four years of high school, talking about fun times, and I felt as though I'd missed out. Suddenly I started accepting party invites, going out on dates, skipping work to hang out with friends."

Eli tried to pull her back into his arms, but she scooted farther away. "That sounds normal. What teenager wouldn't want those things?"

"But I wasn't normal. Our family was going through a crisis and I checked out. Without my money, Dad and Mom worked sixteen-hour days. Hospice came along, but it wasn't the same. We weren't a family anymore, and it was my fault. Mine."

She swallowed back another sob. For some inexplicable reason, she wanted him to feel the same revulsion for her choices that she did.

Car doors opened and shut around them. Engines revved and tires crunched on the gravel drive. The funeral had ended. Would Eli want to terminate this messed-up conversation, too?

"I did the same thing to my family, Christie. You know that." Eli's dark eyebrows met. "No one is perfect."

"True. But I wasn't just imperfect, Eli. I was a selfish monster. The night Bill died was my senior prom—and my birthday. Not that my parents remembered. I was mad that the only thing my mom said to me all day was a reminder to say good-night before I left. Bill was having a bad day and would appreciate a little company."

She ran her hand through her hair, remembering, too late, that she'd put it in a loose chignon.

"I'm guessing you didn't stop in." The timbre of Eli's voice was soft and low.

A bitter laugh escaped her. "Right. I heard him call out as I took a last look in the hall mirror. When a car honked outside, I ran off without even yelling a goodbye." Pain stabbed her chest as if it had just happened. As if she had just realized she'd missed her last chance to see her brother.

She gulped back tears.

"You were jealous of the attention he was getting." The way he said it made it sound more like a statement than a question.

She squeezed her eyes shut. No amount of work she did with cancer patients could ever erase the despicable thing she'd done, the thousand ways she'd hurt her brother—the whole family—the months leading up to his death.

A firm hand tipped up her chin, rough thumbs brushing away the wetness from her tears.

"I hated him," she whispered.

There, she'd said it. For the first time—finally—an admission she hadn't even made to herself. She'd loved her brother and yet she had deeply resented him. But most of all, she missed him. John was right. There were no do-overs.

A trembling took hold of her, a bone-deep chill. Eli caught her in a tight embrace, his hold relentless as she pushed against his chest. Eventually, the shivering subsided and she relaxed in his arms.

"When we got back from the after-prom party," she finally continued, "an ambulance was in my driveway. And instead of feeling upset, I was mad. Can you believe that? Even then, I felt so angry that once again he'd ruined something special."

Eli's voice sounded muffled as he spoke into her hair. "You were in shock."

She pulled her head back and looked at him, his face so blurred it might have been behind a waterfall. She swiped at her eyes. "I was so self-centered. My mother did everything for the funeral while I lay in my room. They made me go to the funeral and I didn't cry until they lowered him into the ground. Suddenly I wanted to jump in there, too. I deserved to die. Not him. I was the horrible person. Oh. God. Not him."

A fresh round of sobs broke free and she buried her head into Eli's chest, mortified to share this with him. He handed her a hankie when she quieted. "Why are you being so nice to me? I'm terrible. Mean-spirited. Uncharitable—"

"Inconsiderate, thoughtless, unkind, insensitive—" Eli cut in. "I know. I've been all of those things, too. But don't you see? We're human, not saints. We mess up. Make mistakes. The important thing is that we try not to repeat them."

"I work hard at it every day. But it's not enough. It's never ever enough to be sorry about the past." She turned her cheek and rested it against his chest, listening to the steady rhythm of his heart.

"You need to stop apologizing," he surprised her by saying.

"How can I when I can't ever make up for what I did? For what I didn't do."

"You can't change the past, and neither can I. So let's work on the here and now. Maybe we could just be better people today. Be here for each other. How does dinner tonight sound… just you and me?"

Shock made her squirm around and look up. "Why would you?"

"'Because the heart wants what it wants or else it does not care.'" He quoted Emily Dickinson. "I wasted too much time not caring—living half a life—until I met you, and I can't go back."

"But I'm—"

"Starting to bug me." He cut her off with a swift, melting kiss. His mouth was firm on hers, unyielding, then he pulled her tight against him. She could feel the rapid beat of his heart, taste the tart sweetness of whiskey on his mouth. She wound her hands into his hair and felt his broad fingers cupping the back of her head. Her heart hammered, and there was a rushing sound in her ears, like beating wings.

She must have made some noise because he pulled back, his hands now on either side of her face, his eyes an exuberant blue.

"I've wanted to do that forever."

She ran a tentative hand up his muscular arm. "Even now?"

"Especially now. May I pick you up at eight? We have lost time to make up."

When she nodded, he laughed, a sharp, happy

sound. He swooped in for another heart-stopping kiss. When he pulled away, her hand rose to her pounding heart.

A knock sounded on the window. Christie scrambled back to her corner of the seat and pinned back her fallen hair.

When Eli lowered the glass, their driver's face appeared. "May I drive you two anywhere?"

"Just the lady, if you would, thanks. I need to catch a cab to Brooklyn."

Eli raised the divide and pulled her into a breathless embrace. When he released her, he said, "Will you be all right? The Vaccaros asked me to stop by and say a few more words about John, but I can go home with you instead."

Christie shook her head. He'd comforted her and now John's family needed him.

Eli's eyes searched hers. "I'll see you in a few hours, then."

"If you're sure."

"I've never been surer." And with a wave he stepped out of the car and closed it behind him.

Christie collapsed against the seat. What had just happened?

"Where to, ma'am?"

She shook her head. Disoriented. Where was she going? For the first time, she hadn't a clue.

It felt as though she'd taken her first step on

a high wire. Her heart's desire waited across from her. As long as she didn't look down, she'd make it.

If she was a believer, a real one now, she'd trust in Eli not to let her fall.

CHAPTER FIFTEEN

"You look beautiful." Eli pulled out a tan leather chair for Christie then moved to the opposite side of their white cloth-covered table. And she was. Under the rainbow prisms cast by Cipriani's elaborate silver-and-crystal chandelier, she glowed. Her turquoise off-the-shoulder dress exposed the graceful expanse of her neck and set off the rich auburn hair she'd worn loose and full. Never had her green eyes looked deeper or more mesmerizing.

"And these are for you." He handed her the wrapped package of red roses he'd hidden in his folded suit jacket. It had felt awkward carrying them that way, but the look of delight on her face was more than worth it.

She buried her face in the blooms then looked up, her white teeth flashing in the well-lit room. "They're beautiful. Thank you so much. But—" her brows came together as she peered once more into the bundle "—they must have cost a lot. There are two dozen."

"And you deserve ten dozen, at least, but

that's all they had left at the shop." He shrugged his jacket back on. "I was late getting back from the wake."

She reached across the table and rested her soft hand on his wrist. "How was that? I'm sorry I didn't go with you. It was selfish not to. I could have—"

"Put on a smile instead of dealing with your feelings—the real ones? Do you think John would have wanted that?" He slid his hand into hers, loving the feel of her silken touch. It comforted him beyond imagining. It *had* been a bit rough at the wake. Telling stories about John had brought out laughter and tears among the attendees. Mostly, he'd missed his good friend.

She peered down at her flowers. "I should have paid my proper respects."

"You did. Going to your first funeral since your brother's...that took a lot of guts. John would have appreciated it." He held her eye, wanting her to acknowledge that she'd been brave. Her breakdown was a breakthrough, her tears a step forward rather than a setback. Even he understood that, and he wasn't a counselor. When she finally nodded, he continued. "As for the wake, mostly it was storytelling. Some really good ones. I'll share them with you, but another time. Tonight let's focus on us."

Christie nodded again and gave his hand a quick squeeze.

"May I start you with something to drink while you look the menu over?" A man dressed in black slacks and a white dress shirt lifted their water goblets and poured water from a pitcher wrapped in green linen.

"Do you have sweet tea?" Christie smiled up at the waiter then quirked an eyebrow at Eli. He held in a laugh. A trendy New York dining spot like this would be the last place to serve their country favorite. Then again, it was the city.

"A Long Island Iced Tea?" The waiter had to raise his voice as a noisy group of what looked like Europeans and models pushed by, jostling him against the back of Eli's chair. The server apologized, but he wasn't to blame. Space at Cipriani's was at a premium.

The lavishly decorated restaurant was long, narrow and filled to capacity with chatting, well-dressed patrons seated in slotted iron-backed booths, small, round tables or at the dark wooden bar. Lighting strips, elaborate antique mirrors and photographs taller than the patrons adorned the walls, while a dropped ceiling contained a collage of snapshots ranging from Sophia Loren to the city of Florence. The restaurant practically screamed Italy—a place he planned to take Christie someday. He smiled at the thought of them together on the coast of Tuscany, the jeweled waters matching her eyes.

"And you, sir?"

He blinked up at the waiter and gathered his thoughts. "A glass of red, the…ah…" He squinted down at the black leather wine list. "The 2007 Sassicaia. Actually, make that a bottle and two glasses."

"Very good, sir." The waiter gave him a polite smile and slipped out of the tight space.

"Is that a good wine?" Christie unfolded her napkin and draped it on her lap. "I've only had the kind out of a box."

He couldn't help laughing, his spirits fizzing like champagne. "Don't think that would make the list here."

She glanced around at the expensively clad diners then down at herself. When she raised her head, her face held a small frown.

He caught her hand in his. "You are the most gorgeous woman in this room."

Her sigh sounded amused. "How do you always know what I'm thinking?"

"Lots of time and effort."

She lowered her water and wiped the peach-colored smudge she'd left on its rim. "And how's that working out for you?"

"Usually, you surprise the heck out of me—so not very well." He picked up a spoon dropped by a man at a nearby table and passed it back. "But I never stop trying."

He earned a double eyebrow lift for that.

"And why not?"

"Can't." He lifted his glass and sipped. "You're all I think about."

"Oh." She dropped her gaze, the pink he adored rising from her neck and flooding her cheeks. If he could spend a lifetime making her do that, he'd die a happy man.

"Do you ever think about me?"

"I—"

A tall glass filled with ice cubes and brown, frothy liquid appeared before Christie, cutting off her answer. He kept his disappointment in check and nodded politely at the waiter after he'd tasted the small amount of wine he'd poured.

"It's great. Thank you." *Hurry along, buster.*

"And you, ma'am?" Was it his imagination, or did their waiter seem to be lingering longer than was necessary over Christie? He straightened her fork and knife—not needed—brushed a piece of nonexistent lint with his table comb—again, unnecessary—and lifted the second wineglass. "Would you like to try the Sassicaia? It's an excellent vintage."

"Not yet. Maybe with dinner."

The server leaned over and straightened her napkin, laying it once more against her lap. "Trust me when I say that—"

"She said, she'll wait," Eli growled. *Paws off.* Suddenly he was glad Christie had led a solitary life before him. She wouldn't have stayed single had she been on the market—and he intended to make sure she stayed off it.

"Very good," huffed the waiter, his formality back in place. "Are you ready to order?"

Christie's hair slid across her creamy shoulders when she shook her head.

"I'm more than happy to tell you the specials, then." The waiter beamed.

Eli held on to his patience while the guy went into his spiel. Then, after a short conference with Christie, he ordered for them both. "We'll start with the Prosciutto de Parma and two spinach, mushroom and bacon salads followed by Pappardelle alla Bolognese and Tagliatelle con Funghi. We'll decide on dessert over coffee. Thank you."

He snapped his menu closed, scooped up Christie's and passed them to the waiter, who tucked them under his arm, still scribbling on a pad as he bustled away.

"It all sounds delicious." She nodded, making her small gold hoop earrings swing.

"I hope you like it." The background restaurant noise of clanging crystal, scraping silverware and exotic accents competed with the soft jazz tune infusing the room. He inhaled the permeating aroma of sweet, fresh basil and leaned back in his chair, his heart full of her and this moment.

"You wouldn't steer me wrong. I have faith in you."

Her words crumbled the last bulwark he'd built around his heart. He leaned forward and felt the round glass table topper press into his suit coat. "And us? Do you believe in us, too?"

She sipped her water, the expression in her eyes so distant he couldn't read it. His heart pounded in his ears. He wasn't a praying man—or a wishing one—but he hoped she was about to say what he needed to hear.

After an impossibly long moment, she lowered her glass and said, "Yes. Very much, Eli."

He closed his eyes, squeezing his lids tight against the rush of joy flooding behind them. Men didn't cry. But it'd been a roller-coaster day. Once again, Christie had proved him wrong about his emotions…as she had about so many things. It was one of the million things he'd grown to love about her.

His hand tightened on his wineglass. *Love.* It was a big word. Funny that he'd never known, until this instant, how deep his feelings for her ran. The forever kind. But he'd wait to tell her. It was too soon and they had plenty of time. Christie had taught him to trust in that. No reason to push it.

Christie raised her glass. "To John, who inspired us to cherish every day, as well as each other." Her smile trembled.

They clinked glasses. When his eyes met hers, her lashes were wet and spiky, the water at the corners mirroring his.

"When I got home from the wake, Becca surprised me with something."

A deafening crash sounded from the kitchen, drowning out his last words.

Christie leaned forward. "What?"

After he repeated himself, Christie gave him a thoughtful look and said, "Children express their grief in lots of ways. Sometimes not the best ways…but with patience—"

"No. Nothing like that." He waved a hand to stop her. "It was a collage of pictures she put on my desktop. She'd snapped shots of John and me at the party."

"Eli. That's beautiful." Christie's eyes widened. "Becca's inherited your talent."

"Let's just hope she doesn't waste it like I did."

She gently nudged his foot under the table. "Oh, so you're too old to go after your dream, to have a gallery show?"

His eyes wandered to the enormous close-up of a laughing man on the wall opposite them. "No…actually the calendar shoot has me thinking about it…that I'd like to go on a trip, take pictures of the countryside the way I used to."

Christie took another sip of her beverage then pushed it away. "Where?"

"I'm thinking a summer trip to Yosemite. Would you come with us?" He was pushing his luck and he knew it. But he wasn't wasting another second with this woman. Not after the week he'd had.

Her hand fluttered to her heart. "I have a lot of time saved at work." She bit her lip. "So I guess they owe me, don't they?"

Her smile unfurled, easing the tightness in his chest.

"Then it's a plan."

Her grin matched his. "A great one."

He raised his wineglass. "To our future."

When they set down their drinks, the waiter returned with their salads.

"Can I get you anything else?"

Eli stared at Christie, barely hearing the guy. Who could concentrate on something as ordinary as food when something much bigger was happening between them?

"Just let me know if you need anything," the waiter murmured, backing away fast.

"He must think we're nuts." Christie picked up her fork and speared a spinach leaf. She returned his smile with a cheeky grin.

"And he'd be right about that," Eli said after chewing a melon ball. It slid down his throat, as tasteless as a stone.

He put his fork on the edge of his plate and stroked her left ring finger. Now that he'd decided to pursue her, that finger wouldn't be empty for long. He knew he wanted to spend all his time with her, to convince her that suffering was in her rearview mirror and happiness paved the road ahead. She'd made a believer out of him, and for that he owed her the world. Hopefully she'd let him give it to her.

"Is something wrong with the food?" She speared a piece of prosciutto-wrapped melon and sniffed it.

"No. I think I lost my appetite." And he had. What he wanted was Christie, an intense awareness of her blocking out all other senses. He smelled the rosewater of her shampoo, felt the softness of her skin, caught every soft, lilting word despite the noisy crowd and had eyes only for her mobile, arresting face. He'd never grow tired of looking at the kaleidoscope of emotions that danced across it.

She put down her fork. "Me, too."

"I wish we were alone. Not with all of these people around."

At her nod, his hand rose in the air, fingers snapping.

"Yes?" The waiter sounded slightly out of breath.

"Something's come up. We'll be taking our meals to go. Oh, and add two pieces of your chocolate cake, as well."

"Very good, sir. I'll meet you at the front." The double doors to the kitchen swished behind him as Eli and Christie pushed to their feet, their eyes clinging.

Eli ignored the burst of pain in his knee as he shook out his leg. The waiter was right, he thought, holding Christie's hand as they pressed to the front of the crowded restaurant, this was very, *very* good.

"Wow. You've got to try this."

They were sitting cross-legged on the faded Persian rug in Christie's apartment, facing each other, a picnic of sorts between them. Candles flickered, transforming her loft from shabby to romantic. She sent Laura a silent thank-you for leaving the candles and matches out before she'd gone to a school function.

She waved a thick forkful of the Bolognese at Eli until he gave in with a husky laugh and opened wide.

"Good, isn't it?" she asked when he closed his eyes, pleasure softening the hard planes of his face. Silvery moonlight poured through the windows and outlined the curves of his mouth, the shape of his cheekbones, the shadow of his lashes, the arch of his throat. She loved it when he looked so relaxed, so at ease—the warrior at peace. In fact, what didn't she love about him? The unbidden thought caught her off guard, freezing her next bite in midair.

Suddenly she didn't know where to look. Not at the expectant blue eyes facing her. He was good at guessing her thoughts. Would he figure out her secret?

She dropped her fork and hurried to the kitchen. As she passed the front door, a sleepy-eyed Angel lifted her muzzle from her dog bed while Sweet Pea dozed.

"Everything okay?" he called.

"Fine," she squeaked. Her hands gripped the cool stainless steel of the sink edge. Love? When exactly had she fallen for Eli? She searched for a recent memory but couldn't stop until she'd gone as far back as the night he'd brought John to the meeting, how he'd shaken out his friend's coat so carefully, the thoughtful way he'd brought everyone treats and drinks. Had she been falling for him even then?

"Need some help in there?"

She almost laughed at that. Help? Yes, but not the kind he thought. Her feelings were deeper than she'd imagined, maybe deeper than she could handle. But they were there, ready or not, and she couldn't deny them. At the very least, she'd keep them to herself. For now. Wait to see how Eli felt. They'd just taken their relationship to the next level. Saying "I love you" would catapult them into the next galaxy. A jump to light speed might leave one of them behind.

Strong arms encircled her from behind. She breathed in the lemongrass and musky smell of him, her heart thumping.

"You've been gone too long," he breathed in her ear.

She felt as if electricity coursed from her sensitive lobe and sizzled through her body. Her lungs trapped her breath and took it hostage. Was there anything more amazing than being held by the man you loved?

She turned and put her arms around his neck. In an instant, his breath quickened, his blue eyes searing hers before he crushed her against him.

"I'm the luckiest man in the world." His voice was low, throaty. "Remember what you said earlier, about feeling like a monster?"

She nodded, burying her face in the firm planes of his chest. Why would he bring that up when things felt so romantic?

He tipped her chin and held her gaze. "Please don't say that again. Don't even think it. You're imperfect. Flawed, a little scarred, but stronger now in a way that makes you the most beautiful woman I've ever met. Inside and out. I wouldn't want you any other way."

It was the most incredible thing anyone had ever said to her. Did she deserve it? An image of Bill came to mind. She could almost picture him giving her a thumbs-up.

Before she had another moment to think, he captured her lips with a kiss so intense it was bruising. Her thundering blood deafened her and her shallow breathing rolled out like a low tide. He tasted like salt and fire as his mouth slanted across hers. She buried her hands in his thick hair, drawing him closer still.

His mouth left hers and traveled along her cheekbone. She could feel the erratic beat of his heart against her chest. His arms held her tight, as if he never meant to let her go. She rained kisses on his neck, his jaw and finally on his lips.

Suddenly, an aching tenderness replaced their earlier frenzy. They needed to explore, to know each other. When he returned her kiss, his hand stole into her hair and wound her tresses with his fingers. Their kisses deepened slowly, softly, the intensity growing between them once more…a single match that had ignited a blaze.

She knew he was strong, but it still surprised her how easily he carried her to the living-room settee and laid her down gently on the scattered pillows. His body slid over hers in one smooth gesture. She inhaled his breath as their mouths moved against each other, every kiss drawn out now, lingering, exploring. Her hands drifted over his back then rose to his shoulders and the muscles of his arms.

At last, he drew himself up on his elbows. Now he was looking down at her, and his expression had changed in the flickering light, his blue eyes darkened to indigo. The rawness of his open, vulnerable expression undid her.

Warmth overflowed her heart, filling up the cracks and wounds she'd held inside. She sighed and buried her hands in the thick strands at the nape of his neck. How had this miracle happened? It seemed beyond imagining, beyond wishing. Yet here she was, with him, the only person who'd made her feel complete. Whole. As if she deserved this moment with him.

"Christie," he murmured in a voice that was both rough and soft, his eyes blazing. His fingers shook as they trailed down her cheek to her lips, outlining the shape of her mouth. "I never thought…imagined…it would be like this. So incredible. It's… You're… This is perfect. Everything I ever wanted. Wished for."

"Me, too." She matched her hand to his, loving the way his fingers curled over the tops of hers. "I'll never forget this moment." And she wouldn't. As long as she lived.

He bent down, his lips brushing her cheek lightly, and still that light touch sent shivers through her body, making her tremble. His mouth swept across the hollow of her temple then traced her cheekbone.

She pulled him down and lost herself against his mouth. He kissed her gently, carefully, but she didn't want gentleness, not when they'd waited this long, and she knotted her fists in his shirt, pulling him harder against her. A low groan sounded in his throat, then his arms circled her once more, gathering her against him, and they rolled over on the settee, tangled together, still kissing. There were cloth-covered buttons digging into Christie's back but she didn't care. All that existed was Eli; all she wanted, breathed, felt, hoped and saw was Eli. Nothing else mattered.

A cuckoo emerged from a clock, squawked and retreated—another of Laura's aunt's hand-me-down decorations. Eli sat up with a groan. "I have to leave. Promised Mary I'd be home by midnight." The gloom turned him into the romantic, shadowy prince of every girl's fairy tale. Yet they'd each been the hero in their love story. Had rescued each other.

She smoothed back a strand that had fallen in his eyes. "So, Prince Charming's about to turn into a pumpkin?"

"You won't get rid of me that easily." He bent down and gave her a leisurely kiss full of promise. "I'm going to be around for a long time."

"Eli," she whispered, her heart aching with the truth of it. The future loomed ahead, as bright as the eyes shining down at her.

He pulled her to her feet then against him once more…so close that her feet trod on his. His arm wrapped around her waist and he waltzed her toward the door, humming something low and sweet. When she pressed her ear to his chest, his heart beat with a steady, reassuring thud.

"I wish you didn't have to go." She turned and unbolted the door. He nuzzled her neck and wrapped his arms around her from behind. "Shoo, mister. I can't focus." And it was true—her fingers fumbled on the third lock and slipped on the chain.

"Can't," he groaned when the door swung open at last.

"At least we have our jog tomorrow." She twirled around, rose on her tiptoes and planted a swift kiss on his square chin, loving the rough feel of his regrowth.

His eyes lit up. "We have more than that." He captured her lips in a last, lingering kiss then stepped out into the hall. "We have forever."

CHAPTER SIXTEEN

"RIGHT THIS WAY, Mr. Roberts." Four weeks later, a nurse in tan scrubs ushered Eli into a spacious office smelling of wood polish and leather. His dress shoes echoed across tiles striped by midafternoon sunlight slanting through the blinds. "Please have a seat and Doctor Cruz will be with you shortly."

Eli sat before a cluttered desk and glanced at bookshelves overflowing with medical tomes. He tugged at his tie, wishing he hadn't had to dress up in the heat. "If she's busy, I'm happy just to drop this off." He held up a large manila envelope. "I thought, as head of Oncology, she'd like a copy of the pediatric-patients calendar."

The nurse's tight smile softened as she spoke through the crack of the shutting door. "She'll appreciate that and wants to chat if you don't mind waiting."

"Of course."

His shoulders relaxed against the warm seat. After his three-o'clock business meeting he'd surprise Christie at work and give her a copy, as well. It had been a month-long endeavor, and he was proud of how they'd all pulled together. He'd already mailed a copy, along with Becca's research paper, to her health teacher. Mission accomplished.

He slid out the calendar. Even better, with his distribution connections, they'd raise a lot of money for cancer charities. Time to celebrate over dinner, family-style.

He smiled.

His new normal.

How had a month passed so quickly? He recalled his first date with Christie, the impromptu picnic on her apartment floor, the tender moments that had rocked his world. It'd been the best night of his life.

He opened to the last page, his fingers tracing over her name in the acknowledgments. Christie Bates. How would it look as Christie Roberts? His smile widened. Better. Much better.

It was too soon to propose. But he'd waited long enough to share the feelings he'd discovered at Cipriani's. He loved her. And not in a candlelit-dinner, please-pass-the-wine-and-smell-the-roses kind of way. That was a movie with a different script.

No.

He loved her for the study in contrasts she

was…the self-possessed woman who saved John's life but needed her rabbit's foot to enter an elevator, the optimist who lifted every spirit but held in her own doubts. She was the tender supporter of children, the ailing and the home-less who turned into a spitfire with wannabe bad boys, dance moms and chess pros alike. She was tough, vulnerable, smart and goofy—even when she didn't mean to be—and prone to pho-bias that made him want to shield her from the world as well as share it with her.

He thumbed through the calendar, his hand stopping on February. It was his favorite shot and one Becca had envisioned. Her new friends Vanessa and Jonah stood silhouetted against the New York skyline, the setting sun bathing them in shades of gold, bronze, rose and lav-ender. Their clasped hands and touching noses screamed "young love." Forever love. Their wish, he read, was to spend every minute they had left together.

He blinked his stinging eyes as he recalled that emotional day, the children clamoring for their moment in the sun, Christie, Tommy and Mary rushing to assist. Though the biggest help of all had come from an unexpected source. Jacqueline.

His jaw had nearly hit the floor when his

ex-wife arrived with assistants from *Faire du Charme* magazine and a couple of outfit racks. According to Christie, Jacqueline's response to the voice-mail request to help Becca with her project was that she would "try."

The central air came on and he lifted his head, letting the cool breeze flow across his heated face. After a moment, he returned to flipping pages and was moved once more by the publication. Jacqueline had outdone herself on her last job in the States before accepting a London-based promotion. The designer duds made the patients glow with a confidence the ravages of disease couldn't touch. And Becca's pictures, ones he'd merely assisted with, had captured their unvanquished spirit and beauty.

After Jacqueline had taken an exhausted but thrilled Tommy and Becca for a rare sleepover, he'd questioned Christie. How had she coaxed Jacqueline to help the family? Playing to someone's strength, Christie had confided, made it easier for them to step out of their comfort zone. He needed to have more faith.

Perhaps that was how he'd fallen for the optimist, getting to know Christie through his family until he'd trusted her enough to step from behind his walls. Tonight he'd tell her how much that meant to him and that he loved her. She deserved that and more.

The door opened and Dr. Cruz slipped inside, a stethoscope dangling from the pocket of a white coat worn over a navy dress. She clutched a bundle of thick charts and radiology sleeves that hid the lower half of her face.

"There," she exclaimed as she dumped the contents on her heaped desk and dropped into her chair, her helter-skelter gray hair looking more static-filled than usual. "Hello, Eli." She extended a hand. "It's been almost six months."

"Closing in on two years cancer-free," Eli added, shaking her clammy hand. It was a significant milestone. Twenty-four months of remission boded well for a healthy future, one he could now look forward to spending with Christie and his kids. "Our final checkup is in September." Nearly in the clear.

"Yes. But I'm glad you stopped in early." She adjusted her slipping glasses, the dark circles under her eyes making him wish he hadn't added to her schedule today.

He rose and handed her the calendar. "My daughter made this for her health class, and I wanted to give you one. A thank-you for all you've done." There were many people he owed for getting him through these difficult years. Dr. Cruz was at the top of that list.

Although she turned the pages, her eyes looked distant, unfocused. Guilt swept him once more. He'd interrupted her rounds. A doctor's day was long enough without soon-to-be-former patients dropping by.

"I don't want to take up your time." He grabbed his briefcase.

She waved him back down in his seat. "This is wonderful. Really. Thank you." Her voice sounded thick with emotion.

"I'm glad you like it." He watched her glance down at her mounded desk. Was that his name on a white radiology folder?

"Dr. Sullivan sent these films over."

Eli's knee stopped jittering, surprise washing over him as she strode to a wall-mounted metal box. Dr. Sullivan? His family doctor? Why would he do that?

She slid some X-ray film into the apparatus and flicked on a light switch. Bones—his knee, he supposed—glowed into relief. He'd given in to Christie's pleading and gotten the sports injury checked out last week. Had been waiting for the results.

"Eli. Your cancer is back. My secretary was

going to call you today to set up an appointment."

Her words swam to him as he sank deeper and deeper under their crushing weight. No. This must be a mistake. He'd encountered these kinds of injuries during training.

But wasn't that how they'd found the osteosarcoma in the first place? another voice whispered in his mind. Yes, but... His thoughts stumbled to a halt, the house of cards he'd carefully stacked crumbling to the floor.

He pinched the bridge of his nose and squeezed his eyes shut, his heart pounding hard. Harder. So hard he imagined it pressing against his damp shirt. Was it possible to both want Christie here and feel relieved that she wasn't?

"Eli?" Dr. Cruz called, but he was already drifting away with the tide.

A hand dropped on his shoulder and he could smell hospital rounds on her: disinfectant, latex and hand sanitizer. He scrubbed at his eyes and looked up at her concerned face, the lines of it crisscrossing in worry. "Did you hear what I said?"

He nodded. It was the best he could do.

"Would you like me to call someone?"

He rubbed his temples. Not Christie. Of all people. Not her. Yet she was the first person, besides his children, who'd truly cared about him since his grandparents had passed on.

"No," he said at last. "It's just me."

After a moment of shuffling papers—time he was grateful for as he strove to corral his runaway emotions—she said, "Given your history, Dr. Sullivan thought it prudent to have additional pictures taken along with a CAT scan."

Eli undid his tie and yanked it free. He'd thought the tests a bit overboard for his injury, but he'd been so busy editing the calendar, so caught up in spending time with his daughter, that it hadn't signified.

Her heels clicked across the floor back to the films. The electric whir of the light projector illuminating his X-rays was the only other audible noise. Suddenly he wished he were back at the Little Red School House with Principal Luce, listening to her sound soother or the clacking metallic balls...anything other than this oppressive vacuum of sound broken by the frenetic beating of his heart.

"As you can see, you have a recurrent tumor above your right patella which is causing you the knee discomfort." She pointed to a swirling white cloud on the X-ray.

He took a deep, shuddering breath. "So, what

are we talking about? Another surgery? More chemo?"

"Possibly." She slid back into her chair, steepled her fingers below her chin and stared at him with tired eyes. "Although I'm afraid it would be of little help."

Air rushed from him. "What do you mean?"

"It's metastasized to your femur and hip joint. Given the aggressive progression since our last X-rays, and the size of the tumors, I'm afraid your prognosis is not good."

The unvarnished truth coldcocked him, a sucker punch he hadn't seen coming when he'd walked in here with hopes and dreams for a future that wasn't ever going to happen.

He gulped past the cotton lining his mouth. "So are you saying—" his brain grappled with the news "—there's nothing to do?"

"We could try to replace parts of the femur with titanium again, although the tumor in the hip is particularly difficult and may not be operable. Additionally, there is a very good chance that the cancer will appear in your lungs soon. As such, you are considered Stage Three, rapidly approaching Stage Four, cancer."

The punch turned into a total knockout. His future down on the mat, gasping for breath.

Eli rubbed his wet palms across his thighs, darkening the fabric. It was too much to take in.

"My sincere apologies, Eli. For everything. We had such high hopes, but I'm afraid we're running out of options." She ran a hand through her hair. "I've got a list of other specialists if you'd like another opinion or to explore some of the alternative therapies."

As if any of them would have better news. Dr. Cruz was one of the best in the country. And as for alternative therapies? He wasn't going to start visiting shamans and hypnotherapists to try to remedy a cold truth that wasn't going away.

"How long do I have?" His voice cracked as if he'd turned thirteen again.

"Six months to a year." She pushed some forms his way. "I sincerely apologize for asking you to think of practical matters right now. As soon as you can, however, you'll need to put your affairs in order."

"My affairs?" he echoed, stuffing the paper work in his briefcase without looking. He'd entered a numb space where her words couldn't reach.

"Your will. A health proxy. Guardianship for your kids. Those kinds of things." Her small brown eyes peered anxiously behind rimless squares of glass. "Joan, your counselor, will be able to help."

Eli rose and looked around for his suit coat until he realized he'd never removed it.

"Thank you, Dr. Cruz. I'll be in touch."

"There is an experimental trial starting next week." Her words stopped him before he got to the door. "It's a departure from our traditional treatments and has no proven results beyond lab animals. But as head of the oncology department, I can pull a few strings to get you on the list."

And raise false hopes that would be dashed again? "No. But thank you for the offer. Goodbye." With a pang, he realized it was the first of many he'd be saying.

He shut the door then strode, puppetlike, out of the office, past the reception desk and out onto the bustling street.

Death didn't scare him. If he faced this last battle alone, he would be able to hold his head high and leave the world without a backward glance. But his kids? The woman who now held his heart in her hands?

They made the stakes so much higher. Regret cut through him like a surgeon's scalpel. Eyes burning, he forced one foot in front of the other, knowing he had a lot of work to do. His hopes and dreams may have died in Dr. Cruz's office, but that didn't mean he could just roll over and die, too. First, he'd have to find a way to make this easier for the people he loved. And that was going to kill him a whole lot faster than any tumor.

CHRISTIE HUNG UP her monkey-ears stethoscope, sank into the soft chair behind her desk and kicked off her Keds. Phew. A long day. She stretched her aching toes and glanced at her iPhone. Five o'clock. She'd have to hurry if she wanted to get in some quality home-shopping time…or was tonight her baking night…?

Whoa.

When had her schedule flown out the window? And at what point had she stopped caring?

She scrolled through some pictures, finding all the answers she needed. There was one of Eli, his blue eyes twinkling as he snuggled the kids during an outdoor screening of *Kung Fu Panda 2,* another of Becca making a face as she tested cheese at a farmers' market and a third of Tommy pointing at wallabies on a trip to Prospect Park Zoo.

The most recent picture, one taken by Mary before they'd gone to a Broadway revival of *Annie,* showed their heads mashed close, arms entwined, grins matching. Christie sighed. It had been an amazing night. No wonder she'd lost track of her daily agenda. Her life was so full these past few weeks she couldn't imagine ever returning to the old, lonely schedules she'd kept.

Her thumb pulled down the last text bubble on the ongoing conversation she and Eli held every day. She'd sent it at two o'clock, wishing him well on his appointment with a new client. Funny that he hadn't answered. She tapped her comment screen and began to type when a knock sounded.

"Come in," she called. The door swung open. Eli.

Her heart leaped and she jumped to her feet. What was he doing here? Maybe he'd had a solo appointment with Joan this week to discuss his family's progress. He'd been diligent about keeping those therapy appointments, for Becca's sake and his.

A strange look on his face checked her forward momentum. Instead of rushing into his arms, she moved toward him awkwardly, not sure where to put her hands. She shoved them in her pockets and toyed with the penny she'd picked up on her rounds.

"How is everything?" she asked when the silence stretched past the breaking point.

"Fine." He smiled, his cheeks lifting stiffly as though pushed by invisible fingers. Something was definitely off. Her stomach roiled. He looked handsome, but he definitely didn't look fine.

Funny how she'd gotten so good at reading him, yet this was a side of him she hadn't seen.

"Sure about that?" She extended her hand but he only squeezed her fingers before pulling out of range. Her heart plummeted at his brief, icy touch.

"Look, there's something I've been meaning to tell you, Christie, and it's not easy."

Her throat constricted and she managed a nod. Where was he going with this?

He peered at the ceiling. "I think we should stop seeing each other."

Her fingers clutched her lucky charm necklace, palm pressed against her fluttering heart. Bile rose in her throat and she fought off a spinning sensation that made her grab a chair.

"Excuse me? I mean, say that again," she gasped. He couldn't be suggesting what she thought he meant. Suddenly, the necklace pooled in her hand, the delicate clasp broken.

His eyes fled hers. "After talking with Joan

today, I've realized that my focus now needs to be on my family. The timing isn't right for a relationship."

A silent scream sounded in her head. This wasn't happening.

Eli rubbed the back of his neck. "Please understand that I—I—" His voice wobbled for a moment then steadied. "I care about you very much. But we're in two different places in our lives. You're young. Single. I'm sure you'd like your old life back. No more helping us through crises."

Her old life? Her free-falling emotions landed with a thud and bounced back, fire engulfing them. She'd lived a half life before the Robertses entered it. And Eli had always seemed so happy when they were together.

"You can't be serious." She moved closer until she stood toe-to-toe with him. Why wouldn't he meet her eyes? And what right did he have to look hurt? Last time she'd checked, she was the one getting dumped. "So, basically you have no further need of my services?"

"I'm sorry." He locked gazes with her for a minute—long enough for her to know he was honest about that much, at least. "But I've got to move forward with my life and my family, on my own."

"Was that all I was to you—someone helping you through rough patches?" She threw out her arms and knocked a paper-clip holder off her desk. When Eli bent to pick up the rainbow of colored plastic, she shooed him away. "I need answers. Not a cleanup."

He limped to the large window overlooking the street, his shoulders bunched. After giving her such feeble excuses, he was turning his back on her? It registered that his limp was more pronounced today, but anger and hurt chased her concern away. Instead, her skin heated, her telltale splotches appearing with a vengeance.

When he spoke, his voice sounded low and ragged. "You know you were more than that to me."

She rushed to the window and leaned against the warm glass, wishing the slanting sun didn't leave the upper half of his face in shadow. His eyes. They would tell her the truth if only she could see them.

"Then why are you doing this?" His unyielding biceps felt like stone, cold and hard beneath her touch. He flinched away.

"Because it's time. We both knew this couldn't last forever. We worked out our issues and now we can move on."

Anger exploded inside her like a fireworks

show gone haywire, every missile firing at once in a torrent of blinding, sizzling light.

"Why wouldn't I think it could last forever?" She jabbed a finger into his chest, making him step back. "You said we had forever, that I was special. We were special. Two imperfect people who were perfect for each other. Was that just some lie to keep me around? To make sure I helped Becca?"

She paced to her file cabinet, grabbing its cool steel sides.

"No. It's not like that."

She wheeled around and pressed her back against the metal tower. "Then how is it? Explain in a way that makes sense."

When he stepped out of the shadows, his eyes focused on a spot behind her left shoulder, a tic appearing high in his left cheek. "I need someone who sees the world the way I do. I can't be a wide-eyed optimist all the time. It's not good for me or my kids."

Realization stiffened her spine. "Is this because of Jacqueline?" His eyes fled hers. "Are you blaming me because she moved to London after I invited her to the shoot? I'm sorry that the kids got their hopes let down again. Really sorry. But that's her. Not me."

Eli stuffed his hands in his pockets and shook

his head, his expression pained. "It's deeper than that. I need a realist and that's difficult for you."

His words struck her like a slap against the cheek. He knew why she needed to hang tight to her optimism with both hands. She whirled to face the window. How dare he bring up her past? Use her secrets against her? The facade she'd constructed over a lifetime started to crack. Fall away. "I should have known this wasn't possible."

"What wasn't possible?"

"Happiness."

"Christie." His voice was softer now, pleading. It reminded her of the old Eli. The one she'd loved. At least she'd waited to say those words, and he'd never know how she felt. There was some dignity in that. "You'll find happiness. Just with someone else. Someone who can make you happy for the rest of your life."

Like you could have, she thought and then shook her head. It was over. Truly over.

"Can't we part as friends?" His voice rose. Urgent. "Say goodbye on good terms?"

"That doesn't sound like something a realist would do." She was being childish but didn't care. Her head began to pound and she rubbed her temples. "Besides, friends don't treat each other this way. And we were more than that," she whispered. "So much more." Suddenly she couldn't stand him being there, sharing space with her, when he wasn't *with* her. "Please go."

A rush of stale hospital air signaled he'd eased open the door. "I'm sorry," he said, his voice hoarse. "Goodbye." The door clicked shut, the soft sound reminding her of her brother's wake, the coffin closing. The End. An eternity of pain for those left behind.

She stumbled to her desk chair and collapsed into it. Her fingers dug in her pocket for the penny then hurled it at the door. It pinged off the surface and bounced to the carpet. So much for good luck. So much for anything she'd believed in.

Her head dropped to her hands and she bent at the waist, rocking, her grief too deep for tears. A deep trembling overtook her instead.

Where had she gone wrong? Had she misplaced a foot a moment before leaping from the tightrope into Eli's arms? Another shuddering heave overtook her. Instead she'd fallen in a broken heap. Pieces of her everywhere. Too scattered to pick up and move on.

So she didn't move. She ignored Joan's knock at the door, the janitor's request to vacuum and her ringing cell. Her eyes drifted to her bookcase. It was crammed with knowledge to help her patients. Ironic that none seemed to apply to her.

She wrapped her arms around herself and watched the city sky turn from gold to rose, lavender to indigo and finally, to an inky, starless black that matched her mood. Something inside her had vanished over the horizon, as well, the light in her disappearing, replaced by a rolling emptiness she hadn't felt since her brother died.

She'd always known that hurting Bill and her parents would come back to haunt her. She'd tried to outrun her own wickedness, atone for it every way she could. But in the end, she'd been caught. Punished. She was losing the best thing she'd ever had, the love of a wonderful man and two kids she adored as her own.

And right now the only thing that surprised her was that she had never seen it coming.

CHAPTER SEVENTEEN

CHRISTIE ROLLED OVER and groped for the ringing cell phone on her bedside table. After working back-to-back double shifts—an epic fail in distracting her from thoughts of Eli—she could have been asleep for hours or days. Her bleary eyes focused on her phone, noting the time—11:00 a.m.—and the caller. She bolted upright with her heart going like a trip-hammer, the covers pooling in her lap.

"Hi, Becca." She strove to keep her voice steady. How had Eli explained her absence these past three days? It broke her heart that she'd lost the children along with Eli. She pulled a crumpled tissue from beneath her pillow and swiped at her nose.

A hiccuping sob came through the speaker followed by "Christie, I'm scared."

"What's going on?" Fear unfurled in her chest. Eli might not want her in his life, but it didn't mean she'd ever stop caring about the kids. "Where's your father?"

"At his lawyer's office and I'm watching

Tommy until he gets back. But he was in a hurry and forgot his iPhone and there's a text message from his doctor. Something about an experimental treatment for his cancer—" Her words dissolved in a watery gulp. "He's sick again. I know it."

Christie's pulse sped, beating against her eardrums. Had his osteosarcoma returned? Suddenly she found it hard to breathe as she recalled his hurt knee. Hadn't it struck her, the night they'd broken up, that his limp seemed worse? She should have questioned him, seen a connection between the ailment and his decision to end things. Distracted by his words and her hurt feelings, she'd focused on the piece instead of the puzzle.

She swung her legs over the side of her bed, eyes scanning the gloom for clean clothes. "Becca, I'm on my way. Don't say anything to Tommy until I get there."

"Too late," she cried. "You're on speaker."

"I want to talk to Christie," Tommy snuffled in the background. Her heart squeezed at the way he said her name—*Krithee*. Adrenaline rushed through her. She had to get there.

Now.

She punched on her cell's speaker and grabbed a pair of sweats and a tee from her laundry pile.

"Tommy. I'm here. Listen, I'll be there very soon."

"I want Daddy. I want Sweet Pea," he wailed. "And why have you been gone? Don't you like us anymore? 'Cause I miss you."

Her eyes burned and she blinked back a rush of tears. How could she have been so blind and selfish when Becca and Tommy needed her? "I miss you and Becca very much. I promise I'm on my way. Okay?"

"Yes," Becca gasped. "But don't hang up."

"I'm not going anywhere." At least not until Eli told her to. Right now the kids needed her and that was all that mattered—that and the possibility that Eli was dying and had been too stubborn and proud to tell her. The room seemed to tilt and whirl, and she grabbed her bedpost to steady herself. It'd been impossible imagining her life without Eli. Now…to imagine *life* without Eli…Becca and Tommy without their father…it was too much to take in.

She would not make the same mistakes she had with Bill. No way. Not happening.

With a swift yank, she pulled on her clothes, beads of perspiration rising on her forehead. "Becca, can you make Tommy something to eat? Maybe some Frosted Flakes?"

"Can I have Honey Nut Cheerios instead?"

Tommy's voice steadied a bit and she breathed a sigh of relief. A little normalcy went a long way for kids.

"We've only got the regular kind left. Dad hasn't gone shopping in a while."

Christie strode into the living area and whistled for Sweet Pea, tripping over Laura's shoes on the way. "I'm sure he's had a lot on his mind."

"Yeah. Nothing he bothered sharing with us. Typical." Becca's anguished voice now sounded angry. Seesawing emotions were normal. Expected. But it pained her to hear the children struggle to make sense of such complicated issues on their own.

With a scratching of canine nails on wood, Sweet Pea scampered to the door, her ears flapping. Christie grabbed the fabric pet carrier and settled it across her chest.

"Is Christie here yet?" she heard Tommy ask as she attached the dog leash, her pup's brown eyes darting to the door.

"On my way, Tommy." She wrestled her dog into the carrier, snatched her keys and slipped outside, the smell of garlic from her foodie neighbors permeating their shared landing.

"We're out of milk," muttered Becca. "Figures."

"Fix yourself something—sweet tea, maybe—

and put peanut butter on a spoon for Tommy. He can dip it in the bowl and lick off the Cheerios." It had been her brother's favorite snack, she recalled with a pang.

Yet for the first time in a long time, a memory of Bill made her smile, too. Somehow, she thought he would approve of her sharing the peanut-butter-and-Cheerios trick.

She zipped down the stairs, her feet skimming the treads, Sweet Pea snuggled in the holder against her chest.

Out in the early-morning heat, she flagged down a cab and jumped inside, inhaling the familiar taxi scent of hair spray and exhaust.

"Broome Street. And quickly," she ordered, and the vehicle swerved into traffic, earning them a few sharp honks. *Please let Eli get home soon.* She scooted back against the leather and buckled her pouch-encased dog beside her. Hopefully he wouldn't be upset to see her. But his children needed answers, and so did she.

"Why is Dad lying to us again? I hate him," Becca hissed, but it was Christie's own voice she heard. Her resentment toward her brother pouring from this young girl's mouth.

Christie's mind raced, her training spinning the dial to unlock the right answer. It landed on honesty, her best shot.

"I was angry with my brother, too, Becca."

"The one who had leukemia?" she asked softly. A spoon clanked against what sounded like glass. She'd made the tea. Good. Mundane tasks helped during stressful times.

Christie glanced out at the gray morning, the city bathed in sepia shades that matched her mood. "Yes. His name was William but we called him Bill."

The cab lurched to a whiplash stop, construction bottlenecking the road ahead. She grabbed Sweet Pea, who slid as her carrier strap broke.

"Why were you mad at him?"

Christie rested her forehead against the glass and watched the current of people streaming down Lafayette Street. How many secrets were hidden in that mob? How many hopes and wishes, too?

"I think I was mostly angry at the cancer… what it did to him. To our family."

A noisy gulp sounded, then "You had to give up dance."

"Yes. And other things, too. That's what I despised, really. Not Bill."

"Oh," Becca sighed. "I've been mad at Dad for a long time."

Christie released her tight grip on the door

handle when traffic resumed moving. "It's okay to feel that way."

"But not at him. I'm terrible." Becca's low sob cut through Christie's heart. "He can't help being sick."

Although he could help how he handled it. Why, why, why hadn't he told her that night in her office? She had to think he'd known. That he'd been making a misguided attempt to spare her some heartbreak. Or worse, that he didn't think she could handle another cancer battle after the way she'd broken down at John's funeral.

"No. He can't. And you're human, not terrible." She craned her neck around a delivery truck. "I'm almost there."

She rapped on the plastic divider, read the meter and slid some bills under the opening.

Heat radiated in waves above the sidewalk in front of the Korean deli. She tugged at a sniffing Sweet Pea, raced up the steps to Eli's building and hit the buzzer.

"Christie!" Tommy's voice shrieked over the intercom.

"Yes. It's me."

The door unlocked with a long buzz. She jerked it open and stepped inside. Her eyes darted between the elevator and the stairs. One was slower, the other pure terror. A glance at her panting spaniel, however, had her heading to the iron gate. The little dog would never make it up those flights and there was nothing she could do to repair her carrier at the moment. With a shaking finger, she jabbed the up button. Facing her worst fear was child's play compared to Eli's cancer returning.

The doors slid open, and with a hard yank the rattling metal folded in on itself. She stepped inside the confined space and dug in her purse for her rabbit's foot. Missing. She breathed deep and forced herself to stay calm when the elevator rose.

The elevator bumped to a halt and the doors slid open. After releasing a deep breath, Christie heaved back the tarnished grate. "I'm here," she called then slipped her phone into her pocket and rang the bell.

Minutes later she snuggled the kids on the couch, the cartoons on mute.

"Is Daddy going to die?" Tommy asked, his sticky fingers twining with hers. Christie's stomach knotted but she kept her face neutral, her smile reassuring.

She squeezed his hand. "We can't know anything until he comes home."

"So maybe he won't be sick!" Tommy's gap-toothed smile blazed then faded. "But Becca said—"

Her eyes met Becca's. She gave the girl a small nod, hoping she'd understand her silent plea to reassure the boy.

"I was mad, Tommy," said Becca. "When I read the text, I thought he was hiding stuff from us. Like before. But Christie's right. Dad needs to tell us if he has cancer again."

Tommy wiped his nose with the back of his hand. "That makes me scared." He glanced up at Christie, his brows, nearly the same color as his pale skin, knotting. "Is that bad? Daddy's brave but I'm not."

She cupped his soft, dimpled chin and said, "No. All feelings are okay. And I think you are very brave." Her gaze flew to Becca, who gave her a small smile. "When your dad comes home, you should tell him how you feel."

"You won't leave us, will you, Christie?" His warm body curled up on her lap, one hand now tangled in her hair, the other wrapped around a content Sweet Pea.

When she shook her head, her swishing hair reminded her she'd never combed it. "No." She gave Becca a meaningful look. "I'm not going anywhere."

The children sighed, their bodies relaxing

against her. Yet the sound of the key in the lock had everyone tensing. Eli.

He strode in, tall and devastatingly handsome. He didn't look sick…. He looked like the man she'd fallen in love with. His blue eyes blazed at her, shocked.

"What's going on?"

Christie spoke over her pounding heart. "Eli, Becca and Tommy have something they want to ask you."

Although Becca's fists clenched in her lap and her mouth opened, only tears escaped her.

Eli rushed to her, but Tommy's words stopped him cold.

"Daddy. Are you fibbing about cancer? 'Cause that makes me sad. And scared." He looked her way and she patted his leg. Brave boy.

"What?" Eli dropped to his knees before them. "Who told you that?" She flinched under his accusing gaze.

"I did." Becca spoke up. She paced to the kitchen and held up his iPhone. "You forgot this when you hurried out of here. Dr. Cruz left you a text message about some experimental treatment…for your cancer."

"You read my private messages?" Eli stood, his face pale.

Becca's lower lip stuck out. "How else could I find out anything? First you stop seeing Christie—without talking to us—and now this."

Eli dropped into a chair and pinched the bridge of his nose. "I was trying to protect all of you." His gaze flew to Christie, a pleading expression in its blue depths.

He'd broken up with her rather than tell her he had cancer again. The full impact of the news washed over her, dragging her into a whole new riptide of doubts. Fears. Hadn't he trusted her to be there for him? She tucked those emotions aside, knowing the kids came first.

"You can't protect us from the truth. It comes out anyway." Becca returned to the living room and crossed her thin arms over her trembling body. "Is it true? Is your cancer back?"

Eli gestured for the kids to come closer. Tommy handed over Sweet Pea and leaped onto his father's lap while Becca perched on the arm of the chair, Eli's arm wrapped around her. A deep longing seized Christie, a wish to join them, no matter what Eli's news was. She didn't want to run as she had from Bill or even from John's funeral. She wanted to give comfort as much as she received it—not to make up for what she'd done, but to be with them, join them on their journey…wherever it led.

"Yes," Eli sighed. "And it's worse than before."

Tommy buried his head in his father's shoulder and cried.

"I'm here, Little Man." Becca rubbed her brother's back, her cheeks tributaries of tears. She turned to her father. "But you're going to get treatment, right? This experimental thing?"

Eli shook his head. "I don't know."

What? Christie's stroking hands stilled in Sweet Pea's fur. She understood why patients chose to pass on with dignity. But he had to keep fighting for the children's sake. Maybe a small part of her wished he would have fought for her—for them—as well.

Becca shot to her feet. "Then you're just going to die? Didn't you tell me not to be a quitter?"

"Daddy—" Tommy raised his wet face "—I'm only little. But I love you a lot. Please get better. I need you."

Eli glanced from his furious daughter to his pleading son then finally back to Christie. Their eyes met for an anguished moment and she saw everything she needed to know—fear, pain and much more. When had she learned to read him so well? If only she'd used those skills the other night in her office instead of hiding her head in the sand...refusing to see what had been right in front of her. She gave Eli a nod, encouraging him silently. And then, like a light emerging behind storm clouds, she saw his expression clear. A new determination fired through his gaze.

His shoulders squared and he pulled Becca onto his lap so the squealing children collapsed into a tangled ball of limbs. Sweet Pea barked in delight at the chaos.

"Fine. I'll try. But no promises."

"No," Tommy said. "But I'm still going to wish."

"Me, too." Becca kissed his cheek. "Thank you, Dad."

Christie swallowed back the fierce desire to be there with them, wrapped in the warmth of this family. But she scooped up her dog and stood. She'd done her job and gotten the family back on track. Now she needed to go home and grieve on her own. It'd been tough holding it together this long.

"Eli. I'm so sorry and if any of you need anything—" her gaze swept over the suddenly still group "—please call. If the trial is the one I heard about, the first round of treatment should be over in time for your trip to Yosemite."

"Will you wait for me outside?" Eli's eyes searched hers.

She nodded, gave the kids each a kiss that

ripped her heart in two then slipped out the door. This wasn't about her anymore. It was about what Eli needed, even if that meant letting him go.

A moment later, Eli joined her. The familiar smell of him—lemongrass and musk—flooded her senses with a longing so fierce it was a physical ache. If only she could dial back the clock and rush into his arms one last time.

He ran a hand through his hair and shifted his weight to his left leg. "I'm sorry. I should have told you. It's just that I—"

She held up a hand. They were past apologies. "I understand. You thought I couldn't handle this, would let you down."

Sweet Pea wriggled and she set down the dog.

Eli's eyes flashed at her, surprised. "No. I wanted to spare you. Make it easier on everyone."

He reached for her then stuffed his hands in his pockets, a defeated look on his face. "I'm grateful you'll be around for the kids when I'm gone. It means a lot."

"Try to think positively," she said over the painful tightness in her throat. "The trial might help and—"

"Please, Christie. That's your way of thinking, not mine. I'll join the experiment for the kids. But the reality is I've got six months to a year. The sooner I come to terms with that the better."

Christie wiped the rush of wetness from her eyes. "I see." Inspirational quotes ran through her mind, motivational thoughts that helped her patients live with cancer rather than die of it. But this wasn't what Eli wanted to hear and that was all that mattered.

"My thoughts are always with you, Eli." Never had she spoken truer words. "And I'm here whenever you need me." *Please need me,* she added silently. *Want me. Trust me.*

She pushed the elevator button and forced herself not to say more. It would only make things harder. Breaking up with her must have been difficult, something he'd only do if he felt he must. They'd cared so deeply. Had come so close to love.

"Wait. I'll ride with you. I know how you hate the thing."

"Thanks, Eli. But I'll take it from here." She led Sweet Pea inside then pulled the gate across. "And please take care of yourself."

His image, a wounded man, yet a warrior still, wavered as the doors slid closed. She made sure she hid her tears until the elevator was well out of sight.

Four weeks later, Christie sat at the White Horse Tavern's round wooden table, her fork pushing an anchovy across the top of her Caesar salad.

"Your Eli sure is a fine-looking fellow." Gran lifted her glass of Guinness. "Let's drink to his health."

Christie raised her glass but not her eyes. It'd been difficult keeping her secret from her perceptive grandmother. But so far, she hadn't felt ready to talk. She couldn't bear adding Gran's disappointment to her own.

"To Eli." Their glasses clinked and she braced herself for the usual minefield of questions she'd have to step carefully across. One misplaced foot and her secret would blow up in her face. She took a sip of the dark liquid.

"So tell me what you did this week." Gran's green eyes watched her over the rim of her glass. Gran adjusted the lace collar of her aquamarine dress then waved a napkin in front of her face.

Christie smoothed her white eyelet skirt then dabbed her napkin in her water glass and pressed the cool cloth against the back of her flushed neck. Thank goodness her sleeveless navy blouse had a high neckline, which hid the worst of her telltale splotches.

"The usual. Work. Support group. Oh, and I finally got the Amaya Holiday Tiny Tot doll on the Home Shopping Network, Tuesday. They ran a Christmas in August special." Christie felt a bit of happiness at the thought, though completing her collection of Marie Osmond dolls didn't make up for losing the Roberts family. She missed them so much. Sometimes her mind ran over the spot they'd occupied in her heart like a tongue searching for an extracted tooth. They were gone, in Yosemite now for that long-delayed family vacation Eli had wanted. Yet her soul still refused to accept that even when they came home it wouldn't be to her.

She chewed a salty bite and stared at a group of men and women crowded around the dart board. They laughed and jostled, cheering and catcalling to one another. How strange it felt to watch happy people when she felt so wretched.

"Amaya?" asked Gran. "I was hoping to hear about Eli, Becca and Tommy." She waved her fork like a maestro.

"Oh. Nothing new to report there," she said in a rush then stuffed her mouth full of chicken, the tangy dressing barely registering as she chewed.

"Are you certain of that?" Gran's eyes narrowed.

"Tell me about the seniors' center." Christie stalled after swallowing her tasteless bite.

"That trick won't work with me every time, young lady," her grandmother warned.

A Bob Dylan song, "It's All Over Now, Baby Blue," blared on. Fitting. Christie squirmed and blocked out the lyrics, distracting herself by making a triangle with her fork, knife and spoon.

"The two of you are so happy together. And the children, they're absolutely precious and need a mother like—"

"Just stop," Christie whispered and waved her white napkin in defeat, the reminder of all she'd lost too painful to hear. It was a miracle she'd lasted this long without Gran figuring everything out.

Gran's lotion-soft hand descended on hers, a whiff of rose perfume rising from her wrist. "I'm sorry, dear. You see, I've tried to give you time to deal with this, but I've run out of patience waiting for you to tell me the truth."

"The truth?" Christie echoed, stalling. She signaled the bartender for another round. Their second.

"Yes." Gran gripped her other hand. "You're skinny as a rail, you've got eye circles so dark they're black and you haven't smiled—a real one—in weeks. Of course I knew something was wrong."

Christie forced a grin when an elderly man entered the bar and waved their way. Gran, however, didn't bother flirting. Her eyes stayed on Christie, the expression compelling her to speak.

"Now tell your gran like a good lass."

Her eyes stung and she took a deep breath. "Eli broke up with me a month ago."

Gran's hands tightened on hers. "The idjit. Why would he throw away the best thing to happen in his life? His kids loved you and he seemed so happy."

"He was. We were. But then his cancer came back." Her hoarse voice was interrupted by the thunk of glasses on their table, beige froth seeping down the sides. "Thank you," she whispered to the bartender, who took one look at her and scurried away with a quick nod.

"No," breathed Gran. "Then why are you here and not with him?"

"Because he wants to handle this on his own."

"Without you? Or your help with the children? Why would he be so foolish?"

"He doesn't think I can handle it."

"Why? You work with cancer patients and families every day. More importantly, you love them. I could see it at the party."

Her eyes welled and she dabbed at them with her napkin. "I told him about Bill. Eli thinks I'll let him down, too." She cleared her throat and shook her head. "He doesn't want to put me in that position again."

Knowing Eli and his generous, thoughtful spirit, that probably came closer to the truth.

"And what do you think?"

"I know I don't want to hurt him the way I hurt Bill."

Gran dug inside her oversized purse, pulling out spare nylons, a rain hat and a Fodor's book about the Caribbean before producing a care-worn envelope, the recognizable handwriting on its cover making Christie gasp.

Bill.

"This is the last letter I got from your brother before he passed. He wrote it the day he died. It was in my mailbox when I flew back from the funeral." She slid on her reading glasses, unfolded the sheet and cleared her throat.

"Gran, don't. Please."

She didn't know if she could handle this right now.

"You need to hear this, my darling girl. Trust me."

At Christie's nod, Gran took a sip of her beverage then began.

"Dear Gran,

Not a lot of energy today, but it's exciting here anyway. Christie's prom is tonight. I hear her running up and down the stairs, asking Mom to borrow her curling iron or heels. She sounds excited, which makes me glad. It stinks that she's worked so much and hasn't had much fun. For tonight at least, Christie gets what I've hoped for all along, a chance to be happy and normal like other kids. Imagining her in the blue dress Mom showed me makes me feel like maybe she'll be okay when I'm gone.

I love you, Gran. I'll write when I can, though I've been feeling kind of off lately.

Keep sending the soda bread. It only lasts about a day when we get it.

Good night,

Bill"

Gran lowered the paper, her fogging glasses slipping down her damp nose. "Don't you see, sweetheart? He was happy you were enjoying your last year of high school. He didn't want you to work or ignore friends. The way I understand it, seeing you live a normal life gave him the courage to finally let go."

Christie took a deep breath that hitched on a watery sob. Could it be true? All these years she'd regretted that night, never knowing she'd made Bill happy in spite of herself. A weight nudged from her shoulders and fell away.

"Thank you, Gran."

"Don't let old ghosts hold you back from your future, my girl." Gran sipped her ale, holding Christie's gaze. "I never knew you carried that kind of guilt around or I would have shown you that letter a long time ago." She patted her purse. "I keep it handy because I like to have him close."

Her warm smile made Christie sure that Bill was nearby. A fulfilled spirit that didn't resent her after all.

"I never knew..." Christie's voice hitched again, but she finally felt free to think about her future now that she wasn't focused on the past.

"So the question is...what are you going to do about it?"

Christie smoothed her hair and wiped her tear-stained face.

"Hurry." She shouldered her purse. "I've got a plane to Yosemite to catch."

She couldn't cure cancer. But there was another hurt, one she and Eli shared, and she would do everything in her power to fix it.

CHAPTER EIGHTEEN

"GOOD NIGHT, DADDY," Becca and Tommy called. They headed toward their three-room tent in the glow of the dwindling campfire. Flashlights bobbed like fireflies around their site as fellow campers at the California state park readied for bed.

"And don't stay up too late," added Becca. "Tomorrow morning is the kids' scavenger hunt." The sound of a raising zipper cut through the static hum of cicadas and grasshoppers.

"Got it." Eli poked at a couple of fallen logs in the flaming pile. They'd been looking forward to the group activity for days. It was the last one before they headed back to New York, where more treatment and his latest radiology results awaited. "Love you," he called over his shoulder.

"Love you!"

"Hey, that's my pillow," he heard Becca grump from behind nylon walls.

"Finders keepers," argued Tommy. "I want the fluffy pillow."

"Then you should have brought one." His daughter. So wise.

Eli enjoyed hearing them talk about normal stuff. He hadn't made cancer off-limits, but he hoped they'd talked about it enough that the kids didn't spend too much time worrying. It sure didn't sound as though it occupied their minds now. The bullfrogs' deep bass was no match for the sibling tempest brewing inside the tent. The grunts of what sounded like a tug-of-war floated in the crisp wilderness air.

"Didn't have room 'cause I needed to bring Rexie."

"Yuck. Get that dinosaur away from me. It's filthy."

"Rexie is going to bite you."

Eli suppressed a chuckle, warmth spreading through him at the thought that they'd always have each other…and Christie.

"If that thing comes any closer I'll— Ahhhhhh! Dad!"

"Knock it off and go to sleep," Eli growled, his smile seeping into his voice. "Tommy, give your sister her pillow and borrow mine from the other room."

"Yes, Dad," they chorused, and after a few more scuffling sounds, finally all was quiet.

His world was temporarily at peace. But this

was the calm before the storm. His life's visa had nearly expired. He pulled on a sweatshirt against the first chill of a late-summer evening. It heralded autumn—the dying season.

Soon color would blaze across the countryside, nature's last gasp before winter's killing frost. And he could relate. He'd been taking pictures nonstop, wanting to immortalize every minute of this amazing trip. He'd taught Becca and Tommy what he could about lighting, framing, angles and lenses. But it was the spontaneous moments of fun—jumping into a warm spring fully clothed, making daisy chains on a hike, discovering Tommy's first fossil and a geode for Becca—they'd remember. The only legacy that mattered was the love he gave and the memories they made. Now that Christie had taught him to open up about his feelings, they'd poured from him like a broken faucet he never wanted to fix. And while worried, the children had never seemed happier.

Adjusting a blanket beneath him, he crossed his arms behind his head and stared up at the twinkling night sky, wishing Christie were here. When wind rustled through the trees, carrying the scent of pine and wildflowers, he imagined her in his arms, her soft hair against his shoulder, her deep green eyes gazing into his.

But that was all he could do. Imagine. Having her here for real would have been too selfish. She'd only be reliving her painful childhood through him. And he wanted so much more for the woman he loved.

And yet…she would have loved this vacation. He couldn't deny the guilt that sneaked up on him at odd times of the day when he thought about how much he would have enjoyed looking for shooting stars with her at night.

He scanned the inky sky, searching for one. Which one was John's? Which one would be his? He'd know soon. While he'd survived the first round of the aggressive experimental treatment, a deep exhaustion dogged him. Now he gripped banisters when climbing steps, gasped for breath when carrying in groceries and napped after finishing graphic-design projects. Not that he'd expected to feel better. He'd done the trial for the kids, wanting them to know that he loved them enough to battle for his life.

And he had Christie to thank for making him realize that, too. It blew his mind that she'd promised to be there for his children, even after he'd broken her heart.

A spark popped from a log and he shepherded the logs into a tidy heap again. He inched closer to the diminished heat, appreciating it all the more since it would soon be out. Had he been wrong to spare Christie with his stilted attempt at a breakup? He wasn't so sure. And now he'd lost her for good without ever having the chance to tell her how much he loved her.

She might not deserve to deal with his cancer, but that should have been her choice to make, not his. She wasn't the same person she'd been when Bill died. Yet, he'd treated her like her eighteen-year-old self rather than the woman who worked with pediatric oncology patients and support groups alike. The woman who'd helped Becca through her crisis and taught Tommy—and him—that it was okay to admit their fears.

She was the strong one. Maybe she didn't recognize it, but he did now. He should have had more faith in her…in them. Maybe it wasn't wrong, or selfish, to want her with him at the end, to have her in the last picture he took of this world before leaving it.

He sat up in the growing darkness, aware that he'd let the fire go out. He kicked sand on the last embers, letting them hiss and turn black. Too late.

A star streaked across the sky and he wished on it for a miracle, a Hail Mary pass that somehow, some way, Christie would forgive him and stay with him until the end.

His head dropped into his hands. Stupid, idiotic dream. He'd done irreparable harm and it was all too late. He hadn't been given time to make mistakes like this. Game over.

CHRISTIE'S GRIP ON her backpack tightened when the morning shuttle bus swung past a wooden sign that read Upper Pines Campground. After an eight-hour flight and two bus rides, she felt exhausted and exhilarated. In minutes she'd locate Eli's campsite and see him, Tommy and Becca again. Would they be as thrilled to see her as she was to see them? The kids, definitely. Eli…she wasn't sure.

When they'd said goodbye, he'd seemed sad but unwilling to trust her enough to stay by his side. She raised her chin and watched children race around the campsite holding nature items and papers. A scavenger hunt. Hopefully, like them, she'd find what she was searching for. Eli's trust and love.

Her heart skipped a beat when the bus slowed then stopped with a high-pitched squeal.

"Ladies and gentlemen, you'll need to check in at the ranger's station before I take you to your sites. No need to rush. I'll be waiting." The grizzled driver's teeth appeared in a smile over his thick, salt-and-pepper beard.

No need to rush? She was already four weeks late. Gran said absence made the heart grow fonder and hopefully that was true in Eli's case. He'd had plenty of time to think this month, as had she. Did she dare hope he'd seen things differently by now? Reconsidered his decision to shut her out of his life? She clambered down the stairs. If not, she'd have to make him understand that she was here to stay. For everyone's sake, including her own.

When the park ranger looked up Eli's reservation and confirmed that her name was listed, she breathed a sigh of relief. They'd made the travel plans so long ago. Thankfully Eli hadn't thought to remove her from the approved guest list.

Back on the bus, her heart sped as the tires churned up the log-lined dirt road. Colorful tents, cloth-covered picnic tables and metal food chests mixed with towering sequoias, the Sierra Nevada granite cliffs a postcard of a backdrop. She glanced at a number nailed to a white fir tree as they left a loop and turned down another. One hundred and fifty four. Only twenty sites to go and she'd be stepping off the bus. Would she be stepping into Eli's arms?

"This is me." She swayed down the narrow

passageway when site #174 came into view. When the doors wheezed open she took a deep breath and plunged out, momentarily blinded by the sun bursting through the cloud cover.

She blinked the spots from her eyes and lowered her bag.

"Christie?" A familiar voice sounded behind her, making her heart squeeze. "What are you doing here?"

She whirled around and there he was, thinner and paler than she remembered, but as gorgeous as ever, his piercing blue eyes searching hers. The brilliant sunshine outlined him in light—already an angel.

Instead of answering she burst into tears. The flight, the bus rides and now seeing him. It was too much. Here she was, falling apart, every inch the weak girl he thought her to be. But she couldn't help it. She loved him so much.

"Shh, sweetheart." Eli dropped his water bucket and drew her close. He was shivering and the wind ruffled the flannel shirt he wore over a faded T-shirt. "Shh. It's all right." His large hands cupped her face, his thumbs brushing the steady stream flowing from beneath her lashes.

"No. It's not," she finally gasped and pressed her wet face against his chest. This was not the strong entrance she'd hoped to make. What a mess. She'd reinforced everything he'd thought, justified every reason he'd given for sending her away.

"Let's talk." With a firm hand on her waist, he guided her past his large green tent, a picnic table decorated with a mug overflowing with wilting dandelions and three fold-out chairs set before a fire pit. The smell of burned wood, charcoal and bacon wafted through the morning air. The peaceful quiet was broken by the sound of calling birds. Where were the children?

"Becca and Tommy—"

"Went with my neighbors and their kids on a scavenger hunt. We have a few minutes before they get back."

She swiped at her nose and followed him to the rear edge of his campsite. He sat on a log in the midst of a thicket and she joined him, partly so they could be on the same level and partly to disguise that her knees were shaking.

They were not far from each other but he was holding back, she could tell. She wanted to reach out to him but kept her hands still, her voice steady. Time to dig deep, show him the strength that would make him trust her to stick around for the long haul.

"Eli. I've missed you and…and…" Her voice stumbled over the words jostling to be heard.

He opened his mouth but she held up a hand. She might lose her nerve if he interrupted and she'd waited too long to speak from her heart.

"I came here to tell you that you were right. I wasn't strong enough. But not in the way you think." She pressed a finger against his parting lips, her eyes begging him for patience. After a moment, his shoulders relaxed and she continued.

"Agreeing to leave you seemed like the right thing to do. You wanted it, and I honored that. But I should have considered how much you need me and I need you. Or that the children depend on us both. I know you think I can't handle your cancer because of what happened with Bill." She paused, and her stomach turned over, a sick, wrenching flip. "But I'm not eighteen anymore, and I'm not scared. I want to be a part of your journey. Wherever it takes us, however long and hard the trip. Because though we might lose our way, we won't have lost each other. And that's what counts."

She stood and gazed down at his bent head. "I came out here because I never should have left you in New York. I wanted you to know that I'm sorry."

She halted again, and this time the silence

stretched out between them, longer and longer, a thread pulled impossibly tight.

When Eli looked at her, his eyes were overflowing. "*You're* sorry? I owe *you* an apology." He leaped to his feet and closed the distance between them. "I should have never asked you to go."

"What?" She blinked at him in surprise, her heart soaring. Was he happy she was here? Wanted her after all?

"I never should have doubted you, Christie. It was my past, my issues that messed with my head. It had nothing to do with you and Bill."

He lifted a hand as if he meant to touch her face then put it down hastily. "Staying with me should have been your decision to make, not mine."

They looked at each other in silence for what was probably minutes but felt like hours. What to say? She couldn't speak for the emotion overwhelming her. Finally, he continued.

"I was pigheaded and shortsighted. Mostly took the coward's way out. When you love someone, you trust them, believe in them, tell them how you really feel. You taught me that and I didn't listen."

Relief and gratitude exploded in Christie's heart, the shattered pieces coming together again to form a stained-glass version full of light. He loved her. She pressed her hands to her flushed cheeks, her fingertips covering her eyes.

"You love me," she repeated, more to herself than him.

He gently lowered her hands and kissed her with an aching sweetness that stole her heart. "From almost the first moment we met. That sappy quote—what was it, something about oaks and roots? Your optimism drove me crazy, but then you jumped in and saved John's life. You were so calm and capable. I knew you were special and it scared the hell out of me. I wasn't ready to let someone back into my life. But the more time we spent together, the way you helped Becca, Tommy and me, my feelings grew."

She'd never dreamed he would feel that way. Not in her most hopeful visions of this trip. Joy, impossible and fragile, took root in her heart in spite of everything.

"And now?"

"Now I love you, Christie Bates." He kissed each of her palms then pressed them against his cheeks.

"Say that again." She couldn't hear it enough.

"I love you. More than I can say. My body

might quit, but this—" he tapped his chest "—is yours. Forever."

"I love you, too."

His eyes lit up and he gathered her in his arms. She could hear him breathing now. His eyelashes tickled her cheek and their lips were a whisper apart then not apart at all. They brushed lightly then with firmer pressure, their kisses intensifying until he finally pulled back and stared at her, his eyes full of adoration and joy. They leaned together, breathless and content.

"I'm so happy," she said at last, her head now pillowed on his shoulder. "Whatever happens. We'll face it together."

He tipped up her chin and gazed down at her, his expression sober. "I don't think the trial is helping my cancer."

Concern rose but she kept it from reaching her eyes. "You haven't seen any signs? Your tumors are the same?"

A line formed between Eli's brows. "I don't have the radiology results back yet. But some people lost their nails, which means the treatment is working...for them."

She twined her hands in his and squeezed. "Eli. Everyone responds differently. The important thing is that you keep trying. For the kids and for us. And I'll be right beside you every step, no matter how dark that road gets."

A smile ghosted across his face and he buried his hands in her hair. "Thank you. I thought I could do this alone, but I know now that I can't. I need you—"

She silenced him with a butterfly kiss that ignited a firestorm. His mouth traveled across her cheek and jaw before he captured her earlobe, murmuring endearments into the hypersensitive flesh. She moved restlessly against him, a shivering desire to be closer than close. His arms banded around her, his heart galloping in time with hers. Suddenly, they couldn't touch or feel enough. She stroked his broad shoulders and rippling back as his hands skimmed along her neck and down to her waist.

Finally, he pulled back, breath ragged, and tucked a lock of hair behind her ear. "Christie, I don't believe your superstitions and struggle with that hope stuff. But I believe in you. In us. That's where my faith will always lie."

Christie's eyes welled—happy tears, for the first time in a long time. Despite Eli's prognosis and the difficult road ahead, she felt a sense of relief that drowned out everything else, including the worry about how quickly his health would deteriorate and how the kids would handle it. What mattered most was that they were together, and Eli wanted her, had faith in her. She felt him turn his head and lightly kiss her hair.

"You're my guardian angel." She both heard and felt him whisper it against her hair. "We have something few people ever find, and from here on out my life, such as it is, and my heart are yours—always."

She brushed away her tears and took a deep breath. These sounded like vows, ones they might never get to speak in a formal ceremony, so she wanted to get it right.

"I'm the luckiest woman in the world and so thankful that you're sharing the rest of your life with me, no matter the length. You're the light of my life and I love you, Eli. I know things might get rough. But that makes our love even more precious to me. From now on there is no more you. And no more me. Only us. And we'll handle what comes our way as best we can—together."

He pulled her in for a searing kiss that left her breathless, her head in a whirl.

"Christie!"

Tommy and Becca!

They turned and held out their arms for the rushing children. Her heart nearly burst. It'd been so long since she'd seen the children she loved as her own. How beautiful they were, flushed and tan, their shrieks ringing from the treetops.

Tommy nearly knocked her over when he leaped, his arms and legs wrapping around her monkey-style. She staggered back, got her footing then held out an arm for Becca. The teenager hugged Christie hard, though it wasn't until Eli joined in that they landed on the ground in a giggling heap.

"Nice," Becca laughed, spitting out a pine needle. She stood and brushed dirt from her bare knees.

Eli pulled Christie to her feet and wrapped an arm around her waist. "Kids. Christie came all this way to be with us. For good."

"And you're not doing anything stupid again, like letting her go?" Becca playfully punched her father's shoulder.

He made a show of rubbing his arm and grinned. "Not a chance."

"Yay!" Tommy leaped and waved a fistful of dandelions in the air. "I've been picking these every day, Christie." He shoved the crumpled bouquet her way. "Can we blow on one and make a wish?"

"Sure." She pulled out one with an intact white head, its seed pods fully sprouted.

The group crowded around her. "One, two, three…"

A collective burst of air sent the white fuzz flying, some sprinkling pine boughs like snow while some floated on wind currents, disappearing into the sun.

"Wow!" Tommy exclaimed, turning in circles until he fell on the ground laughing. "It worked. Daddy's cured!"

Eli crouched down and faced his son, his expression calm and reassuring. "We won't know until I finish my treatment, Tommy." He pulled up his son and gathered them all in a tight hug. "But we can have hope. That's all we need."

Becca nodded and rubbed her eyes. "Can we have hot dogs, too? For lunch."

Eli laughed and shook his head. "Always hungry. Sure, Becca-Bell. Let's get the fixings."

Christie and Tommy trailed behind them. It filled her heart to see the father and daughter, their shoulders brushing, their closeness evident in the way they joked and horsed around on their way to the picnic table.

Tommy stopped her before they left the trees and reached for a piece of dandelion fluff in her hair. "Is hope better than a wish?"

"I believe it is. But it's good to have both, don't you think?" She nestled him against her side.

He nodded and grinned up at her, the buds of two new front teeth peeking from his gums. "What did you wish for, Christie?"

She tapped his nose and smiled, her eyes meeting Eli's as he struck a match, the tiny flame cupped in his large hands.

"The very best kind...a wish for tomorrow."

* * * * *

REQUEST YOUR FREE BOOKS!

2 FREE INSPIRATIONAL NOVELS
PLUS 2
FREE
MYSTERY GIFTS

Love Inspired

YES! Please send me 2 FREE Love Inspired® novels and my 2 FREE mystery gifts (gifts are worth about $10). After receiving them, if I don't wish to receive any more books, I can return the shipping statement marked "cancel." If I don't cancel, I will receive 6 brand-new novels every month and be billed just $4.74 per book in the U.S. or $5.24 per book in Canada. That's a savings of at least 21% off the cover price. It's quite a bargain! Shipping and handling is just 50¢ per book in the U.S. and 75¢ per book in Canada.* I understand that accepting the 2 free books and gifts places me under no obligation to buy anything. I can always return a shipment and cancel at any time. Even if I never buy another book, the two free books and gifts are mine to keep forever.

105/305 IDN F49N

Name	(PLEASE PRINT)	

Address		Apt. #

City	State/Prov.	Zip/Postal Code

Signature (if under 18, a parent or guardian must sign)

Mail to the Harlequin® Reader Service:
IN U.S.A.: P.O. Box 1867, Buffalo, NY 14240-1867
IN CANADA: P.O. Box 609, Fort Erie, Ontario L2A 5X3

**Are you a subscriber to Love Inspired books
and want to receive the larger-print edition?
Call 1-800-873-8635 or visit www.ReaderService.com.**

* Terms and prices subject to change without notice. Prices do not include applicable taxes. Sales tax applicable in N.Y. Canadian residents will be charged applicable taxes. Offer not valid in Quebec. This offer is limited to one order per household. Not valid for current subscribers to Love Inspired books. All orders subject to credit approval. Credit or debit balances in a customer's account(s) may be offset by any other outstanding balance owed by or to the customer. Please allow 4 to 6 weeks for delivery. Offer available while quantities last.

Your Privacy—The Harlequin® Reader Service is committed to protecting your privacy. Our Privacy Policy is available online at www.ReaderService.com or upon request from the Harlequin Reader Service.
We make a portion of our mailing list available to reputable third parties that offer products we believe may interest you. If you prefer that we not exchange your name with third parties, or if you wish to clarify or modify your communication preferences, please visit us at www.ReaderService.com/consumerschoice or write to us at Harlequin Reader Service Preference Service, P.O. Box 9062, Buffalo, NY 14269. Include your complete name and address.

LIDIR13R

REQUEST YOUR FREE BOOKS!

2 FREE CHRISTIAN NOVELS
PLUS 2
FREE
MYSTERY GIFTS

HEARTSONG
PRESENTS

YES! Please send me 2 Free Heartsong Presents novels and my 2 FREE mystery gifts (gifts are worth about $10). After receiving them, if I don't wish to receive any more books I can return the shipping statement marked "cancel." If I don't cancel, I will receive 4 brand-new novels every month and be billed just $4.24 per book in the U.S. and $5.24 per book in Canada. That's a savings of at least 20% off the cover price. It's quite a bargain! Shipping and handling is just 50¢ per book in the U.S. and 75¢ per book in Canada.* I understand that accepting the 2 free books and gifts places me under no obligation to buy anything. I can always return a shipment and cancel at any time. Even if I never buy another book, the two free books and gifts are mine to keep forever.

159/359 HDN FVYK

Name _____ (PLEASE PRINT) _____

Address _____ Apt. # _____

City _____ State _____ Zip _____

Signature (if under 18, a parent or guardian must sign)

Mail to the Harlequin® Reader Service:
IN U.S.A.: P.O. Box 1867, Buffalo, NY 14240-1867

* Terms and prices subject to change without notice. Prices do not include applicable taxes. Sales tax applicable in N.Y. This offer is limited to one order per household. Not valid for current subscribers to Heartsong Presents books. All orders subject to credit approval. Credit or debit balances in a customer's account(s) may be offset by any other outstanding balance owed by or to the customer. Please allow 4 to 6 weeks for delivery. Offer available while quantities last. Offer valid only in the U.S.

Your Privacy—The Harlequin® Reader Service is committed to protecting your privacy. Our Privacy Policy is available online at www.ReaderService.com or upon request from the Harlequin Reader Service.
We make a portion of our mailing list available to reputable third parties that offer products we believe may interest you. If you prefer that we not exchange your name with third parties, or if you wish to clarify or modify your communication preferences, please visit us at www.ReaderService.com/consumerschoice or write to us at Harlequin Reader Service Preference Service, P.O. Box 9062, Buffalo, NY 14269. Include your complete name and address.

HSPDIR13R

REQUEST YOUR FREE BOOKS!

2 FREE INSPIRATIONAL NOVELS
PLUS 2
FREE
MYSTERY GIFTS

Love Inspired

HISTORICAL
INSPIRATIONAL HISTORICAL ROMANCE

YES! Please send me 2 FREE Love Inspired® Historical novels and my 2 FREE mystery gifts (gifts are worth about $10). After receiving them, if I don't wish to receive any more books, I can return the shipping statement marked "cancel." If I don't cancel, I will receive 4 brand-new novels every month and be billed just $4.74 per book in the U.S. or $5.24 per book in Canada. That's a savings of at least 21% off the cover price. It's quite a bargain! Shipping and handling is just 50¢ per book in the U.S. and 75¢ per book in Canada.* I understand that accepting the 2 free books and gifts places me under no obligation to buy anything. I can always return a shipment and cancel at any time. Even if I never buy another book, the two free books and gifts are mine to keep forever.

102/302 IDN F6CY

Name	(PLEASE PRINT)	
Address		Apt. #
City	State/Prov.	Zip/Postal Code

Signature (if under 18, a parent or guardian must sign)

Mail to the Harlequin® Reader Service:
IN U.S.A.: P.O. Box 1867, Buffalo, NY 14240-1867
IN CANADA: P.O. Box 609, Fort Erie, Ontario L2A 5X3

Want to try two free books from another series?
Call 1-800-873-8635 or visit www.ReaderService.com.

* Terms and prices subject to change without notice. Prices do not include applicable taxes. Sales tax applicable in N.Y. Canadian residents will be charged applicable taxes. Offer not valid in Quebec. This offer is limited to one order per household. Not valid for current subscribers to Love Inspired Historical books. All orders subject to credit approval. Credit or debit balances in a customer's account(s) may be offset by any other outstanding balance owed by or to the customer. Please allow 4 to 6 weeks for delivery. Offer available while quantities last.

LIHDIR13R

ReaderService.com

Manage your account online!

- Review your order history
- Manage your payments
- Update your address

---

*We've designed
the Harlequin® Reader Service
website just for you.*

Enjoy all the features!

- Reader excerpts from any series
- Respond to mailings and
  special monthly offers
- Discover new series available to you
- Browse the Bonus Bucks catalog
- Share your feedback

Visit us at:

ReaderService.com

RS13